Noah

The Craigdon Family Dynasty

Book Seven

CHRIS TAYLOR

LCT Productions Pty Ltd
18364 Kamilaroi Highway, Narrabri NSW 2390

ISBN. 978-1-925119-86-2 (Paperback)

Noah is a work of fiction. Names, characters, places, brands, media and incidents either are the product of the author's imagination or are used fictitiously. Any resemblance to actual persons, living or dead, events, or locales, is entirely coincidental.

Published in the United States of America.

Books by Chris Taylor

THE MUNRO FAMILY SERIES
The Profiler
The Investigator
The Predator
The Betrayal
The Deception
The Negotiator
The Christmas Vigil
The Ransom
The Defendant
The Shooting
The Maker
(Available in Audio)

THE SYDNEY HARBOUR HOSPITAL SERIES
The Perfect Husband
The Body Thief
The Baby Snatchers
The Final Bullet
The Debt Collector
The Lab Test
The Stolen Identity
The Cliff-top Killer
The Likeable Fraudster

THE SYDNEY LEGAL SERIES
An Accidental Murderer
At the Hand of Her Father
A Woman Scorned
Lies and Deception
Ordinary Evil
The Ties That Bind
The Perfect Crime
A Toxic Inheritance
Malicious Love

THE CRAIGDON FAMILY SERIES
Callum
Joel
Isabella
Nicholas
Sophia
Flynn
Noah
Logan
Elizabeth

THE BARRINGTON FAMILY SERIES
Broken Lives
Broken Promises
Broken Bonds
Broken Spirits
Broken Vows
Broken Minds
Broken Dreams
Broken Hearts
Broken Homes

THE FAIRFAX FAMILY SERIES
A Cattleman in Disguise
A Cattleman's Quest
A Cattleman's Daughter
A Cattleman's Secret Baby
To Catch a Cattleman
The Doctor and the Cattleman
To Rescue a Cattleman
A Cattleman's Heart
For the Love of a Cattleman

BACHELORS AND BRIDES SERIES
Matilda
Austin
Farrah

Benjamin
Verity
Denver
Ebony
Tyrone
Willow

Chris Taylor writing as
BELLA CHRISTIAN

THIS IS WHERE IT ENDS SERIES
(in order)
Jessie's Story
Ryan's Story
Holly's Story
Sarah's Story
Veronica's Story

Get a FREE book when you sign up for Chris Taylor's
newsletter at: www.christaylorauthor.com.au

Love Audiobooks? Check out Chris Taylor Books on audio
on Audible.com, Amazon.com and Apple Books.

Join Chris Taylor's Facebook reader group/fan page and be
among the first to receive news of book releases, read and
review books prior to release and other amazing offers. Join
Now at: www.facebook.com/groups/1758023621144744/

Find out more about all of Chris Taylor's books, by visiting her
website at: www.christaylorauthor.com.au

Dedication

This book is dedicated to Cherise Fourie. Your story touched my heart. It is for you and readers like you for whom I write. Thank you for inspiring me to be the best writer I can be.

And as always, to my husband, Linden. My best friend, my soul mate. I love you to the moon and back.

Acknowledgments

As usual, no book comes into being without a lot of help and support by my friends and family. A world of thanks must go to my wonderful editor, Pat Thomas. Thank you for everything that you do to make my stories even more amazing than I could ever dare to dream. To former Detective Superintendent Michael Kilfoyle, thank you for lending my story credibility. Any mistakes are wholly my own.

To Mary and all of the team at Miblart, thank you for the fantastic book cover. To my sister, Nicole Guihot and to my friends, Ally Thomson and Sue Ricardo, thank you for your excellent editorial comments, proof reading skills and suggestions. I hope you like the final result.

To Amy Atwell, Kirby and the dedicated team at Author EMS who are so much more than book formatters. Amy, once again, thank you for your magic.

To the fantastic writer organizations such as Romance Writers of Australia, Romance Writers of America and Romance Writers of New Zealand for all the help, support and encouragement they offer new and aspiring writers, including me.

To my readers, thank you for your support and love for my stories. Your encouragement and enjoyment make this journey all worthwhile.

And lastly, to my friends and family, especially my husband and children. Thank you for putting up with late dinners and even later conversations as I've emerged day after day from the sometimes scary but always enthralling world I've created on my computer.

Chapter One

Deep inside his chest, Noah Craigdon felt the heavy beat of the house music thumping from the DJ's speakers. It was Friday night and he was with his younger brother in a nightclub in the city. The Pitt was exactly the kind of place Noah usually avoided. He was quiet and shy—some would say reserved—and the noisy, crowded nightclub was completely out of his comfort zone.

But that was the point. On the advice of a girl he'd once thought he was in love with, he was determined to get out more and meet women, prospective partners. It was like Jayde had suggested: This would be a numbers game. The more women he met, the more chance he had of finding his soul mate.

The nightclub was popular with cops and other first responders. Paramedics, doctors, nurses, firefighters—they all seemed to gravitate to The Pitt. Loud music, dim lighting, the press of bodies. The beer flowed, wine glasses clinked and sparkled, catching the overhead lights.

The pool table in the back was well-used. Any arguments were quickly stifled. The patrons were slick and well groomed. Women with long flowing hair, artfully applied makeup; guys with loose collarless shirts and designer jeans. There was a frantic sort of energy permeating the room that came from a crowd was enjoying some downtime from stressful, difficult jobs.

Noah had talked Logan into coming with him. His brother had never had a problem with women. They flocked to him like teenagers flocked to Snapchat. Logan and Flynn were very alike in that way. It was Noah, the middle brother, who'd always been the odd one out. It usually took every ounce of courage he had to even look a girl in the eye, let alone start up a conversation.

The only place he was confident in a social setting was on the dance floor. Which didn't make a lick of sense, seeing it was the one place where even the most confident of people could come unstuck. But Noah had always had perfect rhythm and the music transported him to another place, somewhere far away from his usual awkwardness.

They found a spot at the far end of the bar, away from the loud music and settled onto bar stools. Logan got the first round of drinks. Noah took a sip of his cold beer and sighed.

"Oh, yeah. That tastes good," he said and then grinned.

Logan managed a brief smile that looked more like a grimace. It was about as jovial as he got these days. What seemed like a lifetime earlier, Logan had been a competitive sailor, racing yachts. But a bad accident had resulted in serious injuries. He suffered numerous fractures to his femur, his tibia and his fibula and unfortunately, some of the broken bones hadn't set very well. He'd been left with a permanent limp and was no longer lithe enough to race competitively. Logan often said he knew exactly how Tiger Woods felt.

Logan now designed and built super yachts for the family company, headed by their father, Archie. Even so, three years down the track, Logan was still down on everything. To make matters worse, Logan had recently been jilted at the altar.

Noah swallowed a sigh and took another sip from his beer. "How's work?" he asked.

Logan shrugged. "The same as always. Dad's still pressuring me to take up a managerial role in the company."

"Would that be so bad? You love Craigdon Super Yachts."

Logan's response was swift and passionate. "I love being in the thick of it, designing them, building them from the ground up. Not managing employees, paying bills, fighting with contractors. I don't want to be stuck on the phone all day! That's the reason I put Nicholas in charge of Craigdon Enterprises. I'm not cut out for that kind of thing." He paused and then added in a bewildered tone. "I still don't have a clue why Uncle Henry left me his company."

Noah considered his response. His cop instincts were telling him there was a chance Logan might have been the product of an affair between their uncle and their mother. Noah had no evidence to base his suspicions on and so he remained quiet. Instead, he responded by saying, "We've opened an investigation into Mom's death."

Logan compressed his lips and nodded. "I still can't believe Uncle Henry was drunk behind the wheel when they crashed. I mean, what the hell? How come we've only just found out about this? And why the hell were they driving together that late at night anyway? Where had they been? Did anyone bother to ask?"

Noah shrugged. He had all of those questions and more filling his head, but as yet he had no answers. He was determined to get to the bottom of what had happened and bring to justice those involved in covering it up. If that's what had happened. The jury was still out on that.

He sighed and took another sip from his glass. "You heard from Flynn lately?" he asked, referring to their oldest brother.

"No. Since he and Jayde hooked up he's never around. I left a couple of messages for him. He hasn't called me back."

Noah refrained from commenting and chugged down the rest of his beer. Logan eyed him speculatively.

"Didn't you bring her to Callum's wedding?"

Noah pretended confusion. "Who?"

Logan rolled his eyes. "Jayde."

"Oh, Jayde. Yeah."

"And?"

"And what?"

Logan continued to regard him steadily. Noah grimaced. "There's nothing to tell, Logan. Yes, I liked her, but she didn't like me. At least, not in that way, and that's okay. You can't help who you fall in love with."

"You're right. But who's looking to fall in love?" Logan's face twisted with bitterness. "Been there, done that. It didn't work out so well. In fact, she ran off with her best friend, remember? So from now on, I'm done with love. A little lust works just fine for me."

Noah felt a moment's sympathy for the shabby way his brother's long-term girlfriend and fiancée, Virginia Maxwell, had treated him, but already Logan was looking meaningfully toward a couple of attractive, twenty-something women who stood together a little further down the bar. Noticing the attention, the girls smiled and waved. A moment later, they moved closer to the brothers and regarded them with friendly smiles.

"Hi, I'm Amy," said the blond, zeroing in on Logan.

Reluctantly, Noah turned his attention to the brunette and forced a smile.

"I'm Brittany," she said, flashing a set of perfect white teeth.

"Noah," he mumbled. Logan nudged him with his elbow. Noah ignored the subtle intrusion and managed another weak grin. "Um, can I get you a drink?"

Brittany moved closer. Her generous breasts brushed against his arm. Embarrassed, he quickly turned away and flagged down the bartender. He ordered another beer and ascertained from Brittany that she was drinking gin.

"Plus soda water, and don't forget the lime," she added with a wink.

Noah tried to rustle up some interest at the frank promise in her eyes, but it wasn't forthcoming. Swallowing a sigh, he ordered their drinks and wondered how soon he could call it a night.

Logan leaned toward him and wiggled his eyebrows. "Having fun, bro?"

Noah grimaced. "Sure."

Logan gave him a wry smile. A moment later, he grabbed Amy by the hand and despite his permanent limp, started heading toward the dance floor.

"Come on, Noah. Brittany wants to dance," Logan threw over his shoulder.

The brunette stood there with an expectant look on her face, batting her false eyelashes. Noah groaned beneath his breath. He was going to kill his brother. The last thing he wanted was to spend any more time in Brittany's company. She was pretty enough, but she wasn't doing it for him and that wasn't anybody's fault. Before he could get away with a mumbled excuse, Brittany had taken his hand, her face lighting up with enthusiasm.

"Yes! Let's dance! I *looove* to dance!"

With reluctance dogging his every step, Noah allowed himself to be led onto the dance floor. The music was loud and fast with a rhythmic techno beat. Before he realized it, his body began to move—his feet, his hips, his legs. It was like he had no control over them. With a sigh, he relaxed and gave himself up to the music.

Brittany was a terrible dancer, but what she lacked in style and technique, she made up for in enthusiasm. She draped her arms around his neck and pressed herself against him. She wiggled and jiggled and spun around, laughing as she stumbled and would have fallen if he hadn't reached out and caught her. He wished she was the kind of girl he could get into. There was plenty to like. But the only quickening of his pulse when he looked at her was from the exertion of the dance.

Simple, rhythmical, mesmerizing. He moved with effortless grace. People stepped out of the way to give him room and to watch him, a mixture of envy, disbelief and enjoyment on their faces. Noah became oblivious to all of them once he was caught up in the beat of the music. Sweat gathered on his forehead and ran down the sides of his face. He distractedly pulled off his glasses and swiped at the perspiration with the back of his hand.

Logan leaned over and said something in his ear, but Noah couldn't hear over the music. He shrugged and Logan mimicked getting a drink and Noah gave him a thumbs up. Logan's dance partner went with him and Brittany quickly followed. Feeling a little foolish out there on the dance floor alone, he same to a sudden stop.

And then another woman materialized before him. She was so beautiful, his breath caught in his throat. Her long dark hair blazed blue-black in the spotlights. She wore a sparkly crop top covered in beads that dangled low across her taut stomach. A tiny glittery skirt that barely covered her butt made up the rest of her clothing. Four-inch black heels that almost looked dangerous, elevated her to just below his shoulder.

Her toned legs were shapely and tanned. She took his hand and put her other hand on his shoulder. His hand automatically came to rest just above her hip. The music changed to a tango and before he knew it, they were carving up the dance floor with a swishing of skirts and a flash of feet. His heart pounded, both from the exertion and the exotic woman he held in his arms.

Who is she and where did she come from?

It was obvious she was a dancer. An instructor, perhaps?

Or maybe she'd just been born dancing. Her coloring hinted at South American heritage, or maybe Spanish. It was hard to tell in the dimness, but there was no mistaking her beauty or the aura of confidence that surrounded her and sparkled in her dark brown eyes.

Noah lost all sense of time and place, like he usually did when he got caught up in a dance. The woman continued to match his every step, lithe and rhythmical in his arms. At last the music came to an end and they both stopped and stood staring at each other, breathless. Applause broke out around them. When Noah could finally speak without gasping, he held out his hand.

"Hi. I'm Noah."

"Ayla Rodriguez."

They smiled at each other. The warmth in Ayla's gaze flustered Noah and he quickly looked away. She turned and made her way off the dance floor. He sighed in relief and after a moment's hesitation, followed her. She came to a halt near an empty table and sat down, looking up at him expectantly. Nerves swirled in his gut. He swallowed hard and surreptitiously swiped sweaty hands down his jeans before perching abruptly on the seat opposite her.

"So, Noah, do you come here often?"

Her eyes sparkled with good humor. He sucked in a breath and did his best to sound normal.

"Not really. This"—he waved a hand around the crowded room—"isn't really my thing."

Her eyes widened in surprise. "You could have fooled me. I won't believe you learned to dance like that by watching videos on YouTube."

He laughed. Her relaxed attitude eased a little of his tension. "You're right. I took dance lessons for years. Jazz, tap, rock 'n roll. I pulled on my first pair of dance shoes when I was four."

She looked at him with admiration. "No wonder you're so good. So, do you dance professionally?"

He laughed and shook his head. "No. Not even close. I stopped lessons when I got to high school. It wasn't cool for a teenager to be attending dance classes. Especially not a teenage boy."

"Too bad. You're very talented."

He blushed with pleasure. When he was young, his mother had often praised his dance ability, but she was his mother. It was her job to ensure he had a healthy ego. Coming from this beautiful stranger, it really meant something. "Thank you. You're not so bad yourself."

It was her turn to duck her head in embarrassment. "Thanks. I'm no Solange Acosta, but I enjoy it."

He eyed her quizzically. "Solange Acosta? I don't think I've heard of her."

"She and her partner, Max van de Voord, won the Tango World Championships in 2011. They're from Argentina."

"You know a lot about it."

She shrugged. "What can I say? I like to tango." Once again, laughter glinted in her eyes.

Noah's pulse rate picked up its pace. He swallowed against another rush of nerves. "Where did you learn to dance?"

"My parents are from Uruguay. They migrated to Australia when I was eight. I'd already spent enough time in my home country to feel the rhythm of the tango in my blood. My mom and dad love to dance and they've always loved the tango. They were happy to teach me. I fell in love with it, too."

"Is it hard to find dance partners?" he asked, curious.

"Sometimes, although there are a couple of fantastic Central American dance clubs in the city that are as mad about the tango as I am. I go there fairly often. I can usually find someone who wants to dance. Who knows? Maybe I can even convince you to join me."

She smiled and his heart skipped a beat. *Oh, God. This is ridiculous. We've only just met and I'm in love. What if she has a boyfriend? Oh, hell, she might even be married.*

His gaze slid to her hands. *No rings. Okay then, hopefully not married. What the hell am I doing? We've only just met! Get a grip!*

Noah cleared his throat in an effort to get control over his wayward thoughts. "So, what do you do for a living?"

"I'm a cop."

He started in surprise. "Really?"

"Yeah. Why, do you have a problem with cops?"

"No, of course not. I'm a cop, too."

Now it was her turn to blink in surprise. "Really? I would never have pegged you as a cop."

"Why not?" he asked, curious and slightly offended.

She shrugged. "I don't know. You seem too…normal. Not hardened enough."

He gave a half-laugh. "I guess that's a compliment. The truth is, I haven't spent much of my career out on the street. I spent the first few years in general duties, but now I work for the Law Enforcement Conduct Commission. I'm a detective on the investigative team."

Her expression sobered. "The LECC?"

"Yes. The newest version of Internal Affairs."

"Wow. Investigating fellow officers isn't everyone's cup of tea."

He kept his expression carefully neutral. "I enjoy it."

"Good on you."

"So you don't have a problem with it?"

She shook her head. "No, of course not. You guys have a job to do, just like the rest of us."

He pulled a wry face. "Not all cops see it that way."

"You're right. A lot of them see you as traitors."

He tensed. "If cops didn't do the wrong thing, there'd be no need for us to investigate their behavior," he protested.

She held her hands up in a sign of surrender. "Hey, you'll get no argument from me, but it's not always as clear cut as that, is it? Our job isn't always black and white."

"It is in my world. There are rules. They're there for a reason. If you break them, you should expect to be punished. That's the society we live in."

"I wish I had the faith you seem to have in the system," she said softly.

He stared at her. She sounded so…disillusioned. He opened his mouth to question her further, but she merely waved him away and laughed. It sounded forced.

"So, does Noah have a last name?"

He blushed. "Yes, of course. Craigdon. I'm Noah Craigdon."

Something in Ayla's demeanor changed. A shadow crossed her face. A long second later, it seemed she made a conscious effort to clear her troubled thoughts. She smiled, but it looked forced.

"Craigdon. Are you related to Joel and Jett Craigdon?"

Noah blinked in surprise. "Yes, I am. They're my first cousins. Do you know them?"

"Yes. I went through the Academy with Joel. I don't know Jett so well, but I've met him once or twice through Joel."

"Wow. Small world," Noah murmured and was grateful both of those cousins were already spoken for.

And then she nudged him with her elbow. "Look at the two of us! It's Friday night! Who wants to talk about work? We're meant to be having a good time."

Noah let the subject slide even though he was keen to know more about what had dampened her mood. He hoped it wasn't something he'd said. It seemed where women were concerned, he was always stuffing things up. He swore inside his head.

"Would you like a drink?" he asked.

"Thank you, but no. It's getting late. I should go." With that she pushed back her seat and stood. She held out her hand. "It was really nice meeting you, Noah."

He stood and shook her hand. She had a sure, firm grip. "You too, Ayla." He wanted to say more, maybe even ask for her number, but by the time he found the courage, she'd slipped her hand out of his and had disappeared into the crowd. He was left to curse his cowardice and wonder if he'd ever see her again.

Chapter Two

Noah arrived at work the following Monday morning with a spring in his step. Though he hadn't made any effort to return to The Pitt or otherwise track down the beautiful Ayla over the weekend, she'd consumed his thoughts for more hours than he cared to admit. All sorts of fantasies had gone through his head and though he wasn't sure if he'd ever see her again, their encounter had been fun and for the first time since Jayde had chosen his brother over him, Noah felt hopeful for the future.

To be fair to Jayde, they'd never been a couple. They'd attended his cousin's wedding together and Noah had hoped she felt as strongly about him as he did her and that their friendship would become more. But that wasn't to be. Her heart belonged to Flynn.

Since Noah had come to terms with her choice, he was okay with it and wished his brother much happiness. Now that he'd met Ayla, he felt far more positive that his soul mate was still out there and that maybe, just maybe he'd find his dream woman some day.

Tossing his briefcase on his desk, he hung up his jacket in the locker that stood in one corner of his office and then went searching for caffeine. He found his partner, Declan Munro, standing before the coffee machine, mug in hand.

Declan turned and greeted him with a friendly smile. "Craigdon! Good of you to drag your sorry ass in here."

Noah merely gave him the finger. Declan chuckled, taking the rude gesture in the spirit it was intended. At forty, Declan Munro had started to gray at the temples, but he still stood shoulder to shoulder with Noah and was as fit as any of the investigators on their team.

Six years earlier, Declan had worked as a detective for the Australian Federal Police in Canberra. His career had fallen apart when he'd been investigated by their Internal Affairs department for police corruption. Fortunately, he'd managed to clear his name and not surprisingly, he'd requested a transfer. He'd ended up in Sydney at the LECC a few years before Noah. They'd been partnered together when Noah came onboard and over time had become firm friends.

Declan wasn't into dancing, but he loved something else Noah enjoyed—fast motorbikes. Declan owned a Ducati 1199 Panigale. A beast of a machine that went like the wind. With his million-dollar inheritance, Noah had recently treated himself to a cherry-red Honda Fireblade. He couldn't wait to take it out on the motorway and open up the throttle.

Noah filled his cup and wandered back toward his office. Declan followed him and threw himself down on the chair opposite Noah's desk. Though his office was situated in the middle of the building and had no windows, the décor was nice enough—especially for government digs.

The carpet was new with a pleasant geometrical pattern. The furniture was predictable, but comfortable and clean. The best thing about it was he had the office to himself. A luxury that was largely unheard of for the average cop.

Declan sipped at his coffee and then cleared his throat. "Tell me more about your mother's case."

Noah took the seat behind his desk. He'd brought the case to his superior in the hope the LECC would decide to open an investigation. Fortunately, after providing his boss with the scant details he had, his boss had agreed it was worth looking into. When he'd expressed concerns about Noah's family connection, Noah had quickly agreed Declan could take on the role as lead investigator.

Noah had no problem with Declan taking charge. The two of them worked closely together. Declan would ensure Noah was included in any investigations. In fact, so far Declan had been more than generous with his willingness for Noah to get involved.

"At this stage, we only have the word of a known criminal—John Hassad—that my uncle was drunk behind the wheel when he crashed the car in the accident that killed my mother. If there's any truth to that claim, you have to wonder why evidence wasn't brought forward to substantiate it. Why none of us were told about it. Why my uncle was never charged…"

Declan frowned. "If what Hassad says is true, you're looking at one hell of a cover up. Cops who've kept quiet for reasons known only to themselves, maybe even bribery involved." Declan sighed and then added, "It's not like it hasn't happened before."

Noah nodded grimly. "Right. That's why we need to get to the bottom of this. I've taken the liberty of putting in a request for the old police file. We need to head over to the records department to collect it. Do you want to ride with me?"

Declan grinned. "Sure. Beats sitting around here. Let's go."

The Corporate Records & Logistics Department was located in Parramatta, not far from the police headquarters. All of the New South Wales police records relating to archived cases were kept there on site. As Declan started the ignition of the unmarked police vehicle and entered the stream of traffic heading west, Noah pulled out his phone and called ahead to let the records department know they were on their way.

Traffic was slow as people made their way to work. When they came to a stop at a set of lights, Declan sighed with impatience. He tapped his fingers on the steering wheel. He scratched his nose. Finally, he turned to Noah.

"So, what did you get up to on the weekend? Anything exciting?"

"Actually, I went out clubbing with my brother. The Pitt."

Declan looked at him without comprehension.

"It's in the city," Noah added.

Declan shook his head. "Never heard of it. I'm a married man, remember? Three kids under six. I can't remember the last time I went to a nightclub."

Noah shot him a look of sympathy. "Poor old man."

"Hey! Steady on the old! I'm only forty."

"So, what did you get up to on the weekend? Twister?" Noah grinned.

"Ha, ha. Smart-ass. In fact, I took the twins to the park and played soccer. Gave their mom a break. Ran off a bit of their energy."

Noah kept his expression somber. "Sounds super exciting. How old are they?"

"Three. And my daughter is five."

Noah pulled a face. "Ouch."

Declan smiled with amusement. "That's exactly how I felt when I was your age."

"How long have you been married?"

"Nearly six years."

"You sound…happy about it."

"I *am* happy about it. Chloe's the love of my life. I couldn't imagine what it would be like to live without her. God, did I just say that? I'm such a sap. Chloe would fall over herself laughing if she heard me."

"She sounds like one hell of a woman."

"She is. One in a lifetime. You got a girlfriend?"

"No."

"Boyfriend?"

"Hell, no. I like women well enough. It's just…" His voice petered out. He flushed with embarrassment.

Declan shot him a look. "It's just what?"

Noah's embarrassment deepened. Declan continued to throw him expectant looks. Noah shrugged. "I get tongue-tied whenever I get near them. Especially one I like."

Declan grinned. "Man, you need to get out and meet more of them. Practice, if you like. It gets easier the more times you do it. It's even easier if you practice with girls you're not into."

"So you're suggesting I go up to some random female and start up a conversation?"

"Why not?"

"Because it's weird."

"Why? You're in a nightclub. People who go to nightclubs are looking for a mate. Everyone knows that."

"Maybe I just like to dance."

Declan rolled his eyes. "*Puhlease*! Are you *sure* you're not into guys?"

Noah's cheeks heated. His thoughts immediately went to Ayla. "No, I'm definitely not into guys."

"So what did you do at The Pitt?"

"I hung out with my brother, Logan. Had a few drinks. Danced."

"With a woman?"

"Of course."

"Well, that's good. It's a start. Did you share any conversation?"

"Yes. We did. In fact, she was really easy to talk to."

"So I take it you weren't into her?"

Noah flushed again. "To the contrary. I was very into her."

"And yet you were able to carry on a conversation with her?"

"Yes."

"So sometimes you can manage it," Declan replied, his brow creasing in thought. The lights turned green and he hit the accelerator. The car leaped forward. He shot Noah a measured look. "Maybe you overthink things, mate? Get yourself into a panic? The thing is, talking to women all comes down to practice. Like I was telling you."

Noah nodded in agreement. Declan was the second person to encourage him to put himself out there and meet as many women as he could. Perhaps it was good advice after all. By heading out to The Pitt last Friday night he'd met Ayla and that was a good thing. Too bad he hadn't asked for her number. Still, she knew he worked for the LECC and she'd told him she was a cop. She also knew two of his cousins. It shouldn't be too hard for her to track him down if she wanted to. That was the question. Would she want to? Was she as into him as he'd been into her? He wished he knew. Of course, there was nothing stopping him from tracking her down. If he could scrounge up the courage…

An hour later, they arrived at the records department. An attractive young woman in her twenties sat in a chair behind the counter. She greeted them with a big smile. Declan took one look at her and turned and gave Noah a meaningful look of encouragement, followed by a wink.

Noah was immediately filled with nerves. His palms turned sweaty. His cheeks flooded with heat. Declan stood back, forcing Noah to approach the woman behind the desk.

"G-good-morning. I'm D-detective Craigdon. This is Detective Munro. I called earlier. We're here about the C-craigdon file."

While Noah blushed furiously, Declan stepped forward and shook the woman's hand.

She glanced at Noah. "I was the one you spoke to. I took the liberty of locating the file. I have it here." She handed a file across the counter. Noah took it from her. It was much thinner than he expected for an accident that had resulted in someone's death.

"Th-thank you," he mumbled.

Declan rolled his eyes. Noah steadfastly ignored him. He tucked the file under his arm and bid the woman a muttered farewell. The bright morning sunshine hit him full in the face as he walked out of the building and headed toward the car park.

"What the hell was all that about?" Declan asked, chuckling.

Noah pretended innocence. "What?"

"That. In there. Didn't you listen to anything I said? There was a gorgeous woman in there. You had every opportunity to flirt with her and you failed miserably. You looked like you were about to face your executioner." Declan shook his head slowly from side to side, his expression somber. "Boy. You sure weren't joking when you said women tie you up in knots. You need more practice than I thought."

And then he gave him a friendly slap on the back. "Never mind. There'll be plenty of other opportunities. Lucky you have me. I haven't met a woman I couldn't charm. Just ask my wife. We met while she was investigating me for police corruption."

Noah's eyes widened. He shook his head and chuckled. "Why doesn't that surprise me?"

Declan winked. "It's all in your manner, mate. There's an art to approaching women. One I happened to perfect. Trust me, you're going to be able to observe and learn from the best."

The two men laughed. With that, they climbed into their car and headed back the way they'd come.

Superintendent Ayla Rodriguez sat at her desk at police headquarters and dealt with the pile of emails that had come in over the course of the weekend. In her position as Chief of Staff for Police Commissioner Kevin Beechwood, it was her responsibility to deal with any emergency that might arise in relation to her boss. Given Kevin's flagrant disregard for the rules, hers was no easy task.

Right now she was formulating a response to an enquiring journalist who appeared to have way more information about the commissioner's personal life than she should. Ayla wondered about the woman's source. Then again, maybe the journalist had been following him. It wasn't hard to do, given Kevin's flamboyance and desire to see and be seen. It was the bane of Ayla's existence keeping his name out of the papers.

And then she thought about her Friday night. The way she'd spent it clubbing with her friends, and in particular, her time at The Pitt. At the thought of Noah Craigdon, her cheeks grew warm. He was a cop, so he understood the job like lay people couldn't. He was also nice. And cute. And he loved to dance. Not only loved it, he was good at it. Such a contradiction. Sweet and shy, but amazing on the dance floor. So confident, so sexy. A heady combination. The only problem was, he was a Craigdon.

The door to the commissioner's office opened and Kevin strode out. In his mid-fifties, he was of average height and average build. His gray hair sported a short military cut. A soft paunch spilled over the top of his trousers. Today he was clean-shaven, but he went through periods where he grew a beard. The beards made him look decades older. Ayla could never work out why he did it.

He came up to her and tossed a file on her desk. "I heard whispers the LECC might be looking into the motor vehicle accident involving Henry Craigdon," he said without preamble.

Ayla's stomach lurched at the mention of the Craigdon name, but she forced herself to keep her expression blank. "Really? Why would they be interested in a case that happened more than ten years ago?"

His lip curled up in disgust. "Who knows? They must have plenty of time on their hands. Or a limitless budget. Frankly, either scenario is plausible. This new LECC is a joke. They think they're going to identify every single case of serious police misconduct in this state. Ha! They're babes in the wood. The Police Integrity Commission couldn't keep a handle on all of it. What makes them think they'll be any different?" He paused and gave her a pointed look. "You haven't said anything, have you?"

She flushed and briefly lowered her gaze. "No, of course not."

His gaze remained hard. "Good. You're happy in your position as my chief of staff, aren't you?"

"Absolutely. It's a dream job."

He nodded, his lips compressed. "Yes, it is. And it can disappear in a heartbeat. Life's like that. You can never take it for granted. Don't you forget that."

With that, he turned on his heel and left, leaving Ayla staring after him, confused and shaken. Dread formed in the pit of her stomach.

What the hell was that all about?

Chapter Three

There were scant few pieces of paper that made up the decade-old investigation into Henry Craigdon's motor vehicle accident. Noah and Declan had the entire contents of the file spread across Declan's desk. Declan picked up the police report produced at the time of the incident. He scanned the opening lines and then frowned.

"Kevin Beechwood was the officer in charge of the station that night."

Noah looked at him in surprise. "The same Kevin Beechwood who's the current police commissioner?"

"Yep."

"You're kidding!"

"Nope."

"Great. That complicates things. Now what do we do?"

Declan shrugged. "We do what we always do. We examine the evidence, see what we come up with. You already indicated there's no guarantee Hassad was telling the truth."

"True. He's far from a credible witness. But I understand the conversation in question occurred with Hassad's daughter. It was nothing more than casual talk. She didn't know about the events he spoke of. She didn't know the people involved. At the time, Hassad had no idea his daughter was a cop. There was no motivation for him to lie to her. The way I see it, he was merely passing on information in the course of an idle conversation and therefore, it's more likely he told the truth."

From the moment Noah's brother, Flynn had told him about the conversation Jayde had had with her father, a feeling of cold foreboding had permeated Noah's gut. There had been so many unanswered questions surrounding his mother's death. That conversation had crystalized into a determination to open the investigation.

Still, Declan looked unconvinced. "Yeah, maybe. Don't forget Hassad isn't exactly a pillar of society. I'm not sure how much stock you can put into him telling the truth."

Declan scanned the report again. "It says here Sergeant Joseph Bettino was Beechwood's second in charge that night. He attended the scene with Beechwood and provided a police statement. What do we know about him?"

Noah reached for another piece of paper. "I did some digging into his background—thirty-four years of age, divorced, father of two. He's the non-custodial parent. Lives in Concord. He's currently on paid stress leave from the police service."

Declan nodded and looked at the police report again. "According to this, the accident occurred at 2318 hours on Saturday, 10 April, 2010 on McDonalds Road, Pokolbin." He looked at Noah. "Do you know it?"

"No."

"It's an area in the Hunter Valley, famous for its wineries. About two-and-a-half-hours' drive north of Sydney. Nice place to stay for the weekend."

"I'll take your word for it," Noah replied.

Declan flicked through the other papers on his desk. "Let's see what else we have here. Statements from Beechwood as the officer in charge, Bettino as the 2IC, a report from the police mechanic…" He scanned the contents. "No mechanical fault with the vehicle. Then there's a draftsman's drawing of the scene of the accident to scale, including a handful of photos of the scene. We also have a report from a Dr Richard Mitchell of Maitland Hospital pronouncing Janelle Mary Craigdon dead on arrival."

He looked up. "I'm sorry. I hope this doesn't stir up bad memories."

Noah bit his lip and shook his head. "It happened a long time ago. I still miss her, of course, but the pain of that day has faded with time. I must admit, this has brought things back again, but I need to know what happened. All these years, I believed my mother died in a tragic accident. My uncle insisted that was the case. Maybe he was telling the truth, but after what Hassad told his daughter, now I'm not so sure. It's time to expose the truth, once and for all."

"What were they doing out there together?" Declan asked. "Were they on a business trip? Did your mother work for him?"

"No. She didn't work for him. We were shocked when we were told where she was killed and that she was with Uncle Henry. We still have no idea why she was with him. She'd told my father she was staying with a girlfriend for the weekend." Noah didn't want to think of the other possible alternative…

He scrubbed at the whiskers on his cheek. "Harriet Young was a good friend of my mother's and had apparently been recently released from hospital after surgery. My mother said she was going to look after her for a couple of days until the woman's older son could fly down from Brisbane. Dad didn't think too much of it. He knew Harriet had undergone surgery for '"women's problems"' as he put it. The only thing was that Harriet lived in Northbridge, a long way from the Hunter Valley."

"Did anyone speak to her afterward to find out why your mother wasn't with her there?"

"No. Not as far as I know. We were all too traumatized.

None of us were thinking straight. I was only eighteen. My younger brother was only fifteen. We were in shock. Plus, we believed Uncle Henry. He'd never given us a reason not to."

"Were any of you interviewed by the police at the time?"

"No. Except Dad. He was the one they informed about Mom's death. Dad was the one who told the rest of us."

"How many of you are there?"

"I have an older brother and a younger brother. And I just found out I have a half-sister."

Declan merely raised a single dark eyebrow. Noah flushed. "S-Sophia. She's… She's my dad's daughter to…Elizabeth Craigdon." He finished in a rush and stared hard at the floor, willing his embarrassment to cease.

Declan frowned. "Elizabeth Craigdon? Isn't she—?"

"Yes. My aunt. Married to Henry Craigdon."

Declan responded with a low whistle. "Wow. And I thought my family was complicated!" He grinned and Noah slowly grinned back, relieved the awkward moment had passed.

Declan returned his attention to the police report. "According to this, your mother wasn't wearing a seatbelt. She was thrown through the windscreen and died from severe head trauma at the scene."

"Is that supported by the autopsy report?" Noah asked.

Declan flicked through the papers and came up with nothing. "It isn't here."

Noah frowned. "The matter would have been automatically referred to the coroner because of the death. There would have been an autopsy."

"I'm not saying there wasn't one. I'm only saying it hasn't been included in the police file."

"I'm going to request a copy of the autopsy report. I want to get a clearer picture of how my mother died."

"Fair enough."

Once again, Declan referred to the police report. "It says

here that mandatory drug and alcohol tests were performed on the driver at the Maitland Police Station. The results were negative."

Noah felt a momentary surge of relief. At the same time, he wondered why John Hassad had lied to his daughter.

"So it appears John Hassad wasn't telling the truth after all," Declan mused, voicing Noah's thoughts.

"Seems so," Noah agreed, though the feeling of foreboding in his chest hadn't eased. "I guess the negative test results explain why we were never told my uncle was drunk." A moment later, he shook his head, baffled. "John Hassad lied. The question is, why? What did he have to gain?"

Just another mystery I have to unravel…

Declan continued with the report. "Apparently the driver indicated he'd swerved to miss a kangaroo. He lost control and hit a tree."

Noah frowned. "Swerving to avoid an animal is contrary to traffic laws and involves criminality. Why weren't any charges laid?"

Declan shrugged. "It looks like the matter was deemed to be an accident where no fault was attributable to the driver and the case was closed. There's no indication whether a civil suit was instigated by your family. Do you have any information on that?"

"No. The family didn't sue."

And that was that.

Declan gathered the scattered papers into a pile and replaced them in the file. "Where to from here?" he asked.

Noah looked at him grimly. "I can't shake the feeling something's not right. We only have the word of the two police officers there that night that my uncle's results were negative. I'm still not convinced Hassad was lying. I get that he's far from squeaky clean, but the circumstances surrounding his conversation with his daughter need to be taken into account.

He had no reason to lie to her. On the other hand, you and I have seen countless times when a police officer's been tempted to stretch the truth. My gut's telling me there's more to this. I've learned to trust it."

Declan agreed. "So what do you suggest?"

"We need to talk to the two officers who were there that night."

"Who's first?"

Noah smiled without humor. "Might as well start with the man at the top."

"Beechwood?"

"Of course."

Declan groaned. "I thought you'd say that. Beechwood has a reputation for being a bit of a dick with an ego the size of Sydney Harbour. He's not going to welcome our intrusion."

Noah grinned, filled with anticipation. "Just the kind of interview I like to do."

"And yet you look like you couldn't even swat a fly," Declan mused.

Noah winked. "You're a decorated police officer. You should know better than to judge a book by its cover."

"I'll call and set up an appointment," Declan muttered, reaching for the phone.

As Ayla tackled the huge pile of letters in her in-tray, her thoughts kept returning to Noah. It had been five days since she'd met the sexy cop and she couldn't seem to get him off her mind. She still hadn't decided if she wanted to track him down. They hadn't exchanged numbers, but he wouldn't be hard to find. After all, he'd told her he worked for the LECC. They only had one head office in Sydney. It was in the city, about a thirty-minute drive away.

Did she want to track him down?

It would most certainly indicate her level of interest. Did she want to show her hand like that? But how else would she get to see him again? More importantly, did she even *want* to see him again?

At twenty-nine, she was well past the impulsiveness of youth, and she was also mature enough that she was past playing games. She liked him, was attracted to him. She enjoyed the short time she'd spent with him. She wanted to get to know him better. That should be all that mattered.

Decision made, she reached for the phone. At the same time, she tapped the keys on her keyboard and opened a search engine. She typed in the words "LECC" and was rewarded with their contact details. Before she could put her plan into action, the receptionist appeared before her, an expectant look on her face.

"Ayla, there are two investigators from the LECC waiting outside. They don't have an appointment, but they asked to see the commissioner."

Ayla stared up at the woman and her heart skipped a beat. *No, it can't be. Just a coincidence. That's all.*

Gathering her wits, she gave the receptionist a smile. "Send them in, Sarah. I'll see them now."

A few moments later, Sarah returned to Ayla's office. Behind her followed Noah Craigdon and another man, equally tall and broad-shouldered. Both men had that somber look about them that told her they meant business. This was no idle meet and greet.

With an effort, she got her pulse rate under control and offered them a bland smile. "Gentlemen. What can I do for you?"

It was the unfamiliar officer who stepped forward. "I'm Detective Declan Munro. This is Detective Noah Craigdon. We're here to see Commissioner Beechwood."

"What about?"

Noah cleared his throat. "We're looking into a traffic accident involving the death of Janelle Craigdon that happened ten years ago. The commissioner was the officer in charge of the investigation at the time."

His words echoed through her head. She was still trying to come to terms with the reality that the man who'd filled her thoughts since the previous Friday night was now standing before her. Then the import of what he'd said registered.

All of a sudden, she felt lightheaded. She recalled her boss mentioning the rumor that the LECC had started looking into the Craigdon MVA. Now two stern-faced investigators from the Internal Affairs department stood before her asking to see her boss. One of them was named Craigdon.

Oh, God. What if he's related to the deceased? What a cruel irony that would be…

She fought hard against the urge to plug Noah's name into a search engine and see what she could find. All of a sudden, it seemed imperative to know his connection to the case she'd tried so hard to forget. But now wasn't the time with the two detectives regarding her with a mixture of annoyance and impatience. She blinked hard and did her best to hide her discomfort.

"Ten years ago? Why the sudden interest?"

"Do you mind letting the commissioner know we're here?" Noah asked, neatly sidestepping her question. He gave her a level look. They both knew he had no obligation to reveal anything about an LECC investigation.

"O-of course."

Seeing him there, in his professional capacity, threw her off balance. Her normally unruffled demeanor deserted her. It was all she could do to remain calm and unaffected, particularly given she wasn't sure where he fit in with everything. For reasons of his own, Noah was also struggling. He lowered his gaze and shuffled his feet and then looked at her again.

Their gazes caught and held for what seemed like an eternity. She saw the questions in his eyes, but was helpless to answer them. When he finally looked away, she felt shaken, afraid, confused.

"I-I'll let him know you're here." With that she turned and headed straight for her boss' office.

As they waited for Ayla to return, Noah shot a surreptitious glance in Declan's direction, hoping his partner hadn't noticed the temporary shock that had surged through him the moment he'd spotted Ayla. She'd told him she was a cop. She hadn't told him she worked for the police commissioner. He needed a moment to adjust.

She looked different than the vivacious woman he'd met the previous Friday night. The woman with the long hair and sparkly, barely there outfit. Today she wore a tailored designer suit. The pale pink jacket was fitted. The matching skirt fell to just above her knees.

All perfectly sophisticated and proper. Nothing like the spontaneous, wild firecracker he'd danced with. Of course, her grace and poise were just as evident in the suit as it had been in the nightclub, but that's where the similarity ended. Instead of her long hair loose and flowing, it was tucked into a neat bun that sat on the back of her neck and secured with pins. There wasn't a hair out of place.

When Ayla returned, her expression looked decidedly strained. Noah couldn't help but wonder what effect news of their arrival had had on the commissioner. Surely he had to wonder why the LECC had chosen to investigate such an old case. No doubt he'd pester them with questions.

"Commissioner Beechwood will see you now," Ayla said tightly and then turned and led the way back to Beechwood's office.

She opened the door and stepped back to allow them to enter then pulled the door closed behind them. The office was large and airy. It was fitted out with rich wood paneling and large glass windows. Sunshine poured through the window behind the commissioner's head.

The walls were decorated with several paintings in gilded frames. Next to them were similarly framed citations and awards, including one where the commissioner had been delivered the keys to the city of Parramatta. A floor-to-ceiling bookcase overflowed with books and smaller framed pictures along with other knickknacks and collectibles lined the shelves.

Beechwood greeted them with forced civility, but they'd expected that. No one wanted a visit from the LECC, particularly when it involved opening an investigation into one of their old cases. The commissioner indicated they take a seat on the studded leather couch that matched the style of the seat behind his desk. Noah and Declan did as they were asked.

"Gentlemen, my chief of staff tells me you're here about the Craigdon investigation."

Declan nodded. "Yes."

The commissioner nodded. "I must say, I'm surprised. What would you want with that old matter? It was an open-and-shut case."

"So you remember it?" Noah asked.

Beechwood shrugged. "Not in any great detail, but I remember enough to know there was nothing untoward about it."

Noah and Declan shared a glance, but neither man commented. Instead, Noah asked, "Do you remember who worked that investigation with you?"

The commissioner screwed up his face in thought. "I think it was Joe Bettino. He was a young sergeant, still wet behind the ears. If I recall correctly, Maitland was his first country posting." He smiled fondly.

"Where can we find him?" Declan asked.

Beechwood paused. "I don't know. We lost touch some time ago." His tone was dismissive. Then he stood and moved around his desk. "I'm sure you can appreciate how busy I am. It was nice meeting the two of you. I wish I could help you out with Bettino, but I haven't seen the man for almost a decade."

It was obvious the meeting was over. Noah and Declan stood. Noah pulled out a business card and offered it to Beechwood.

"If you remember anything you think might help us, give us a call."

The commissioner took the card and merely offered him a tight smile.

On the way out, Noah couldn't help but look toward Ayla. She sat upright behind her desk, her gaze fixed on the computer screen in front of her. He tried to catch her eye, offered her a brief wave but she either didn't see him or deliberately ignored him. The stab of disappointment was almost overwhelming.

⌒

Ayla stared at her screen and pretended to tap away at her keyboard until Noah and his partner had left. She was trembling with fear. Two officers from the LECC had arrived on her doorstep. Albeit, they appeared to have the commissioner in their sights, but what if they dug deeper? Discovered the truth? It would be the end of her.

While the investigators had been occupied with the commissioner, she'd searched for Noah online. Though he had no presence on any of the social media channels she tried, there was the odd mention of him in the social pages in connection with his more prominent relatives, the family of the late Henry Craigdon. His uncle. What was worse, she'd found an old newspaper article that made brief mention of the car accident Henry had been involved in that had resulted in the death of his brother's wife. *Janelle Craigdon.* Noah's mother.

Her vision darkened. Noise filled her head, blocking out everything else around her. She sat frozen in her chair.

This is a nightmare…

She couldn't believe her past was coming back to haunt her. She'd worked so hard to keep it buried. She thought it would stay that way forever.

Most people assumed she'd slept her way to the top. She was the youngest chief of staff ever to hold the position. Most people were in their late-thirties—even older—before they could be considered for such an important role.

She couldn't care less what people thought of her morals. How she got to where she was now was so much worse than performing sexual favors for her superiors. She dreaded anyone finding out the truth.

Chapter Four

*E*lizabeth was grateful for the large umbrella that shaded the table where she sat at the outdoor café half a block from the Sydney Harbour Hospital. She'd arranged to meet Isabella and by some small miracle, her daughter had managed to juggle her schedule.

In between her work as a surgeon, her recent engagement and plans to move to Queensland to be closer to her fiancé, it had been hard to pin Isabella down. But Elizabeth had finally managed to accomplish it and she couldn't wait to see her daughter again and catch up over coffee. Particularly since Isabella had let mention over the phone the night before that she and Raine had gotten engaged. Elizabeth couldn't wait to hear all the details.

They normally caught up at the café inside the hospital, but the early January day was so perfect in all its summer glory, Elizabeth had opted for outside. With the sun now beating hot through the umbrella, she thought she might regret her decision.

Elizabeth checked her watch. It was a few minutes past the appointed meeting time. Still, it wasn't unusual for Issy to be late. Especially while she was at work. Dealing with sick patients was her priority and sometimes taking her break got pushed a long way down the list. Elizabeth hoped this wasn't one of those times. She checked her phone for messages, just in case. There was nothing.

When she looked up again, Isabella had materialized among the crowd of pedestrians heading to lunch. She strode down the footpath toward the café, oblivious to the appreciative glances she drew from those around her. She'd ditched her white lab coat and was dressed in an expensive-looking, short, black fitted skirt and pale blue, silk blouse, together with oversized designer sunglasses and four-inch stilettos. She looked every inch the sassy, successful, wealthy young woman she was. At first glance, she could be mistaken for a sophisticated model with attitude. Only Elizabeth knew how kind and generous and disarming her daughter could be. She was so proud of all Isabella had achieved.

"Mom! How are you?" Isabella greeted her with a smile and a kiss on the cheek.

Elizabeth stood and gave her daughter a hug. "Congratulations! Another wedding to plan. I do so love a good wedding." She held her daughter away from her. "You're looking well. Positively glowing. Being engaged agrees with you."

Issy's smile widened as the two of them took their seats. She held her hand out for her mother to see. A two-caret solitaire diamond on a plain gold band adorned Issy's ring finger.

"Oh, darling! It's gorgeous! I'm so thrilled for you and Raine!"

Isabella looked down at the ring and grinned. "Thank you, Mom. Raine chose the ring himself."

"Well, he outdid himself. That man always had good taste."

Issy chuckled. "You're right. He chose me, didn't he?"

They laughed together. Elizabeth was filled with relief. They'd all had a tough year since the death of Issy's father. It was nice to see her so happy.

A waitress appeared and took their orders. As soon as she'd departed, Elizabeth leaned over and covered her daughter's hand with hers.

"I want to hear all about the proposal. Were there roses? Champagne? Did he get down on one knee?"

Isabella shook her head and smiled. "Mom! You're worse than Sophia! When I called her last night with the news, she refused to let me go until she had every last detail."

"We're just so happy for you, Issy. And excited. Can you blame us? I didn't get to hear any of the details when Sophia and Jarrod got engaged. It was all I could do to prise out of her the reasons for her hasty marriage. Even then, she didn't tell me the truth. I had to get that from Jarrod."

"He's a good man," Issy agreed.

"The best. So right for Sophia. Like you and Raine. I never met a couple more suited to each other."

Issy pulled a face. Elizabeth frowned in alarm. "What is it, honey? What did I say?"

"Nothing, Mom. Raine's great. He's perfect. But his life's in Brisbane. I… I'm not sure I want to leave Sydney."

Elizabeth stared at her daughter in concern. "But… You love each other. You're meant to be together."

Isabella sighed and rested her chin in her hand. "I know, Mom. And I love Raine so much it kills me to think like this. But I'm a Sydney girl. Everyone in my family lives here. I've never lived in another city. And Brisbane…" She gave a little shudder. "It's just not the same."

Elizabeth sat forward and once again covered her daughter's hand. She squeezed it reassuringly.

"I understand what you're saying, honey and you have very valid concerns. But your job is more mobile than Raine's. He has his company in Brisbane. His brother is his business partner. They've spent years building their reputation, gathering a list of clients. That kind of thing doesn't happen overnight and it takes so much work to achieve. Picking up roots and moving their business to Sydney would be a monumental task."

Issy nodded grudgingly. "I know. That's what's driving me crazy! I already have job offers from two hospitals in Brisbane. I could start work tomorrow if I wanted to. But a part of me wants Raine to love me enough to be willing to give up everything—including his business."

"Oh, honey! Of course he loves you enough. He's asked you to marry him!" Elizabeth shook her head slowly from side to side. "To expect him to give up his business… To move to Sydney and start again… It's too much."

Isabella's eyes flared with temper. Her jaw set in a determined line Elizabeth knew all too well.

"But, why Mom? Why should *I* be the one to give up a job I love, leave my family, my hometown? Why shouldn't it be *him?*"

Elizabeth sighed quietly. "I already told you, Issy. Your job's so much more mobile than Raine's. If he were a doctor or a nurse or a…a plumber… Then, of course you'd have so much more to work out. It wouldn't be a given that you'd be the one uprooting your life. But the fact is, he's none of those things. What he does can't just be picked up and plunked down somewhere else. Not without a lot of hard work and effort. It could take him years to establish himself here in Sydney." She looked at her daughter in earnest. "Do you really want that for him?"

Issy's shoulders slumped on a sigh. "No. Of course not. I don't know why this has suddenly become so important to me. Right from the start I knew that if things got serious between us, it would be me who'd make the move to another state."

She looked up and it broke Elizabeth's heart to see tears glistening in her daughter's eyes.

"I guess…with the engagement…things have become so real. I'm going to marry Raine. I'm going to be his wife. And that means leaving my family, my life behind and moving to Brisbane."

"Do you love him, Isabella?"

Her daughter stared at her. "More than I dreamed possible. I can't imagine life without him."

Relief flooded through Elizabeth. She smiled. "Then you have your answer. When you love someone like that, you'll do anything to keep them happy."

Isabella gave her a skeptical look. "Is that how it was with you and Daddy?"

Elizabeth closed her eyes briefly against a barrage of memories—good, bad and ugly. She managed a sad smile. "Sometimes. In the beginning, at least."

Their coffees arrived, along with the quiche and salad ordered by Isabella and the chicken and avocado sandwich Elizabeth had ordered. When the waitress left, Isabella sighed again.

"I can't believe so many of your children are willing to take such a leap of faith. Callum with Grace. Joel with Sheridan. Jett and Danielle. Nicholas and Harper. Sophia and Jarrod. And now me. All six of us, Mom. And yet we knew better than anyone that you and Daddy had fallen out of love a long time ago."

She pursed her lips in thought. "I wonder what it is that keeps us hoping for the best. Hoping that our love will last the distance when yours and Daddy's didn't. Are we being naïve? Foolish? Or are we that much in love we're prepared to throw common sense to the winds and give it our best shot?"

Elizabeth's heart clenched in pain at the cynicism on Isabella's face. Once again, she reached for her daughter's hand and squeezed it.

"Don't judge your relationship with Raine by what you know of ours. Though I loved your father very much, we were never a love match. I was twenty-seven, but in many respects I was as innocent as a young girl. I'd only had one other relationship before your father came along. I didn't have enough experience to know the difference between love and infatuation."

Isabella frowned. "But what about your parents? Your mother? Didn't she offer you any advice? Counsel against rushing in? She must have been able to see something didn't seem quite right."

Elizabeth compressed her lips against a rush of emotion and shook her head sadly. "No. My mother was so pleased I'd caught the eye of such a handsome, wealthy suitor. At twenty-seven, she'd been concerned I'd remain a spinster all my life. Especially after David."

The name fell off Elizabeth's lips. A split second later, she gasped. She couldn't believe she'd mentioned him. After all these years. And to her daughter, no less. She snuck a peak at Isabella, hoping there was a chance her daughter might not have heard. Isabella stared at her. Her mouth gaped, her eyes were wide with surprise. Elizabeth's heart sunk.

"Who's David?"

Isabella closed her mouth and then narrowed her gaze on her mother. "Who's David?" she asked again.

"He's no one. Someone I knew a long time ago."

"How come I've never heard of him?"

Elizabeth waved away her question as if it were of no consequence. "He was a boy I dated back when I was young. He was no one."

Isabella's curiosity was aroused. Until now, she'd never given any thought to her mother's life prior to meeting her father.

She sure as hell hadn't ever heard of any previous boyfriends. For her mother to mention him now must mean something.

She leaned closer. "Don't give me that, Mom. He's not 'no one.' If he was no one, he wouldn't have registered in your memory, especially not in the same discussion. We were talking about love."

Isabella watched while her mother took a bite of her sandwich. She seemed to take an interminable time to chew and swallow it. Then she reached for her coffee and took a sip. When she reached for her sandwich again, Isabella's patience came to an end.

"Mom! You can't just ignore me! Tell me! Who's David?"

Her mother stared down at her hands. Her shoulders slumped on a sigh. "He was my boyfriend. It was a long time ago."

Isabella shook her head, bewildered. "Why have I never heard about him?"

Her mother shrugged. "I was nineteen. A baby. He was my first love."

Isabella felt a rush of warmth. "Oh, Mom! Your first love! What was he like?"

Her mother's expression softened. A sad smile turned up her lips. "He was beautiful."

Isabella stared at her. "Oh, my God! Mom! You really were in love!"

Elizabeth nodded, her expression still filled with sadness and now there was regret. "Yes. I was."

"What happened?" Isabella asked, curious.

Elizabeth was silent for so long, Isabella was certain her mother wasn't going to answer. "Mom?" she prodded.

"Life happened. Things didn't work out."

"But—"

"It doesn't matter, Isabella. It was a long time ago. Long before I fell in love with your father."

Isabella frowned. Her mother's flippant answer felt unsatisfactory, like there was more to this story she wasn't saying. "But—"

"No, Isabella," her mother said firmly. "It's ancient history. Let's leave it in the past, where it belongs." Her mother reached for her coffee and took another sip. "Now, we were talking about you. Have you set a date for the wedding?"

Issy rolled her eyes, but dropped the subject. For all her curiosity, it was obvious her mother wasn't going to reveal any other secrets that day.

"No, Mom. No date yet. I figured I'd get settled in Brisbane before I set myself up for that kind of stress."

"Oh honey! It doesn't have to be stressful! I'll be here, ready and willing to do whatever you need me to do. I can be your wingman…wingwoman… Whatever…"

Isabella burst out laughing. "Thanks, Mom. I must admit, after watching you pull off Callum and Grace's wedding, I think you missed your calling. You could hang your shingle out any day as a wedding planner."

Elizabeth smiled with delight. "You think?"

"Yes, Mom. You were great. It was a wonderful celebration. I'm sure Callum and Grace feel the same way."

"I had a lot of fun, too. I can't wait to sit down with you and start making plans."

Isabella groaned and reached for her coffee. "Mom! I just told you! We don't even have a date yet. Please don't start calling me to talk about colors and fabrics and place settings. All I have time for right now is to concentrate on finishing up my time at the hospital and planning the next adventure in my life."

"Well at least let me throw you an engagement party."

Isabella nodded reluctantly. "Okay. An engagement party. But something small and intimate. Don't go over the top. Deal?"

"Deal."

Issy regarded her mother with suspicion. She'd capitulated far too easily.

"So, have you found a place to live?" her mother asked, deftly changing the subject.

Isabella shook her head. "Not yet. I'm moving into Raine's apartment in the short term. We're going to look for a place together. A place we can call our own."

"That's nice."

Isabella forked in a mouthful of salad. "Soph told me the two of you have patched things up. Is that right?"

"Yes."

Isabella smiled. "I'm glad. I hated it when the two of you were at odds with each other, no matter the cause."

Elizabeth grimaced. "Yes, well I certainly gave her cause."

"I'm not going to argue with that, Mom. But you have to stop beating yourself up about it. Sophia's at peace with what happened. You ought to accept that and move forward."

Elizabeth shot her a grateful look. "Thank you, Isabella. That's very kind of you."

They both returned their attention to their lunch. A few moments passed in silence before Isabella broke it once again.

"I'm still trying to come to terms with what Flynn told us about Daddy being drunk behind the wheel when Aunt Janelle was killed."

Elizabeth grimaced. "I still don't buy that. If he'd been drunk, he would have been charged. There's no doubt about it."

Isabella shot her a sideways glance. "Have you ever wondered why they were together that night, so far from home?"

Her mother didn't answer. Isabella tried again. "Do you think it's possible Aunt Janelle and Daddy were having an affair?"

Her mother's response was swift and adamant. "Archie's certain his wife never strayed."

Isabella started in surprise. "So, you've discussed it?"

Her mother nodded. "Yes. It's not the first time the thought occurred to me. When I raised it with Archie though, he vehemently denied it. There's no way his wife would have cheated on him."

"But *he* did," Isabella said.

Elizabeth's lips tightened. "Yes. But he's adamant she never knew. Right up until she died."

"So what do you think she was doing with Daddy out in the country at that time of night?"

"I don't know. Your father was vague on the details. He'd just been involved in a fatal crash. I thought his unwillingness to provide me with any kind of sensible explanation was because of the trauma of what had happened. Unintentional or not, he *had* caused Janelle's death."

Elizabeth sighed. Her expression grew distant. "It was an awful time, Issy. You can't imagine. We were all in shock, your father included. It wasn't until a few months afterward that I really began to think about it and then I began to wonder why. By then... Well what was the sense?"

Issy contemplated her mother in silence. When she didn't continue, Issy shook her head a little impatiently.

"Did you ever ask Daddy about it? About what he and Aunt Janelle were doing out there? He must have given you some kind of explanation. And if not you, Uncle Archie. Surely he would have had the same questions."

Her mother bit her lip and shook her head. "I asked your father about it, but he never gave me any kind of satisfactory explanation. He told me he was too upset to talk about it. That he wouldn't forget Janelle's dying face for as long as he lived. It was hard to press him for answers when he looked the way he did. Her death devastated him. He might not have been charged with any crime, but that didn't alleviate his guilt."

"I was sixteen at the time," Isabella said slowly. "I remember how awful it was. I felt so bad for my cousins."

"Yes. Logan was only fifteen when it happened. So sad."

"I wonder if that's one of the reasons he's so down on the world?" She glanced at her mother. She gave her a half-smile. "Despite all the times you and I have been at loggerheads, I couldn't imagine what it would be like not to have you around. And to lose you at fifteen…" She shuddered.

Elizabeth reached over and squeezed her hand. Tears glinted in her eyes. "I'm so glad you feel that way, honey. I love you so much, but we've had our differences over the years. I'm so relieved it hasn't affected the way you feel about me. That you'd miss me if I weren't around."

"Of course I'd miss you!" Isabella exclaimed. "Besides, our disagreements usually stemmed from something to do with Daddy. Back then, I wasn't aware of what was really going on. All I felt were the undertones and Daddy had a way of making it appear like everything was your fault. He made it easy for me to believe him."

Her voice caught on a lump of emotion. She was deeply ashamed of how harshly she'd judged her mother. She could only thank God her mother was so kind and generous and forgiving. Knowing what she did now, about how often her father threw her mother's love back in her face, Issy could barely comprehend the hurt he must have inflicted. Being in love herself, it was difficult to imagine how her mother had remained so strong. It only deepened the love and respect Issy felt for her.

Then her mother managed a smile. "Hey! Let's talk about something else. It's too nice of a day to ruin it with sad memories. You haven't forgotten about the ball this weekend, have you?"

Issy rolled her eyes. "Your annual summer ball for our first responders! How could I forget?"

"You'll be there, won't you?"

"At this stage, I can say yes. I'll try. But I'm on call. Anything can happen."

"I guess I'll have to be satisfied with that. Will Raine be coming?"

"Yes. He flew in from Brisbane last night. He's here for a few days."

Elizabeth smiled. "That's lovely. I'm so happy for you, Issy."

"Thanks, Mom."

"What about Nick and Harper? Isn't it wonderful to hear they're engaged?"

Issy nodded and smiled. "Yes. I can't believe he popped the question so quickly! She's his first serious girlfriend!"

Elizabeth nodded. "Yes. But he's twenty-five. Old enough to know his mind. And you've seen him and Harper together. They're perfect for each other."

"You're right. And I'm so pleased for him. For both of them." She sighed and finished her coffee. "I guess love really does make the world go round."

Elizabeth clapped her hands together. "Oh, we could have a double engagement party! Wouldn't that be fun? I could still keep it small. I promise."

Isabella merely rolled her eyes and groaned.

Chapter Five

With a couple of hours before the end of their shift, Noah and Declan decided to pay a visit to Joseph Bettino. According to the police report, Bettino had also been on duty the night Noah's mother died. He'd provided a statement of the incident that was almost a duplicate of the report made by Beechwood. Though Noah wasn't sure what he hoped to achieve by interviewing Bettino, it was something that needed to be done. The commissioner had been less than forthcoming with details of that night. Maybe they'd have more luck with Bettino.

Noah drove the unmarked sedan and followed the GPS directions to Bettino's house. He lived in a quiet neighborhood of similarly aged houses in an older part of town. The inner west suburb of Concord was filled with mostly red brick and tile houses that had been built in the fifties and sixties. A few had been gentrified. Bettino's wasn't one of them. Many of them, including Bettino's, still had the original, low red brick fence across the front boundary of the property.

Noah and Declan climbed out of the car. Noah flipped the latch on the old wrought iron gate. The lawn was overlong and dead-looking. A handful of drooping flowers fought for life amongst the weeds. A cracked and stained concrete path led to the front door.

Noah crossed the verandah and opened the screen door. It squeaked loudly in protest. He rapped his knuckles on the faded wooden door. The paint on the door was cracked and peeling. Two of the panels were broken. The air of general neglect was surprising, given Bettino was still a serving police officer, albeit one who'd been on stress leave for some time.

After waiting a few moments, Noah knocked again. This time, he heard the sound of someone moving down the hallway toward them. As the occupant drew closer, Noah heard the man cursing. An unshaven, unkempt Bettino squinted at them through the screen door. His clothes were dirty and hung off him. He'd obviously lost a lot of weight. Noah barely recognized him from the headshot that had been attached to the man's HR file.

"Whaddya want?" Bettino slurred. He looked at them through bloodshot eyes. His expression was surly.

Noah concealed his surprise. Bettino was clearly under the influence. Alcoholic fumes wafted toward them. Noah cleared his throat.

"Sergeant Joseph Bettino?"

"Who wants to know?" the man snarled.

Noah flashed his badge. "I'm Detective Noah Craigdon. This is my colleague, Detective Declan Munro. We're from the Law Enforcement Conduct Commission. We'd like to ask you a few questions."

"What the fuck is the Law Enforcement Conduct Commission?" Both Bettino's tone and manner had turned belligerent.

"Internal Affairs," Declan supplied.

Bettino's frown was ferocious. "Why the fuck would you want to talk to me?"

Noah glanced at Declan. Noah could tell his partner was thinking the same thing. Bettino was drunk and out of it. It might be better for them to leave their questions for another time, a time when Bettino might be sober and a bit more cooperative. A look of understanding passed between Noah and Declan. Noah turned back to Bettino.

"Listen, we need to talk to you about the death of Janelle Craigdon. I understand it happened a long time ago, but we need to talk to you just the same. When's a good time for you?"

It seemed to Noah that Bettino paled at the mention of Janelle. Then again, the man might have just been experiencing the effects of too much alcohol. A moment later, Bettino pushed open the screen door and vomited all over the verandah.

Declan stepped out of the way of the mess. His lip curled up in distaste. "We'll be back when you sober up, Bettino. Don't go anywhere."

Together, Noah and Declan turned their backs on Bettino and headed for the car. On their way back to the station, Noah stretched his arms above his head and groaned. "Well, that was a waste of time."

"Maybe. We'll see what he has to say when he sobers up."

"*If* he sobers up. Looks like he's been in that state for some time."

"Certainly looked that way. I wonder where his family is. Didn't you say he has a wife and kids?"

"Yeah. Who knows?"

Declan fell silent, concentrating on the late afternoon traffic.

"Thank God it's Friday," Noah muttered.

Declan shot him a glance and grinned. "You got any plans for the weekend?"

"As a matter of fact, I do. My aunt hosts an annual ball this time of year. It's specifically to raise money for our emergency services. All the first responders are invited." He looked at Declan and lifted an eyebrow in silent query. "How about you and Chloe come along? It'll be fun."

"When is it?"

"Tomorrow night. From seven. It's being held at Craigdon Manor. In Richmond."

Declan shook his head. "Saturday night? Nah, sorry. It's the twins' birthday. Chloe's invited twenty or so two- and three-year-olds over. The party starts at three. No doubt I'll have a thumping headache and be ready for bed by seven."

Noah shook his head and grinned. "The joys of fatherhood."

It was the end of another long working week. Ayla was relieved when five o'clock came around. Ever since the visit from the LECC officers, the commissioner had been out of sorts. He'd snapped at anyone who came within hearing distance of him, including Ayla. For all his pretense that Noah and his partner's visit hadn't rattled him, Ayla could tell her boss was on edge. That was enough to have worry gnaw at her insides.

It had taken a gargantuan effort to set her unease aside and accept a longstanding invitation from one of her police colleagues to join him for a drink. Like she'd told Noah, she'd known Detective Joel Craigdon for years, though she'd never asked about his family. Until now, she'd been oblivious to the fact Henry was Joel's father. There was nothing she could do about that now and she wasn't going to end her friendship with Joel because of that.

Though he was a year younger than she was, the two of them had come through the police academy together. That was a time when lifelong friendships were often formed. Her relationship with Joel certainly fit into that category. She hoped he might also prove to be a source of information. After all, he was Noah's cousin.

She spied him seated on a stool at the bar. He already had a beer in front of him. When he saw her coming toward him, he stood and enveloped her in a friendly hug.

"Great to see you, Rodriguez. It's been too long."

"You're right," she agreed and settled on the seat beside him.

"Can I get you a drink?" he asked.

"I'll have what you're having." She grinned.

"Still my kind of girl, I see," he teased.

She laughed. "I heard you got engaged."

Joel's teeth gleamed white against his black beard. "You heard right. Sheridan McClintock. She's the love of my life."

Watching the tender emotion fill his face as he mentioned his fiancée, Ayla felt a pang of jealousy. While she and Joel had only ever been friends and she treated him like a brother, she yearned to have a man feel as deeply about her as Joel obviously did about his fiancée.

"She's a lucky girl."

He shook his head. "Uh uh. *I'm* the lucky one. You know better than anyone what she has to put up with, being married to a cop."

The bartender set down a glass of beer in front of her. Ayla murmured her thanks. She lifted the glass and took a healthy swallow. The beer was cold and yeasty. The froth tickled her nose.

"*Ah*, that tastes so good."

Joel merely smiled and took another drink from his glass. Ayla eyed him with speculation, wondering if she were brave enough to broach the subject of Noah. The man had been constantly on her mind. She wanted to know more about him. Scratch that. She wanted to know everything.

Gathering her courage, she shot Joel another glance and then said as casually as she could manage, "You didn't tell me there was another cop in the Craigdon family."

Joel frowned. "Jett? You've known him for years."

"No, not Jett. Noah."

"Oh, Noah. He's my cousin."

"I see. Your cousin. So your father and his were—?"

"Brothers. Uncle Archie's younger than Dad by two years."

"Is he still alive?"

"Yes. Unlike my father, Uncle Archie's lived a pretty clean life. He doesn't drink to excess and doesn't smoke and generally takes good care of himself. He's sixty-three, but he looks much younger than that."

"And what about Noah's mother? Is she still alive?" Ayla asked, pretending ignorance.

Joel's expression sobered. "No. Aunt Janelle died in a tragic accident ten years ago. An MVA."

"Oh no!" Ayla exclaimed, her eyes widening in mock surprise. "What happened?"

Joel grimaced. "It wasn't long after we graduated from the Academy. Dad was driving. He hit a kangaroo and then collided with a tree. Aunt Janelle died at the scene."

Ayla continued the subterfuge and slowly shook her head. "Wow. That's awful. Noah must have still been a teenager."

"Yeah. We're the same age."

"How sad," she murmured.

"Yeah."

There was a moment of silence as both of them sipped their drinks. Then Joel nudged her in the side with his elbow.

"So, how did you meet Noah?"

Ayla fought to keep a blush from spreading across her cheeks. She busied herself with her glass and fumbled for the right words.

"Um… We… Ah… We met at The Pitt."

"You met at a nightclub? Wow, Rodriguez! I'm impressed."

She felt a spurt of irritation. "What the hell are you getting at, Craidgon? Don't you think I have a life outside of work?"

Joel held up his hands as if to ward her off. "Whoa! Easy! I didn't mean that. I was referring to Noah. I don't think I've ever heard of him going to a nightclub before. If you've met him, you must know how shy he is."

Ayla's momentary flash of irritation eased. She took another sip from her beer and thought about what Joel had said. It was true. Noah wasn't exactly the outgoing type, but she liked that about him. He was quiet and thoughtful and intelligent. And boy, could he dance.

Her pulse leaped at the memory of the two of them moving to the tango. It had been so much fun. It had also been arousing. Tall and broad-shouldered, with dark-blond hair and brown eyes that had gleamed with excitement, there was a lot to like. She knew the emotion had been caused by the dance, but she liked to think just a little of that excitement had been because of her. She certainly hadn't been immune to his attractiveness and she was sure he'd been just as aware of her.

So why haven't I called him? Why haven't I asked him out on a date?

She knew why. He was a Craigdon. Not only a Craigdon, but an officer from Internal Affairs and the son of the woman who still haunted Ayla's dreams. And nothing was going to change that.

"So, you met my cousin in a nightclub?"

Joel's words brought Ayla back to the present with a jolt. She looked up. An assessing gleam filled Joel's eyes. She tried not to grimace.

"Did the two of you hook up?"

Ayla blushed hotly. "No! Of course not!"

Joel continued to regard her with a teasing smile. "Are you sure?"

"Of course I'm sure. We…danced. That's all."

"Ah." Joel gave her a knowing look. "You danced. Well, that I can believe. Noah is one hell of a dancer."

Ayla nodded. "You're right. He said he took classes as a kid."

"Yeah. My aunt was into all that artsy-fartsy stuff. She insisted her sons take dance lessons, singing lessons, music lessons. I think Flynn even had a go at pottery. He sucked at that, but he did it for his mom. She was like that. Aunt Janelle. You wanted to please her."

"She sounds like a nice woman."

"She was. Gentle and soft spoken, but there was steel in her spine. Uncle Archie had turned his back on the family property development business and struck out on his own. He now has his own company. He designs and builds super yachts. In the beginning though, it was tough. They weren't as wealthy as we were. But Aunt Janelle was determined her sons would have the best. We all went to the same private school in Sydney and our families often took overseas holidays together. It was a fun time for a while."

"What made Noah decide to go into the police service?"

Joel shrugged. "I don't know. Maybe you could ask him." He winked.

Once again, Ayla fought back a blush. Burying her nose in her drink, she finished her beer and set the empty glass back on the bar.

Joel eyed her with a grin. "Thirsty, Rodriguez?"

Ayla rolled her eyes. "You wouldn't believe the week I've had. The commissioner's been driving us all insane."

"You can always be reassigned to a station. Do some *real* police work."

Ayla took the comment in the spirit it was intended. She punched Joel lightly on the arm. "I wouldn't want to crowd your style, Craigdon."

Joel laughed and ordered another round of drinks. While they were waiting for the beers to arrive, he asked, "So do you have any plans for the weekend?" He nudged her with his elbow and grinned. "Gonna see Noah again?"

Ayla managed a nonchalant shrug. "Who knows? Maybe I'll go back to The Pitt. The drinks aren't cheap, but they have great music there."

Joel gave her a look of speculation. "I take it you like to dance?"

Ayla grinned. "I *love* to dance. How about you?"

Joel looked horrified. "Hell, no. I have two left feet. Just ask Sheridan."

"What about you? Are you off this weekend?"

"Yeah. Two whole days. Sheridan and I are going hiking in the Blue Mountains. We're taking our dogs. They're not exactly built for hiking, but it should be fun. Then we're attending my mother's Emergency Services Ball."

"What's that all about?"

Joel sighed. "It's one of my mother's pet projects. She's always raising money for some worthwhile cause. Every year she holds a summer ball in the gardens of our family home for all the first responders. Police, firemen, health professionals. I guess with two sons and a nephew who are detectives and a daughter who's a doctor, she sees it as her way to support her family, along with the wider community."

"Sounds like fun. Why the long face?"

"No long face. It's just that Mom expects us all to be there—barring an emergency."

Ayla giggled. Joel grinned. "Hey! You should come!"

She shook her head in a rush of panic, unsure if she were ready to face the possibility of seeing Noah again. "No, I'm fine. I… I have a few things to do."

"Such as?" Joel demanded.

"Such as… Such as…cleaning out my wardrobe of… summer clothes. It won't be long before winter's on its way…" Her face flamed with embarrassment.

Joel gave her a knowing look. "It's all right, Rodriguez.

I won't remind you we're not even halfway through summer. Admit it. You have absolutely no plans whatsoever for the weekend."

His grin took the heat out of his words. She shrugged, feeling helpless. "Okay, you're right. I have absolutely no plans whatsoever for the weekend."

"So you have no reason not to accept my invitation." He shot her a cheeky look. "Who knows? Fred Astaire—I mean, Noah—might just pop in."

Ayla's face flamed. At the same time, her heart skipped a beat. Though the idea of coming face to face with Noah again filled her with panic, she couldn't deny the burst of excitement that flooded through her veins at the possibility. Seeing him again would also give her the chance to ask him about his investigation. It was imperative she know what he'd discovered. Not only for the commissioner's peace of mind, but for hers, too.

Chapter Six

yla felt distinctly out of her depth. Though Elizabeth Craigdon's black tie Emergency Services Ball was meant to highlight the important work done by the first responders, and more importantly, to raise much-needed funds for them, the extravagance of the affair made her feel awkward and out of place.

The crowd of emergency workers, more comfortable in uniforms than glad rags, had been transformed like Cinderella before the ball. In place of the regulation, government issued pants and shirts and boots were ball gowns made of chiffon, satin and lace in every color imaginable. The men looked similarly jazzy. Tuxedos, mostly black, and a variety of colored bow ties and cummerbunds complemented the bright array of dresses.

Uniformed waiters glided over the grass, holding platters of exotic canapés. Bar staff, carrying tray after tray of sparkling champagne, white wine, red wine and beer also made the rounds. Ayla found a quiet spot off to one side of the crowd and took a seat on a concrete bench. She looked around her.

The grounds themselves were stunning. Thousands of fairy lights filled the trees that dotted the acres of manicured lawn. The lights had been woven around the branches and gave the whole area a magical feeling. Neat flowerbeds bursting with color, hedges trimmed to amazing precision, breathtaking water features… The list went on.

Ayla had never found herself in such glamorous and overtly wealthy surroundings and she wasn't quite sure how to handle it. She'd known Joel since their days together at the Academy, but he'd been just another cadet. Cheeky, fun, good looking. He'd worked hard and was a real team player. And though she'd never felt any physical attraction, she'd enjoyed his company on many occasions.

In all the years she'd known him, he'd given no indication he'd come from a wealthy family. Of course that didn't change the way she felt about him. They were still good mates, like they'd always been. She stood and craned her neck above the crowd in an effort to spot him. She saw him surrounded by a group of men who looked quite a bit alike—she guessed they must be related. And then she recognized Sheridan McClintock.

Tall and slim and beautiful, Sheridan could have stepped off the pages of a fashion magazine. Like the late Henry Craigdon, her father had also been in property development. Though Ayla had never met any of the McClintocks, she knew enough from the social pages to know they were as wealthy as the Craigdons.

Joel and Sheridan… A heady mix.

"There you are!"

Ayla spun around and came face to face with her boss. He looked sloppily smart in a rented tuxedo and a poorly tied bow tie. She wasn't sure who'd invited him, but she was disappointed to see him there. As if spending five days a week in his company wasn't enough…

"H-hi, sir. How are you?"

The commissioner smiled benevolently. "Great. Just great. But please, we're at a party! Call me Kevin." He looked around him. "I have to give it to Elizabeth. She sure knows how to throw a celebration."

Ayla blinked in surprise. "I didn't realize you knew her."

He looked away and shifted his weight, burying his hands in his pockets. "Well, I can't say I *know* her. She's Henry's wife, of course."

The look he gave her was chilling in its intensity. Apprehension shivered down Ayla's spine. It was all she could do not to shudder. *As if I could ever forget Henry Craigdon...*

Determined not to show him how much he'd rattled her, she gave her boss a tight smile. "Yes, well she's outdone herself. The place looks amazing. I'm sure it'll be a fabulous party. Enjoy yourself, won't you?"

Without waiting for his reply, she turned and went to leave. He grabbed her by the arm and moved so he blocked her way.

Ayla gasped in both alarm and anger. "Kevin! What are you doing? Let go of me!"

With studied casualness, he dropped her arm, but the menacing look in his eyes didn't fade. She took a step back and came up hard against the bench she'd been seated on a few moments earlier. Beechwood leaned so close she could smell the alcohol on his breath.

"Just don't you forget about that comfortable job you have, Ayla. Keep your mouth shut and you'll continue to do well." He gave her another hard look. "You're a smart woman. I'm sure you understand."

With that, he turned and walked away. Shaken, Ayla took a moment to gather herself. This was the second time her boss had alluded to the fact her job might be under threat. The only thing she could think of was the Craigdon affair.

After all these years and all the efforts she'd made to put that night behind her, it had once again reared its ugly head. The problem was, there was no one she could go to about it. She'd made a conscious decision not to tell anyone about what had happened. How did she expect anyone to take her story seriously now?

The truth was, she was on her own. Beechwood had made himself clear. If she wanted to keep her job, she needed to maintain her silence. She wished she was brave enough to tell him to stick his job up his ass, but that would be foolish. She had no trust fund or generous inheritance. She needed her salary to make ends meet. She supposed she could always get another job, but if the commissioner chose to be vindictive, he could put an end to her career in the police force. She'd be forced to start again.

Recalling Beechwood's smug expression right before he walked away infuriated her all over again. His arrogance incensed her, but she understood where it came from. For ten years she'd kept her mouth shut. Why wouldn't he expect she'd keep silent for another decade…or more?

Drawing in a few deep breaths, Ayla did her best to get control of herself, but the fear and panic coursing through her veins still remained.

I need a drink… Something to calm my nerves…

With that thought in mind, she hurried away as fast as her stilettos would allow her across the deep and fertile grass. Her pulse still raced. Her heart still thumped. With her head down, she strode toward the crowd and plowed straight into Noah.

She cried out in surprise. "Oh, my goodness! I'm so sorry!"

"Whoa!" Noah held a bottle of beer in his hand. Thankfully, he managed to avoid spilling it all over them. And then he smiled. Broadly.

Her heart flipped over. He was so gorgeous. His dark blond hair was slightly damp, like he'd not long ago stepped out of the shower. His eyes were liquid chocolate. A sensual mouth, strong jaw, broad chest. Even his black-rimmed glasses were adorable.

Oh, God. Why does he have to be related to Janelle Craigdon…?

Realizing she was staring, she hurriedly cast around for something to say. "Um, hi. It's… It's good to see you again."

His gaze raked over her black dress. It was a dress she loved to tango in. The top half of the bodice was sheer, skimming over the tops of her breasts. It carried over to the short sleeves. The rest of the dress was satin. It clung to her body like a second skin and ended above her knees in a flourish of ruffles cut on the diagonal. It was far from new, but it fit her well and always made her feel sexy and confident.

When Noah's gaze once again met hers, he looked flushed. "It's good to see you too," he finally responded. "I didn't expect you to be among the party goers."

She looked away, feeling unaccountably nervous. On the dance floor, she was the most confident person in the room, but in the presence of a man who made her heart beat faster, she felt awkward and tongue-tied.

"Thank you. I met up with your cousin, Joel, a few days ago. He invited me along."

"Well, I'm glad he did. It's lovely to see you again." Once again, he shot her an adorable smile. Predictably, her stomach jiggled with another rush of nerves.

He looked gorgeous in a black tux with a pristine white shirt and black satin bow tie. The well-cut jacket only emphasized his broad shoulders that tapered down into slim hips. Ayla looked around for a drink. If she was going to be subject to the full force of Noah Craigdon's charm, she needed to fortify herself with alcohol.

A passing waiter came to the rescue. She reached for a glass of champagne and murmured her thanks. Taking a healthy mouthful, she gave Noah another smile.

"Who'd have thought that out of a city of five million people I'd know some of your family? You and Joel and Jett. How many more are there?"

"Quite a few more, actually. I only have two brothers, but

Uncle Henry fathered seven children. The whole family is here tonight. You can meet as many of them as you like. There are also any number of first responders—doctors, nurses, police, paramedics, firefighters. No one's been left off the list. My aunt has even invited employees from Craigdon Enterprises and volunteers from Jennifer's Kitchen."

She raised an eyebrow in silent question. "Jennifer's Kitchen? What's that?"

"It's a soup kitchen in the inner city. It was started by Jennifer Rawlings back in the nineties. It's now been taken over by my cousin, Callum and his wife, Grace. He's invested millions of his own money into redeveloping the site to expand the kitchen and include affordable housing apartments above it. Grace manages the kitchen."

Ayla listened politely, but remained silent. What she really wanted to know was how Noah was going with his investigation. She could only assume he hadn't yet discovered what had really gone on that night and the part she'd played in it. Still, it didn't hurt to make sure.

Plastering a casual smile on her lips she touched him lightly on the arm. He jerked away as if she'd burned him. She blushed and tried to ignore the tingle that ran across her fingers.

"How's your investigation? Have you made any progress?"

Noah's expression went blank. He gave her a tight smile. He mumbled a vague response about things going well and then abruptly changed the subject.

Ayla's cheeks burned hotter. Questioning him about an active investigation was unethical, particularly when it involved her boss. She wished she'd kept her mouth shut. Now Noah looked at her with vague suspicion and that's the last thing she'd wanted.

In an effort to distract his attention from her gaffe, she grabbed him by the arm once again.

"Listen! They're playing the tango. Let's dance."

Not giving him a chance to refuse, she dragged him toward the makeshift dance floor where couples had already gathered, including Joel and Sheridan. She gave Joel a nod of acknowledgement and he winked in response. She ducked her head.

And then the music took over and she moved into Noah's arms. They danced the intricate steps of the tango as one—graceful, effortless... As if they'd been dancing together for years. Soon the other couples moved away, giving them the dance floor. Oblivious to the curious onlookers, Ayla lost herself in the rhythm of the music and the warmth and strength of Noah's arms.

Noah's body pulsed with excitement. His cock was hard with desire. To hold Ayla in his arms again was agony and ecstasy, all thrown into one. Her body twisted and turned and spun in response to the music and the dance. He held her close, strong and supportive, loving the feel of her in his arms.

He had been surprised when she'd probed him for information regarding his investigation. It could have been merely polite conversation, but he sensed there was more behind her question than that. She knew firsthand of his interest in the commissioner.

Is she running interference for him? Has her boss asked her to find out what she can?

Noah had spied her talking with the commissioner earlier. He had no way of knowing what they'd spoken about, but the truth was, he barely knew Ayla Rodriguez. Despite his wild attraction to the woman in his arms, he had no idea where her true loyalties lay. Better to take a figurative step back and put some distance between them. Though she was only peripherally involved in his investigation, it would probably be wise to stay well away from her.

With that thought in mind, and ignoring the sharp stab of disappointment, when the music came to an end and they both stood panting from exertion, Noah merely inclined his head and politely thanked her for the dance, then turned and melted into the crowd.

Christopher Barrington was restless. He didn't know why the hell he kept turning up at these over-the-top family functions, but he couldn't seem to help himself. He justified his presence by recalling the main purpose of the evening was a fundraiser for the first responders—most definitely a worthy cause. He'd already made a substantial bid on an item in the silent auction.

So why am I still here?

Usually he couldn't stand hobnobbing with the Craigdons. His half-brothers and sisters, their respective husbands and wives and fiancées. Hell, it seemed nearly every one of them had found their soul mates and fallen in love.

It made him sick. All that love and togetherness. As usual, he was about the only one who'd missed out. Of course there was still Logan, looking glum and utterly ill at ease. Christopher might be unlucky in love, but at least he hadn't been dumped for another woman.

Ouch.

He could understand the surly air that followed Logan wherever he went. The poor guy had done it tough these past few years. First he was involved in a serious accident that put an end to his promising professional sailing career and next he was passed over by the love of his life. Even Christopher could drum up some sympathy for that.

The truth was, he *wanted* to be part of this big loving family. He wanted to be accepted by them without question, without reservation. As the illegitimate son of the late Henry

Craigdon, Christopher had never felt like he fit in. Despite Elizabeth's cordial attitude toward him, it didn't make up for the fact his father never saw fit to recognize him as his son. That kind of rejection hurt. It bit deep. And forty years down the track, the pain hadn't lessened one bit.

In more sober moments, Christopher was annoyed by how much he still yearned for the love and acceptance of his father. It was ridiculous. Henry was dead. He could never give Christopher what he wanted—what he needed. It was almost a year since the funeral. It was way past time to set those old hurts aside and get on with his life.

If only it were that easy...

The sound of the band playing a piece of music with a strong syncopated beat pulled Christopher out of his depressing thoughts. He looked across the wide expanse of lawn to where a makeshift dance floor had been set up. Noah was dancing up a storm with a woman Christopher hadn't met. She was short and petite, but what she lacked in size, she made up for in style and movement. Together, their feet moved in unison, following the intricate steps of some kind of Latin dance. The ruffles around the hem of her short black dress flared with each enticing swing of her hips. She looked at Noah like he was a scrumptious treat, totally absorbed in him and the dance. Noah looked equally smitten.

Interesting...

Noah didn't exactly have a reputation for being fast with women. What Christopher knew of his half-cousin was that the man was inordinately shy. Now it was like déjà vu for Christopher. The last formal family gathering had been Callum and Grace's wedding. Noah had brought along Jayde Hassad. Unfortunately for Noah, Jayde had ended up falling for his older brother. Flynn and Jayde were now apparently madly in love. Christopher couldn't help but wonder how Noah felt about that.

Then again, if the way they moved as one on the dance floor was anything to go by, it looked like young Noah might have moved on. And boy, had he moved on with a stunner.

The woman had rich golden skin and dark coloring. She looked like she had Spanish heritage—maybe something even more exotic—like Cuban or Colombian. Her thick hair hung down her back in shiny black waves. It was held off her face with a jewel-encrusted barrette that glinted when it caught the lights. Her generous breasts bounced inside her sheer bodice. Even from a distance, Christopher could see her eyes were sparkling and her lips were a shiny red. She danced the Latin dance like she'd been born doing it. And maybe she had.

Surprisingly, Noah kept up. Christopher seemed to recall something about Noah taking dance classes when he was a kid. They'd certainly paid off.

Intrigued, Christopher waited for the dance to come to an end. He wanted to meet Noah's mystery woman and find out who she was. When the music finished, he started forward, intent on forcing Noah into making an introduction. To his surprise, Noah merely smiled at the woman and spoke a few words then turned and left her standing there all alone.

Seizing his opportunity, Christopher glided close and came up behind her. He touched her lightly on the elbow to get her attention. She spun on her heel and frowned.

"Do I know you?"

Christopher spread his arms wide and gave her his most disarming smile. "Christopher Barrington, at your service."

She looked at him blankly.

"I'm Noah's half-cousin. Henry Craigdon was my father."

Her face cleared a little. "Oh, I see."

"And you are?"

"Ayla. Ayla Rodriguez."

He inclined his head. "It's nice to meet you, Ayla." The music started again. "Would you care to dance?"

She looked like she was about to turn him down. He stepped forward and smoothly took her in his arms. Though he wasn't the caliber of dancer that Noah was, he could certainly hold his own. To his relief, the music was a simple waltz and he began to lead the woman around the dance floor.

Her initial surprise appeared to recede. He felt her relax in his arms. She fell into the gentle rhythm of the waltz and matched his steps with grace and dexterity. Christopher found himself commenting on her ability.

"You're a good dancer. Do you teach?"

She laughed. "No. Dancing's just a hobby, something I like to do to relax."

"You've obviously taken lessons."

She laughed again. "Not as such. I was born in Uruguay. Dancing—especially Latin dancing—is in my blood."

"I see. That explains your coloring."

She touched a hand to her face almost reflexively, but said nothing.

"So, if you're not a dance instructor, what do you do?"

She smiled. "I'm a cop."

His eyebrows rose reflexively in surprise. "A cop? I would never have guessed."

This time she chuckled. "Yes. Well you've only seen me in my glad rags."

He guessed that was her connection to Noah. Perhaps they worked together. He asked her as much.

To his surprise, she shook her head. "No. I work for the police commissioner. I'm his chief of staff."

Once again, Christopher was filled with surprise. She looked no older than thirty. Incredibly young for someone to hold such an important, high-ranking position. His mind went into overdrive.

What's she done to be elevated to such a lofty position so early in her career?

All sorts of nefarious scenarios instantly ran through his head. Either she knew people in high places or there was some other reason for her speedy ascension through the ranks. Already his instincts were humming. Something wasn't right. There was no way little Ayla could have achieved such a promotion on her merits. No, it was obvious someone owed her—or someone close to her—a favor. He was determined to find out who and what that was.

Ayla saw the calculating glint in Christopher's bright green eyes and felt a frisson of alarm. She wasn't sure what she'd said to trigger his suspicion, but it was obvious something had. He'd gone from looking at her with a lazy kind of interest to a pointed and intense regard. Most likely it was the mention of her position in the commissioner's office. Christopher wasn't the first person to react with curiosity and surprise. She'd gotten used to the reaction, but knowing Christopher was related to the Craigdons filled her with disquiet.

She hadn't imagined Christopher's sudden change in attitude. It might be best if she called it a night. The last thing she wanted was to have people asking questions about her connection to the police commissioner and how exactly she'd made it all the way to his office.

Mind made up, she made her excuses to Christopher and hurried away into the night.

Chapter Seven

It was way past late. The half-moon was high in the sky when Noah let himself into his apartment overlooking Manly Beach. Grabbing a beer from out of the fridge, he opened the sliding door and crossed the balcony. He leaned his elbows on the railing, took a sip from his drink and sighed.

Aunt Elizabeth's ball had been a resounding success. More than fifty thousand dollars had been raised. He'd caught up with plenty of family members, including Flynn and Jayde. The two of them looked so happy together. No doubt another engagement was in the wings. He genuinely wished them all the best.

Hours later, he was still feeling restless and discontent and it had everything to do with Ayla.

He'd been disappointed to discover she'd left the ball early. He hadn't even been given a chance to say goodbye. He wondered why she'd departed before the night was halfway through. Was she feeling ill? In pain? Had she been offended by the way they'd parted? He wished he knew.

The truth was, he couldn't stop thinking about her. She was on his mind every second of the day. It was starting to affect his concentration and his sleep and after seeing her again he knew that wasn't going away any time soon.

At the party, it seemed like a good idea to keep some distance between them, but the more he thought about it, the more he wanted to discard that idea. So, she was employed by the commissioner. A man who'd been the officer in charge of the investigation into the accident that had killed Noah's mother. She'd simply asked a basic question that made him uncomfortable and he'd responded by distancing. That didn't mean it had anything to do with Ayla. In fact, there really wasn't any reason why he couldn't see her. She had nothing to do with his investigation, apart from being a contact point for the commissioner.

He smiled as the decision settled inside him. A surge of excitement and anticipation flooded through his veins.

I'm going to ask Superintendent Ayla Rodriguez out on a date…

"Yes!" He punched the air in a show of triumph. He couldn't get the grin off his face. All he had to do was call her and hope like hell she said yes…

Ayla did her best to concentrate on the words beneath the commissioner's harsh tones as they sounded in her ears through the headphones. He'd dictated several urgent memos and she was busying transcribing them. Normally this kind of work was done by the commissioner's executive assistant, but in this case, the memos contained highly sensitive information and he'd delegated the task to her. Though he'd ordered her to get the finished documents back to him pronto, her mind kept straying to the Craigdon ball. In particular, to Noah.

He was undeniably sexy. Even more so on the dance floor. The way he moved, felt the beat… Lessons notwithstanding, he was a natural. He was also so nice. He seemed so genuine. She couldn't deny her attraction. And that was the problem.

He was looking into the very same investigation that still filled her with dread whenever she was forced to think about it.

Worse still, he was related to the victim. Surely that gave him additional incentive to discover the truth.

Over the years, she'd managed to push what had happened to the deepest recesses of her mind, but she'd never forgotten. Now the commissioner had taken it upon himself to remind her. There was no doubt her job was on the line if she breached her silence. The truth was, she needed to proceed with caution where Noah was concerned, but the very thought of holding herself back from him made her want to cry out in protest.

She couldn't deny she really wanted to see him again and spend more time with him. She wanted to get to know him better, and not just on the dance floor. It had been a long time since she'd been in a relationship. Years, in fact. She'd never been one to jump from one relationship to another and though she dated casually, she was yet to find "the one."

But at twenty-nine, she was far from a spring chicken. She longed to find someone to fall in love with. Someone to share her deepest secrets, her joys, her fears. Someone who'd have her back and support her, no matter what. Someone who wanted to stick around for the long haul.

Could that someone be Noah?

The phone at Ayla's elbow pealed, making her jump. She paused the dictation and answered the call.

"Police Commissioner's office. This is Ayla."

"Ayla. It's Noah."

At the sound of his deep voice, her heart skipped a beat. She drew in a swift breath in an effort to control her response.

"Noah. What can I do for you?"

"You left the ball early. I didn't get to say goodbye."

Though his tone held no accusation, she blushed all the same. The truth was, she'd wanted to seek him out and bid him goodnight, maybe even tease an explanation out of him for the abrupt way they'd parted, but she'd also been keen to get out of there in case she ran into Christopher again. The way he'd looked at her, like he could see straight through her. It was all she'd been able to do, to contain her panic.

She cleared her throat and cast around for a response. "Yes. Well, I'm sorry. I… I had a headache," she lied.

"Too bad."

And then she came out with something a little closer to the truth "Of course, after the way you left me on the dance floor… I wasn't sure if you wanted anything more to do with me."

"Yes, well… I'm sorry about that."

He offered nothing more by way of explanation. An awkward silence fell between them. Ayla was the first to break it. "Um, Noah? Is there something I can do for you? Would you like to speak with the commissioner?"

"N-no. The thing is… I… I was wondering if you'd like to go to dinner with me."

His words took her by surprise. She was immediately beset with doubts. His mother…. The investigation… Things could go awfully pear-shaped… Still, she couldn't deny the way her heart skipped a beat at the thought of spending quality time with him.

Isn't that what I want?

"Ayla?"

Heat swept across her cheeks as she realized he waited for her answer.

"Um…sure," she heard herself respond and then wondered what the hell she was doing.

"Great. I'll pick you up at seven."

Ayla reflexively shook her head. Things were moving too fast. "Tonight?"

"Are you free?"

"Yes. I… I guess so. But if you don't mind, I'll meet you there."

"Sure." Noah capitulated easily and gave her the name and address of an upmarket restaurant in the city. She took down the details and as she ended the call, she tried to ignore the flutter of nerves that filled her stomach.

I'm going to dinner with Noah Craigdon…

Once again, a little voice in her head warned her against falling for this man, but she steadfastly pushed it aside. She liked Noah. Really liked him. Okay, so things were… complicated. But she was looking down the barrel of thirty. She couldn't afford to let opportunities like this slip by. She might never get another opportunity to spend time with a man she found incredibly attractive and who she was quietly confident, liked her as much as she liked him. She just hoped neither of them would live to regret it.

The day dragged by. Noah lost count of the number of times he checked his watch. Finally he could stand it no longer. At 1645 hours, he shut down his computer and stuffed his briefcase with a handful of files. If his night went to plan, he wouldn't get a chance to read over them, but he wanted to be prepared, just in case.

He really liked Ayla and he thought she liked him, too. But he'd never been good at reading women. Hell, he'd never been good with women—full stop. From the moment she'd agreed to go out to dinner, his gut had been twisted with nerves. At one point he thought he might be sick. It was utterly ridiculous.

She's just a woman, Craigdon. Get a grip. If I don't, I'll risk winding up becoming a lonely old man with nothing but a dog for company…

Not that he had anything against dogs. He loved dogs, but they didn't exactly take the place of a loving woman.

He climbed on the Fireblade and started the engine. It roared to life. As he made his way across the harbor and joined the queue of traffic heading north-east toward Manly, his thoughts turned to his upcoming date. A fresh wave of nerves rushed through him. He momentarily tightened his grip on the handlebars.

What will we talk about? I should have told Declan. He could have given me some tips. We could have practiced…

He groaned. It was too late now. He was going to have to wing it and hope for the best. At least she should be impressed with the venue. He was taking Ayla to a popular five-star restaurant. It was normal for bookings to be made weeks in advance. Fortunately for Noah, the owner was the brother of a cop buddy of his and he'd managed to pull some strings.

His thoughts turned to his outfit. A tuxedo would probably be over the top. Besides, he'd worn that to the ball. It was still at the drycleaners. Maybe a nice lounge suit would be better. Yes. The light-gray one. And he'd team it with a blue shirt. No, the white one. Then he wouldn't be restricted with the choice of his tie. White went with everything.

He couldn't believe he was wasting so much time thinking about his wardrobe. Of all the dates he'd had in the past—and to be frank, there hadn't been that many—he couldn't remember spending time agonizing over what to wear. It went to show how important Ayla was to him. He wanted to make a good impression. No, scrap that. He wanted to blow her mind.

She'd already seen him in a tux and he was quietly confident she'd been impressed. Though she hadn't said anything outright, the look she'd leveled on him when she'd first run into him had been full of warmth and appreciation. He was sure he hadn't imagined that. And then she'd dragged him onto the dance floor and the magic between them had been unbelievably thrilling. He wanted to feel that again.

Easy, Craigdon… You barely know this woman… Remember Jayde? Not so long ago, you thought you were in love with her… And you didn't know her too well, either. Now she's with Flynn and you couldn't be happier for them…

It was true. He'd fallen hard for Jayde, was convinced he was in love with her. But it was only infatuation and when it became obvious she didn't feel the same way, he'd bowed out gracefully. No real harm done.

But Ayla was different.

Isn't she?

Yes! They'd had a connection right from the start. They shared a passion for dancing and he hadn't imagined the looks she'd thrown his way. Plus, he was more comfortable with her than he'd been with any other woman he'd been attracted to. That had to count for something.

Pushing the doubts and circular conversations out of his mind, he opened the throttle and began to weave in and out of the traffic. Anticipation built inside him with every mile he covered. When he finally pulled into his garage, his nerves were taut with excitement.

Calm down. I don't want to scare her off. It's a first date, not a proposal. Be cool…

Ayla concentrated hard to keep her hand steady as she applied the second coat of dark red lipstick. Nerves and anticipation jangled in her stomach. She'd chosen and discarded several outfits before she settled on the stretch-knit, crimson sheath dress. It hugged her curves. It also fell to just above her ankles and, along with her four-inch stilettos, made her feel taller. At five foot three in stockinged feet, she could do with every extra inch she could get.

She'd spent almost as much time on her hair. She'd started with an upswept style, but decided that looked too formal. Then she'd brushed the long waves out and left it loose. No, not formal enough. In the end, she'd gone with a loose bun, secured low on her neck. She left a few tendrils free to curl around her face.

At last she was satisfied with her appearance. A quick glance at the clock on her bedside table told her if she didn't hurry, she was going to be late. She tossed her lipstick, a tissue, her house keys and her credit card into a small beaded evening bag. Her hand hovered over the box of condoms she kept in her bedside drawer. It must have been more than a year since she'd used one.

Should I pack one, just in case?

Her heart skipped a beat at the thought of making love with Noah. She was sure it would be amazing. He seemed like that kind of guy. Kind and caring. Someone who would make sure she enjoyed the act as much as he did.

And then she decided against taking protection. Though she was undoubtedly attracted to Noah, she'd never been the kind of woman who slept with a guy on the first date and she wasn't about to start now. Besides, their relationship was complicated enough without bringing sex into it, especially this early in the proceedings. If things worked out the way she hoped, there would be plenty of time for that.

Decision made, she snapped her bag closed and headed out the door.

Ayla caught a taxi to the restaurant. On the way, she made a concerted effort to set aside her concerns about getting involved with Noah and was determined to enjoy the night. The doorman welcomed her and took her coat. She gave her name to the maître d' and with a murmur of acknowledgement, the man asked her to follow him. They wove through a maze of tables until he came to a stop beside one adjacent to a large window overlooking the harbor. Noah stood as she approached.

"Ayla. Y-you look lovely," he said and then blushed. He rushed to pull out her chair and almost tripped in the process. His blush deepened.

Oh, God. Can this guy get any more adorable?

It was obvious he was inexperienced with women. He appeared so far removed from the suave and confident men on the movies, or the ones she read about in romance novels. Men who were always in control of every situation, including the women who fell at their feet.

But that's what she found so appealing about Noah. He wasn't an alpha male. And yet, he was so incredibly attractive. Exactly the kind of man she was drawn to…

She spared him any further embarrassment by ignoring what had happened and merely thanked him and took her seat. Noah returned to the seat opposite and picked up the wine list. "Can I get you a drink?"

She nodded. "Thank you. I'll have a glass of Merlot." Noah signaled the waiter.

Ayla took the opportunity to study him. His hair was damp and messy, like it had been combed in a hurry with his fingers. She liked it. His pale-gray suit fit him well and though she preferred the tux, she wasn't disappointed with the way he looked.

Noah gave her order to the waiter and then asked for a beer. "So," he asked, turning back to her, "how was your day?"

"It was okay. Busy. Long." She grinned.

He grinned back at her and her belly flipped over. "I hear you. I thought the day would never end."

He stared at her and she stared back. Her heart thumped. Her throat went tight. For a while, she was at a loss for words. And then the moment was broken when the waiter reappeared with their drinks.

Ayla murmured her thanks and took a grateful sip. The warm, rich wine glided down her throat. She wasn't much of a drinker, especially on a work night, but she wasn't driving home and with her nerves playing havoc with her equilibrium, she felt the need to fortify herself with alcohol.

Perhaps I should have ordered a bottle? No, I don't want Noah to think I'm a lush. Not while I'm trying so hard to impress him…

It was her first time at the restaurant. Her police pay didn't normally extend to fancy places like this. And she definitely wasn't complaining. She loved to dine out. There was something exciting about dressing up and eating scrumptious food while sharing wine and good conversation. And now she got to do that with Noah.

Could it get any better?

Another smartly dressed waiter arrived to take their food orders. Ayla scanned the menu. It was hard for her to decide. Everything sounded so good.

Noah ordered the New York cut basted in a red wine jus and a side of steamed greens and baby potatoes with chives and sour cream. After much back and forth, Ayla finally decided on the stuffed chicken breast with cream cheese, avocado and pine nuts. She added a salad on the side.

After the waiter left, Noah picked up his glass. "I want to propose a toast," he said.

She smiled. "What are we toasting?"

Noah eyed her steadily. "To us."

The intensity in his gaze did funny things to her insides. She swallowed against a rush of nerves at the promise in his eyes. And then she managed to find her voice. "To us," she repeated and clinked her glass to his.

The conversation flowed freely, along with her glasses of wine. Noah restricted himself to just the single glass of beer. When Ayla asked why, he told her he'd ridden there. "I own a motorbike," he explained.

"You could always leave it here and catch a taxi home," she suggested with a cheeky wink.

He laughed. "Thanks for the suggestion, but I sank a fair bit of my inheritance into my bike and I'd rather find it in once piece in the morning."

"What kind of bike do you have?"

When he told her, she whistled, impressed. "That's one helluva nice bike."

He grinned with pleasure. "You're into bikes?"

"You bet. My father's a restorer. He taught me everything I know about bikes. He's been doing it for years. He tracks down vintage bikes from all over Australia and brings them back from the dead. He has a garage full of them. Much to my mother's disgust. She's always complaining there isn't any room to store anything else."

"He sounds like my kind of man."

Ayla nodded. "He'd like you," she said truthfully.

"Where do they live? Your parents?"

"Out a Camden. They have a few acres there."

"Enough room for more than one garage, I hope," he teased.

She laughed. Being with Noah felt so good, so easy. She'd never felt this way on a date before. Not fumbling around for topics of conversation, not wishing for the night to end. In fact, she hoped the night could go on forever.

Their meals arrived, along with another glass of wine. She took a sip and then set it aside and started in on her meal.

"Oh, yum. This is divine," she murmured after swallowing a mouthful of tender chicken.

Noah smiled. "I'm glad. The beef's pretty darned good, too."

They tended to their meals in silence. Ayla savored every bite. When she was finished, she sat back and patted her stomach.

"Oh, my goodness! That was so good! This place deserves every accolade it's received. No wonder it's been reviewed so well. I could eat here every night."

Noah smiled and regarded her with affection. "You're adorable."

She leaned forward and squeezed his forearm. "I think the same about you."

The air between them suddenly became charged as awareness *zinged* between them. Noah's arm felt warm and well-muscled, even beneath his jacket. She wanted to go on touching him, but forced herself to remove her hand. Casting around for something else to say, she snagged on his family without thinking.

"Tell me about your mother."

Noah blinked. For a moment, he looked slightly confused about the abrupt change of topic, but then his expression softened. He sat back in his seat.

"Her name was Janelle. She was wonderful. Warm and kind and loving. Soft spoken. She never got cross. Even when me and my brothers traipsed mud into the house, or dug up the lawn with our motorbikes, or the time we kicked a football and broke a huge pane of glass. Whenever we misbehaved, she'd call us into her sewing room and express her disappointment, but she never raised her voice. She definitely knew what she was doing. Her disappointment affected us more than a scolding ever did."

Ayla smiled softly. "She was a good mom."

Noah nodded. "The best."

"Joel told me she was killed in a car accident. How old were you when she died?"

"Eighteen."

Ayla's heart clenched with sympathy. "Way too young."

Noah's lips tightened. "Yes. I assume you know my current investigation relates to the death of my mother?"

Ayla managed a slight movement of her head that neither confirmed nor denied. To her relief, Noah continued.

"When she died, I was too young and too traumatized to know what questions to ask. I left that up to my father. I trusted him and the authorities to tell us the truth. We all did. But recently I came upon some information that caused me to wonder if we were too quick to accept the official version of events."

Ayla's heart pounded. Tension caught at her throat. Still, she forced herself to ask the question. "Do you think there was something awry with the original investigation?"

Noah merely shrugged. "That's what I intend to find out."

His tone was coolly dismissive. Knowing to push things any further would no doubt raise his suspicions, she changed the subject.

"What's your aunt like?"

Noah smiled. "She's strong and fierce. She's a warrior. Don't get me wrong," he added hurriedly, "I love my Aunt Elizabeth, but she can come across as rather stern at times."

"Unfortunately, I didn't get a chance to meet her at the ball."

He held her gaze and once again, the air between them felt charged. "I'm sure you'll get another chance. This isn't going to be the last time we go out together."

He sounded so certain there was nothing she could do but smile. Particularly when, a moment later his eyes widened and he blushed, as if suddenly becoming aware of what he'd said. And then she leaned over once again and asked, "Would you like to go dancing, Noah?"

Chapter Eight

Noah's belly swirled with nerves. Ayla walked so close beside him he caught the whiff of her exotic perfume every time the slight breeze lifted a few tendrils of hair that curled around her face. Twice their arms brushed and his heart stuttered with excitement. He'd never been so aware of a woman—or so turned on.

Her hand was so close. He wanted to reach for it and twine his fingers with hers.

Is that too forward? What would she think? What if she pulls away? I couldn't bear it if she did that…

And then they'd reached their destination. After all, The Pitt was only across the street from the restaurant. He'd missed his chance. Never mind. She'd invited him to dance. Soon he'd have her in his arms and his customary awkwardness around women would dissolve as he let the music do the talking.

"Here we are," she said and then smiled.

"B-back where it all began." He blushed.

She took his nervousness in stride, not even making a comment. He was filled with gratitude. Reaching for his hand as if it were of no consequence, she led him forward to join the short queue outside the door of the nightclub.

"Would you like to grab another drink first?" Noah asked as they passed through the entryway.

Ayla nodded and grinned. "Sounds good to me."

He found them seats at the bar and ordered her a glass of Merlot. Noah stuck to water. Their drinks arrived a few moments later and they clinked glasses.

"Cheers," Ayla said and then gave him a cheeky wink.

"Ch-cheers," Noah stammered, once again filled with a rush of nerves. He gulped down his drink and encouraged her to do the same. The sooner they were out on the dance floor, the better.

She raised an eyebrow in silent query. "Are you trying to get me drunk, Noah Craigdon?"

Heat stole up his neck and flooded his face. "No! Of course not!" he protested, genuinely horrified she thought that was his intention.

She laughed and casually cupped a hand around his cheek. "Relax! I'm kidding!"

"I'm just eager to dance," he mumbled.

"As eager as I am," she declared and finished her wine in three swallows. "There! I'm done! Let's dance!"

Once again, she took him by the hand and led him to the dance floor. It was fairly crowded, but they found a small space. Ayla stepped into his arms as if it were the most natural thing in the world. His fingers tightened around hers. They stood close, facing each other. Every now and then her breasts brushed his chest. It was delightfully excruciating. He could barely concentrate on the steps. Lucky for him his feet had committed them to memory. He moved her around the dance floor with ease.

And then the music changed to an up tempo beat and Ayla gazed at him with delight. "Are you ready to tango?" she asked and gave him a saucy grin.

His heart turned over and desire flooded through his veins.

He pulled her to him and assumed the position and together they danced up a storm. The crowd faded away until there was nothing and no one but her. She twisted and spun and danced in his arms, her gaze not once straying from his.

The intimacy of it was astounding and he felt it all the way down to his toes. From the way she looked at him, her eyes dark and compelling and sparkling with excitement, it seemed she felt it too. Joy streamed through him, leaving him flushed and breathless. He couldn't believe he'd found a woman who liked him as much as he liked her. At last he realized what it was like to find a soul mate, someone so connected to him it felt like they were one. He wished the moment would last forever.

And then the music stopped and they stood there, smiling like idiots, gasping for breath. At that point, Ayla stepped forward and came up on her tiptoes. She pulled his head down to hers and kissed him hard on the lips. It was over before he fully understood what she'd done and then he yearned for her to do it again. But the music had restarted and all he could do was take her in his arms once again.

They danced for what seemed like hours. It was late when Ayla finally begged to sit down. Last drinks were called by the bartender and Ayla had a final glass of wine. Noah threw back a glass of iced water and wished the night would never end.

The ice rattled in Christopher's glass as he finished the last of his scotch. His gaze moved past the people scattered around the bar and shifted to the crowd gathered on the dance floor. Even though it was a weeknight, The Pitt was full of beautiful people all out having a good time.

It wasn't his usual hangout. He preferred something far less crowded and glamorous, preferably hidden down a dark alley. Harry's Bar was dark and dingy, without a beautiful person in sight. Still, he'd decided it was time for him to take his own advice. He needed to get out more and socialize. If he ever wanted to find a life partner, he had to put himself out there.

As he scanned the crowd he was surprised to see Noah and Ayla there. They sure looked cozy on the dance floor. The way they moved together in perfect rhythm, anticipating the other's each and every step, Christopher was left to speculate about whether they'd danced together before.

And then he remembered seeing them at the ball.

So, it seems Noah might have scored with her after all… With the police commissioner's chief of staff, no less… Interesting…

What surprised him most of all was that his half-cousin appeared to have found the courage to ask the woman out. Noah must really be into this woman. Then again, it wasn't that long ago he'd been stuck on Jayde Hassad.

Jayde was now with Flynn and from what he'd seen at the ball, the two of them were in love. Or at least in lust. They'd had their hands all over each other. Not that long ago, Flynn had been a sworn bachelor. Now it seemed he'd found the one. Whatever. Christopher couldn't keep up.

Still, he couldn't help but wonder if he could use Noah's budding relationship with Ayla to his advantage. Having a contact in the commissioner's office could certainly turn out to be a good thing. He never knew when he might need a favor. But first, he needed some ammunition. Something to hold over her. There was no way she'd gotten to be chief of staff on mere effort. Something far seedier was going on and he intended to find out what exactly.

With that thought in mind, he moved away from the speakers to where there was a little more quiet. Pulling out his phone, he dialed a number. It was answered on the second ring.

"Aaron. It's Christopher. I need your help again."

As Christopher relayed his request for information about

the delightful Ayla Rodriguez, he heard Aaron tapping on the keyboard on the other end of the phone. A few minutes later, Aaron spoke.

"Ayla Rodriguez. Twenty-nine years old. Currently employed as chief of staff to the police commissioner."

"Go further back. Where else has she been stationed?"

There was more tapping on the keyboard and then Aaron spoke again.

"She was appointed chief of staff in 2017. Before that, she was posted at Gosford. Looks like she was there three years. She also did a stint in Wollongong. In 2010, she was stationed as a probationary constable at Maitland."

Bingo. Christopher smiled. After thanking his informant, he ended the call and moved back toward the bar. He hailed the bartender and ordered another scotch and then thought about what he'd learned.

Ayla Rodriguez had been stationed at the same police station and during the same year Janelle Craigdon had been killed. Of course there was no way to prove Ayla was on duty the night Janelle died, but still… It was an interesting development. He wondered if Noah knew.

Yes, interesting indeed. It might be wise to start keeping tabs on little Miss Ayla Rodriguez. Who knew where it might lead?

Outside the nightclub, Ayla pulled off her stilettos and then sighed in relief. "Oh, thank goodness! My feet are killing me!"

He looked down at the four-inch heels and grinned. "Beats me how you can even walk in those things."

She laughed. "Years of practice. Besides, who wants to be five foot three all their life?"

He chuckled and pulled her in against his side. Her head rested against his chest. His arm tightened around her shoulders.

He loved the way she fit snug against him, like she was meant to be there.

"I guess we should call it a night. I'll flag down a taxi and take you home," he offered.

She frowned. "What about your bike?"

"I'm sure it'll be all right."

After the concern he'd expressed earlier, she was filled with warmth that he wanted to extend their evening for as long as possible. She felt the same. Looking up at him, she smiled.

"That would be great, but a taxi isn't necessary. I live not far away. We can walk."

Ayla leaned on Noah as they walked to her apartment. She probably had far too much to drink, but she couldn't remember a time when she'd felt happier. Noah was everything she'd ever wanted in a man. Physically attractive, but he was also kind and smart and interesting. Best of all, he loved to dance. She'd really hit the jackpot.

She refused to dwell on the other. It was too unsettling, too sobering. She was in much too good a mood to let reality intrude just yet. There would be plenty of time for that tomorrow.

"So, where do *you* live?" she asked.

"I have an apartment in Manly."

"Ocean views?"

"Of course."

She smiled, snuggled in close. Noah's arm tightened around her shoulders. She closed her eyes and enjoyed the sensation of walking beside a man she could very well fall in love with.

Fall in love with? Really? But what about....?

She pushed the thought aside. She didn't know if what she was feeling for him was the real deal. What she did know was

Noah Craigdon was special. A man she wanted to have in her life. If only the dark specter didn't hover over them. She was on tenterhooks wondering if and when he'd discover the part she'd played in the cover up after the death of his mother. Because of course, he'd find out. He was smart. And thorough. And he had a very personal and deep motivation to get to the truth. That thought filled her with foreboding.

I should tell him the truth… It's the right thing to do… It would be better coming from me…

Everything inside her protested. The night had been so glorious. She didn't want the wonderful feelings Noah generated inside her to come to a cold and abrupt end. There would be time for confessions later…tomorrow… Or the day after that. Right now she wanted to cherish this time with a man who under different circumstances could very well be her soul mate.

Mind made up, she reached for his hand and entwined her fingers in his. He had nice hands. Strong hands. Confident hands. They held her so well on the dance floor. The memory of their bodies moving against each other sent tingles across her skin. Her nipples pebbled with desire.

All too soon, they arrived at her apartment. Noah came to a halt. Ayla did the same. She moved closer. His eyes flared wide, but he held his ground. Like she had outside the nightclub, she reached up and pulled his head down to hers. She kissed him softly on the mouth. With a groan, he pulled her even closer. She came up on her tiptoes, until she was flush against him. Her breasts were pressed against his chest.

Like a tinder had been struck, his arms tightened around her and his lips opened beneath hers. He kissed her like a man starving. Over and over again. On her lips, her eyelids, her nose. He smelled like fresh pine forest, sharp, woodsy, clean. His biceps bunched beneath her fingers and still their kiss went on.

I'm in heaven…

He kissed as well as he danced. When they finally pulled apart, both of them were breathless. His chocolate eyes glittered with desire.

She stared up at him. "Th-thank you for dinner. And everything," she managed.

His dark gaze was intense. "I'd really like to see you again, Ayla."

Her heart skipped a beat. Elation flooded through her, tempered by a frisson of dread. She forced the dark feeling aside and smiled. "I'd like that, too."

Ayla felt like she walked on air as she made her way up to her apartment alone. She lived on the third floor of a three-story walk-up. The red brick building had been constructed in the seventies, but it was still in good condition. She didn't have a view of the harbor, but she was within walking distance of the shops and it was only a thirty-minute bus ride to work.

She fit the key into her lock and closed the door behind her. Leaning back against the panel, she sighed. A smile tugged at her lips.

I'm in love… Oh, my goodness! I'm in love with Noah!

The headiness of it left her feeling giddy with excitement. She couldn't wait to phone her mom and tell her all about him. Lucia Rodriguez would be thrilled, of course. She'd been praying for what felt like most of Ayla's life that her daughter would find a husband worthy of her. Ayla was certain Noah wouldn't disappoint.

And then the familiar feelings of dread and foreboding she'd been fighting all night overwhelmed her. This time, they were mixed with fear. She'd developed real feelings for Noah, feelings that weren't going to go away. And yet he was in the middle of an investigation that involved her and though he didn't know that yet, it was only a matter of time. And then what would she do? What would she say? How could she explain?

At the time, she'd been given no choice, but the guilt had weighed heavily on her mind. Over the years, she'd managed to push it to the far recesses of her memory, but she'd never forgotten. There had been times over the years when she'd thought about coming clean, telling someone higher up about what had happened. But then she'd been appointed chief of staff and things had gotten complicated. Though she firmly believed her promotion was based purely on merit, there had always been a niggle of doubt.

Noah was an IA investigator. He saw the world through black and white. There was no room for any other color. Definitely no shades of gray. He'd admitted as much the night they met. Now she'd done a foolish thing and was on the brink of falling in love with him. Her world was teetering on the edge. If she wasn't careful, the whole thing might very well blow up in her face and destroy her only chance at happiness.

Her shoulders slumped on a weary sigh. Her jubilation of a few minutes ago, dissolved. She trudged into her kitchen and dropped her stilettos on the floor and her evening bag on the counter. She wished there was someone she could talk to about it, but no one knew except those involved. She hadn't even told her parents. At the time, she'd been too ashamed. Later, all she'd wanted to do was forget it had ever happened. She'd never dreamed it might come back to haunt her in this way.

A part of her wished she could talk to Joel about it. They'd known each other from the beginning, before either of them were cops. At the Academy, they'd been good mates. There were many times when they'd covered for each other, when one or the other had snuck out after curfew to have some fun in the town. They'd never been caught.

And then she thought about it some more. *No.* Though she was sure Joel could be trusted to keep her secret, he was too close to Noah. And after all, what had happened involved

Joel's father. She wasn't sure how he'd react if he knew the truth about the man he had probably loved and admired.

Her thoughts turned to Joe Bettino. He'd also been on duty that night. He was only twenty-four when it happened. A relatively inexperienced officer. To this day, she wasn't sure what had motivated him to look the other way, but he had and, like her, he'd been forced to live with the consequences of his actions. And the guilt.

Yes, Joe might understand. Perhaps she ought to seek him out, find out how he was coping. Ask him if he'd received a visit from the LECC investigators…

Ayla slept in fits and starts and woke feeling tired and out of sorts. Her eyes felt gritty from lack of sleep. Her dreams had been filled with that night in Maitland, when she'd been a probationary constable, fresh out of the Academy. She'd been so eager to make a difference. She cringed at the memory of her naivety.

With a weary sigh, she climbed out of bed and headed for the shower. Sometime during the night, she'd firmed up her resolve to visit with Joe Bettino. With security access to information about the active and inactive police officers who were serving or had served in the NSW police force, it wouldn't be too hard to find him. She hadn't seen him for years, but that didn't matter. They were cops from beginning to end, part of a brotherhood, and even though she was a woman, she'd always felt part of the team. They stuck together, no matter what.

Stripping off her pajamas, she dropped them on the floor and stepped under the hot spray. She let the water run over her skin. She closed her eyes and imagined the feeling was caused by Noah's hands.

Strong and supple and confident, he moved his fingers over

her breasts, squeezing the firm flesh. He held their weight in his palms and teased her nipples with the pad of his thumb. She cried out from the sweet torture.

She opened her eyes and immediately felt embarrassed.

Oh, God. What's wrong with me? Fantasizing about a man in my shower. And not just any man. Noah. The man she lusted for. The man she could love. The man who could quite well end her career…

That last thought doused her arousal like a bucket of ice water. It had been far too long since she'd last had sex. That's all this was. She was just feeling frustrated. She was still turned on from the evening before. The memory of Noah's strong arms. His broad chest. His passionate kisses that had left her yearning for so much more.

With a sound of impatience, she reached for the shampoo and lathered her hair. She scrubbed hard and then rinsed out the suds and started in on the conditioner. After combing her hair with her fingers, she stood back under the shower and let the water do its thing. By the time she got out, she had less than twenty minutes to get dressed and head out the door.

Hurrying, she pulled on her uniform—the regulation navy-blue socks, navy-blue pants and pale blue blouse with her police insignia embroidered on the breast. Next came her sensible court shoes. Though there were times when she wore civilian clothing to work, on days like this when she had an appointment outside the office, she was expected to be in full uniform.

With no time to blow-dry her hair, she twisted the wet hair into a bun and secured it with pins to the nape of her neck. A quick slash of eyeliner, mascara and lipstick and she was done. Grabbing her handbag, she checked for her wallet, house keys and bus pass. All were accounted for. She snagged a red apple out of the fruit bowl on her way past the kitchen. It wasn't quite her usual breakfast, but it would have to do. There was no time for anything else.

Her last thought as she pulled the door closed behind her was of Noah. Despite her inner turmoil whenever she thought about him, her lips tugged upward in a smile.

Noah... So good, so kind, so sexy... So dangerous to her...

With a sigh she flagged down her bus and focused on the challenging day that stretched out in front of her.

Chapter Nine

The week was halfway through before Ayla got the chance to look up Joe Bettino. Fortunately, it didn't take long for her to locate him. His details were listed in the staff database, along with a phone number and address. She debated about whether to call him first and then decided against it. Though he lived the best part of thirty minutes from her Parramatta office, she'd rather turn up unannounced and take the risk he wasn't home than alert him ahead of time to her visit and run into the possibility he'd take off.

On a stroke of luck, she had a previously scheduled meeting with the police minister's public relations people regarding an upcoming announcement on funding. It gave her the perfect excuse to leave the office. With that thought in mind, she knocked on the commissioner's door and reminded him about her outside appointment.

Her boss barely looked up from the papers he had scattered across his desk. She hastily took her leave before he asked too many questions. The meeting with the **PR** people was legitimate. What she hadn't told him was her intention to pay a visit to Joe Bettino beforehand.

Seated behind the wheel of an unmarked police car she'd signed out half an hour earlier, she checked the address she'd taken from the police database against the GPS and looked at the rundown house and yard where Joe apparently lived. It had been a long time since she'd seen him and ten years when they'd last worked together. Though she'd met his wife and family at a police picnic held about six years earlier, she'd never been to his house.

Climbing out, she headed up the cracked footpath that led to the front door. The air of sad neglect that surrounded the place made her wonder at Joe's current state of mind. And then she recalled the entry in his personnel file. He was on stress leave. She hoped he was getting the help he needed.

For a cop to be out on stress leave wasn't unusual. Policing was an immensely taxing job—both physically and mentally—and it often took its toll. Sadly, a lot of cops struggling with the demands of the job didn't get enough help. There just weren't enough resources to go round. It was a problem neither side of government appeared too eager to fix. Instead, they paid out the money to put the officer on stress leave—sometimes indefinitely—and looked the other way. It was no solution.

She knocked on the front door with its flaky paint. It had seen better days. Cracked and peeling, some of it came away beneath her knuckles and landed on the sagging boards beneath her feet. She caught a slight movement of the tattered curtains covering the window that faced onto the street. A moment later, the door opened and Joe stood before her.

Like the house, he was surrounded by a dismal air of neglect. His hair was greasy and overlong. His cheeks were covered in whiskers. His eyes were red. His clothes were covered in food stains. He smelled of body odor and looked like he hadn't washed for weeks.

"Hello, Joe."

His eyes widened with recognition. "Ayla? Is that you?"

"Yes. It's good to see you. It's been awhile."

As if suddenly aware of his bedraggled appearance, he looked away. An embarrassed flush stained his cheeks.

"What are you doing here?" he mumbled.

Ayla gave him a bright smile. "I heard you were doing it tough," she lied. "I thought I'd stop by and say hi."

He shook his head dismissively. "There's no need. I'm fine."

She'd come all this way. She wasn't going to be put off so easily. "Can I come in?"

He stood his ground. A belligerent expression crossed his face. For a moment, she thought he was going to refuse.

"Please, Joe. For old time's sake. I promise I won't stay long." She gave him another smile of encouragement.

With a weary sigh, he opened the door wider and stood back to allow her to enter. As she moved closer, she was overwhelmed by alcoholic fumes. He turned away and headed down a narrow hallway toward the back of the house. As she followed behind him, it was all she could do not to gag. The smell of rotting food, unwashed clothes, and other things she didn't dare identify assailed her nostrils. Joe was in a worse way than she could have imagined.

The hallway opened up into a small combined kitchen and living room. If anything, the stench was even worse in there. Every available surface was covered—piles of newspapers, half-used food containers, boxes of cereal, a bottle of sour milk. Ayla took shallow breaths and did her best to ignore the stench.

"Coffee?" Joe asked.

Though everything inside Ayla protested against it, she merely smiled and nodded. "Coffee sounds great, thanks."

While Joe busied himself in the kitchen, Ayla removed a pile of dirty clothes from one of the chairs and gingerly seated herself at the table. She glanced around and bit her lip against a rush of emotion. She'd had no idea things had gotten so bad for him.

She looked at him. He was spooning instant coffee into two mugs. "Where are Samantha and the kids?"

His gaze remained fixed on the mugs. "She left me more than five years ago. Took the kids."

Ayla blinked in surprise. At least she now had some explanation for his decline. "Oh, I'm sorry. I didn't know."

He merely shrugged. When the kettle boiled, he filled the mugs. He added a teaspoon of sugar to one of them and then looked around for the milk. Spying it on the counter, he picked it up and grimaced.

"Sorry. No milk. It's gone off."

"That's fine," she hurried to reassure him. "I'll take it black."

He carried both mugs over to the table and sat one in front of her.

"Thanks," she murmured.

He took the seat opposite. Once again, she was met with a wave of alcoholic fumes. He cleared his throat of thick phlegm. For a moment, she thought he was going to hawk it right out there, in front of her. Then with a quick glance in her direction, he pulled out a filthy handkerchief from his pocket and spat into it.

She tried not to shudder. Taking a sip of coffee, she forced herself to remember why she was there. The commissioner. Henry Craigdon. The cover up. *Right.*

He eyed her balefully over the rim of his mug. "It looks like life's been treating you all right."

She flushed and was immediately annoyed at herself. She'd worked hard to get where she was. She refused to apologize for her success.

"Heard you were working in the commissioner's office."

She pursed her lips. "Yes."

His lip curled up with disgust. "Good for you."

She instinctively bristled, but forced herself to relax. "What about you? How have you been?"

He glared at her and spread his arms wide. "What's it look like? Do I look like a man who's enjoying life?"

She bit her lip and drew in a slow breath. It wouldn't do to get him offside. Once, a long time ago, they'd been allies. She wondered if she could find that kindred spirit again.

As if following the direction of her thoughts, Joe's eyes welled up with tears. "Fuck." His shoulders shook. He sobbed quietly, dejectedly—like all hope was gone. She bit back a surge of emotion and fought tears of her own.

And then he shook his head slowly from side to side. "I can't believe you're working for him. That prick. I was never the same after that night. I battled forward for as long as I could, but I couldn't take it. The guilt of what I did ate at me; made it impossible to function. What I did that night ruined my career. Ruined *me*."

Memories besieged her. She swallowed against the lump that had lodged in her throat. "Why did you do it, Joe?"

He shot her a look of disbelief. "You know Beechwood better than anybody. I had no choice."

"Beechwood asked you to do it?" She didn't bother to hide her shock.

His lips twisted. "Don't tell me all this time you thought it was *my* idea?"

She shook her head. "I didn't know what to think. To tell you the truth, I've tried not to think about it at all. I've worked hard to put that night behind me."

"Lucky you," Joe muttered.

Ayla ignored the comment. "Why didn't you refuse?"

"Ha!" Joe's bark of laughter was devoid of humor. "Refuse? How could I refuse? He had me over a barrel."

She stared at him, aghast. "You mean he blackmailed you?"

"Aha! Now you're catching on! Of course he blackmailed me. That's his MO. How do you think he's managed to rise all the way to the top? It's not because he's the best cop in the state, that's for certain."

Ayla blinked to clear her confused thoughts, still shocked at the discovery her boss was so corrupt. She'd known there had been something awry that night, but she'd always assumed Joe had taken it upon himself to provide the drug and alcohol samples. At the time, she had no idea Beechwood didn't always play by the rules.

"What did he have on you?" she asked quietly.

Joe sighed heavily and scrubbed at his lank and dirty hair. "I had a wife and young family. A mortgage so big you couldn't jump over it. Day after day we'd carry out drug busts and confiscate suitcases full of money. The temptation was too much. After all, no one would notice if a few bundles went missing. One or two here and there; it was easy."

Ayla's stomach filled with dread. "You stole drug money?"

"Yeah."

"Wow."

Joe hung his head. "I'm not proud of it, but I needed the cash. And I didn't see where there was any harm."

"It was wrong, Joe."

"Yeah."

"I take it Beechwood found out?"

"Yeah."

"He asked you to provide samples for Henry Craigdon or he'd expose you, is that how it went?"

"Yeah. Something like that."

Her gaze traveled over him, taking in the dirty hair, the unshaven cheeks, the clothes that hung off his slim frame. He looked sad, bedraggled, defeated. She only hoped he hadn't also resorted to taking drugs. She surreptitiously checked out his bare arms for signs of track marks. To her relief, she saw none, but she had to make sure.

"You're not using, are you?"

The shocked look that flooded his face appeared genuine. "Using? Hell, no! I've never taken any of that shit." He looked down, his expression filling with shame. "It's bad enough I turned to the grog."

"Have the guys from IA been to see you?"

"Yeah."

She tensed involuntarily. "What did you tell them?"

"Nothing."

A flash of relief went through her. It was short lived. Noah struck her as someone who liked to be thorough. There was no way he'd complete an investigation without speaking to everyone who'd been involved. No doubt he'd return and press Joe for more information.

She took a sip of her coffee. "How old are your kids now?"

"Eleven and thirteen."

"How often do you see them?"

Joe looked miserable. "Once a month, for a weekend. Supervised. The courts don't think I'm a good influence."

"Well, you can't be surprised by their attitude. They're only trying to do the best they can for the children."

"Yeah. But they're my kids! I love them! I'd never hurt them!"

"I know that because I know you, but the court doesn't. All they see is a man struggling to get through each day. That's not a healthy environment for any child."

Joe stared morosely at the table. His shoulders slumped in defeat. "You're right."

She leaned forward and touched his hand. "It's not too late to do something about it, Joe. Only you can decide to pull yourself together and get clean."

A fresh wave of tears filled his eyes. "Yeah."

Her heart went out to him. "Get off the grog," she urged. "Clear your head. Get back to work. Be the kind of dad they can be proud of. They deserve that."

He sniffed. "Yeah, they do."

She took another mouthful of coffee and then set it aside.

There was only so much of the black brew she could stomach. "Let me know if there's anything I can do."

"Thanks, Ayla. You know, I've had countless visits from the police counseling services, all purporting to be concerned, but I feel like you're the first person who's really listened. Who cares."

"Your family cares, Joe. They love you. I'm sure of it. Do this for them."

With another reassuring pat on his hand, she pushed away from the table and stood. Gathering her handbag, she bid him a quiet farewell. She let herself out and headed back to her car. Though she left with a sense of relief that Joe might be able to get his life back on track, she was still troubled.

If and when Noah returned to interview Joe, there was every possibility he'd discover the truth, and her part in it. She was also disturbed to discover her boss' involvement in the cover up. She'd had no idea the extent of his involvement. In fact, if Joe was to be believed, it was Beechwood who'd instigated it.

Despite her efforts to wipe the memories from her mind, she could remember that night like it had happened yesterday. She'd attended the scene of the accident with Beechwood and Bettino. They'd found Henry Craigdon stumbling along the side of the road, not far from the crash site. His eyes had been glazed, his words were slurred. He'd been bleeding.

She'd smelled alcohol on his breath. It was obvious to all of them he was drunk. She was shocked when the breath test had come back negative and Henry had been released without charge.

Now she knew why. If what Joe said was true, Beechwood had a lot to answer for. She wondered what Noah would think when he learned the truth.

Noah took his time reading over the contents of the autopsy report. He still wasn't sure why it hadn't been included in the police file, but he had a copy of it now. According to the forensic pathologist who'd conducted the autopsy on Noah's mother, Janelle had died from severe head trauma consistent with being thrown through a windscreen at speed. Like the police report had indicated, she hadn't been wearing a seatbelt.

Toxicology tests found there were high levels of alcohol and cocaine in her system. The presence of illegal drugs shocked Noah more than anything. His mother hadn't been a drug user. He didn't even know how she'd come by the stuff.

Had Uncle Henry supplied her with them? Is that why she was with him? To score?

He could scarcely fathom it. The woman referred to in the autopsy report with the drugs and alcohol in her system was a stranger. His mother didn't take drugs. Had never taken drugs. And yet, she'd died with cocaine in her blood…

The levels weren't substantial enough to have contributed to her death, but she'd certainly been having a good time. Perhaps that explained why she hadn't pulled on her seatbelt. And yet Uncle Henry's drug and alcohol tests had come back negative. Whatever his mother had been up to, she'd been doing it alone.

The question that continued to niggle at Noah was what had his mother been doing there in the first place? Over the years, Noah had canvassed several options, but nothing he came up with made sense. Now he'd taken the step of opening an investigation, it was time to get answers once and for all.

With that thought in mind, he drafted a warrant for Henry's bank statements and phone records from ten years ago. He wasn't sure what he might find, if anything, but it was a starting place. Flynn had recently informed the family Henry had been a bigwig drug dealer who'd been known to the police. The DEA had never been able to get enough evidence on him to lay charges, but he'd been on their radar right up until his death.

And even after that. Flynn's new girlfriend, Jayde Hassad, had been working undercover until recently, looking into the possibility any of Henry's family had stepped up and taken over from where he'd left off. Fortunately, she hadn't found any evidence of wrongdoing of the remaining Craigdon family members, himself included. The rest of the family had been cleared.

With a sigh, Noah set the autopsy report aside. He needed to talk to Joe Bettino again. The man had been in no fit state for an interview the last time, but maybe they'd catch him sober this time. Bettino was the weak link. It was obvious he was struggling. They needed to push harder and see if he might give them something.

So far, the only conclusion Noah could come to was that John Hassad had lied when he'd claimed Henry had been drunk, but that simplified explanation didn't sit well. He needed more, something concrete. Something he could accept. It made sense the officer who'd been second in charge of the investigation that fateful night knew something.

With that thought in mind, he picked up his phone and dialed Declan's number. His partner worked in another office, a little further down the hall.

"Yep?" Declan answered.

"I'm convinced Joe Bettino knows more than he's saying. I think it's time we paid him another visit."

"Sure thing. Give me fifteen minutes. I'll meet you downstairs."

As Noah hung up, he thought about Ayla. He wondered if she was at work today. *Is she thinking about me? Is she remembering our last time together? Our kisses…*

His body hardened. He could almost smell her sweet

perfume, feel the softness of her hair. Their date had gone so well. He yearned to see her again.

Is it too soon?

He wished he had more experience when it came to women and dating. He didn't want her to think he was desperate. That he'd barely slept since their date. She'd probably laugh if he told her he'd never kissed a woman like that before. Hell, he'd barely kissed a woman at all. He blushed with embarrassment at the thought.

And yet, there was something about Ayla he'd never felt with anyone. A connection. An understanding. Like his inexperience didn't matter. Like they were on the same wavelength. He was impatient to explore it further. He'd call her as soon as he got back from his visit with Bettino.

What if I lose my nerve by then?

The thought popped into his mind. He frowned. It wouldn't be the first time he'd lost his nerve when it came to women. It had been the story of his life. No, he should do it now. Call her and ask her out again while he was pumped.

Taking a deep breath, he once again picked up the phone.

Chapter Ten

yla stared at the screen in front of her. The words on her computer blurred, became unreadable. She'd attended the meeting with the PR people right after she'd met with Joe. Concealing her tumultuous emotions behind a polite mask, she'd asked the expected questions and had agreed to provide them with a statement from the commissioner.

Of course, her boss would expect her to draft it. That was part of her job description. As his chief of staff, her primary purpose was to ensure his life ran smoothly. The only problem was right now she felt so angry toward him she was quite certain she wouldn't be able to thread three sentences together on his behalf, let alone generate a whole statement.

She couldn't stop thinking about what Joe had told her. It was so unfair! Okay, no one had forced Joe to steal drug money that should have been legally confiscated, but neither was it acceptable that the commissioner had exploited him in the way he had. What Ayla still didn't know was what the commissioner gained from such actions.

The most likely explanation was that he was a friend of Henry Craigdon. Or maybe they knew each other on another level. Maybe Beechwood owed Craigdon a favor? Who knew? The truth was, there could be any number of reasons why her boss had forced Joe to falsify the records by providing drug and alcohol samples and passing them off as Henry's.

Dread swirled in her stomach. She was now privy to some pretty damning information. Of course, it was all hearsay, but Joe's story held a ring of truth. She wasn't sure what she should do with it.

Coward… Of course I know what to do with it…

The LECC had opened an investigation into that very accident. She should call Noah and tell him everything she knew, including her part in it.

Okay, so strictly speaking she hadn't done anything wrong, but she'd known at the time something was off and she'd said nothing. She'd gone along with whatever it was they'd arranged. All these years she'd remained silent. The guilt had eaten into her stomach, making her feel queasy.

She should have come forward years ago, back when it had happened. But she'd been a probationary constable straight out of the Academy. She'd been nervous, scared, uncertain. Questioning herself. Questioning everything. There was the possibility she'd been confused about what had happened. After all, she hadn't actually seen any wrongdoing. What if she'd made accusations against her superiors and it turned out they'd done nothing wrong?

And so she'd remained silent. The years passed. Her career continued to progress Somehow it became easier to keep quiet about what she knew. Now she was terrified that if she came forward, no one would believe she'd had nothing to do with it. Especially Noah.

She could have said something to him about it at any time. From the very first moment she became aware he'd opened an investigation. And yet she'd said nothing. If what Joe said was true and the samples had been switched, Noah would think she was complicit. Her career would be over. She'd be lucky if they didn't bring criminal charges against her.

The phone at her elbow pealed. Flustered and on edge, she picked up the receiver.

"Commissioner Beechwood's office. This is Ayla."

"Ayla. It's Noah."

At the sound of his deep voice, her belly somersaulted with nerves. *Oh, God.* He was so good and decent and sweet. Not to mention sexy. She enjoyed being around him. She liked him way too much. And their kisses—so soft and sweet and tender. So passionate. Everything that encapsulated Noah. She forced her thoughts away.

"N-Noah. It's lovely to hear from you. How are you?"

"I'm fine. I can't stop thinking about you. I'd like to see you again. Are you free this Friday?"

Her mind was in turmoil. Ever since their date, he'd been constantly on her mind. He made her feel things she'd never felt before. She longed to spend time with him, get to know him better.

How can I be around him and not tell him everything? How can I stay away?

The agony of her situation filled her with despair. If she went cold on him, he might wonder about her sudden turn around. He might dig deeper into her career. He might discover she'd been stationed in Maitland ten years earlier, serving under Beechwood and Joe Bettino. He was a smart guy. It wouldn't take him long to join the dots and that would be the end of them. Whatever they had between them would be over before it had a chance to take off.

The worst thing was, she had nothing to hide. But that wasn't what he'd think when he discovered she'd been there that fateful night. It was a no-win situation.

"Ayla? Are you still there?"

She sighed, forcing the inward turmoil aside. Keeping her tone purposefully upbeat, she pasted on a smile.

"Yes. I'm still here and yes, I'd love to see you again. Friday night sounds great. How about we go dancing again? I know just the place."

The sun was low in the sky when Noah and Declan found themselves outside Bettino's front door again. They knocked on the wooden panel and waited. This time, the door opened after only a few minutes. Bettino stood before them in fresh clothes. He was washed and clean shaven. The transformation was quite extraordinary. Though his eyes were slightly bloodshot, he also appeared to be sober.

"Sergeant Bettino, I'm Detective Craigdon. This is Detective Munro. We stopped by here earlier in the week."

"Yeah. I remember," Bettino replied. "You're from IA."

Noah's eyebrows rose. He was surprised Bettino had taken in that much. "The LECC," he corrected. "Same thing."

Bettino got right to the point. "What do you want?"

"Can we come in?" Declan asked.

Noah took a step forward. Bettino put up a show of bravado for a short moment and then his shoulders slumped. He shrugged. "Suit yourself."

With that, Bettino turned and led them down a hallway. It opened up into a combined kitchen and living room. Though the stench of rotten food lingered on the air, it was also obvious someone—Bettino?—had made an attempt to clean up. The kitchen counters were bare and smelled of disinfectant. The linoleum floor had been swept clean. Three large garbage bags filled with rubbish stood outside the back door.

"Coffee?" Bettino offered.

Both men shook their heads. "No thanks," Noah said.

Bettino merely inclined his head. He crossed his arms over his chest and leaned against the kitchen counter. "What can I do for you?"

Noah cleared his throat. "I'm not sure how much you remember from our last visit, but we've opened an investigation into Janelle Craigdon's death. She was killed in an MVA ten years ago. Henry Craigdon was behind the wheel. You were working the evening shift at Maitland Police Station the night she died. You and the now Police Commissioner, Kevin Beechwood, attended the scene. You both provided statements."

Bettino's expression remained cautious. "Why would IA be interested in this now? Seems kind of strange. Like you said, it happened ten years ago."

Noah kept his gaze on the man. "It seems new evidence has come to light."

"What new evidence?"

"We have reason to believe Henry Craigdon was drunk when the accident happened."

Bettino frowned. "I'm sure I recall Craigdon's breath test came back negative."

Noah gave him a hard look. "You're right. The police file shows his drug and alcohol readings taken at the police station were negative. We think those results were falsified."

Noah watched Bettino carefully. The man paled at Noah's words. He began to fiddle with a loose thread on his shirt. His gaze darted around the room, settling on nothing.

"You were there that night, Sergeant. What can you tell us?" Declan coaxed.

"Nothing! I don't know anything!"

Noah moved closer. He lowered his voice. "Are you sure, Joe?"

Bettino's gaze became more frantic. "What about the commissioner? Kevin Beechwood? He was there that night, too. Have you spoken to him?"

"Yes, Joe. We have," Declan replied.

"What did he say?"

"He told us to talk to you," Noah lied smoothly. "He said he was sure you were in the best position to answer all our questions."

Bettino's expression grew frantic with fear. "Bullshit. That prick. He's not going to put this on me! It wasn't my idea! He was the one who told me to do it!"

Noah stilled. A second later, a surge of adrenaline rushed through him. He glanced at Declan. His partner made the slightest movement of his head, acknowledging they almost had their man.

Noah gentled his voice to a coaxing murmur. "Talk to me, Joe. Tell me what happened. What did Kevin tell you to do?"

Bettino's gaze moved from one to the other and back to Noah again. He looked scared and trapped. Once again, Noah encouraged him to speak.

Bettino's shoulders slumped. "I didn't want to do it. Beechwood gave me no choice."

"He was your superior officer, right?" Noah murmured in an understanding tone.

"Yes. He was a detective senior sergeant. He was the officer in charge of the station that night. I took my orders from him."

"What did he order you to do?" Declan asked.

There was a long moment of silence. Noah held his breath. They were so close, so close…

Then Bettino began to speak and Noah swallowed a sigh of relief.

"We received a call about a motor vehicle accident out on McDonalds Road, not far from Pokolbin."

"Who made the call?" Declan asked.

"I'm not sure. It might have been made by a passerby."

"Go on."

"We went out to the scene of the accident."

"You and Beechwood?" Noah asked.

"Y-yes."

"What happened next?"

"A man I now know was Henry Craigdon was stumbling along the road. He had a gash above his eye that was bleeding. He was visibly distressed. He kept repeating the name 'Janelle.'"

"My mother," Noah muttered.

Bettino's eyes widened in surprise. Slowly, his expression filled with comprehension. "Fuck."

"Keep going," Declan urged.

"We searched the car. It was pretty badly damaged. It had come into contact with a massive gum tree. The paramedics were already there. There was a woman's body a few yards from the car. It appeared she'd been thrown through the windscreen. She was covered by a tarpaulin. She was already deceased."

Noah swallowed and looked away. Though he'd read the autopsy report and knew the extent of his mother's injuries, it wasn't easy to listen to them being recounted by a man who'd been at the scene.

"What happened next?" Declan asked.

Noah shot him a look of gratitude.

Bettino cleared his throat. "The paramedics treated Craigdon for minor injuries. Then they loaded the female victim into their truck. We took the driver back to the station for mandatory drug and alcohol tests."

"How did Henry Craigdon appear to you?"

Bettino frowned. "What do you mean?"

"I mean, did he appear drunk?"

Bettino paused and then slowly nodded. "Yes, sir. He was slurring his words and stumbling around."

"He'd just been involved in a serious car accident. Is it possible he was suffering from shock or a concussion? You said he had a head injury," Noah said.

"Yes, sir. A minor head injury. He was treated by paramedics at the scene. They deemed him well enough to accompany us back to the station. He sat in the back seat of the patrol car. He smelled quite strongly of alcohol."

"What happened after you arrived at the station?" Declan asked.

Bettino sighed. "Craigdon was put in an interview room. Beechwood drew me aside and told me he'd be conducting the interview. Naturally I stepped aside."

"Did you know Henry Craigdon?" Noah asked.

"No."

"What about Beechwood? Did he have any previous connection to Craigdon?" The question came from Declan.

Bettino shrugged and shook his head. "Not that I knew of. He certainly didn't volunteer information to that effect. He told me he'd conduct the interview and I didn't think any more of it. He was the senior officer, after all."

"So, Beechwood interviewed Craigdon. What happened next?" Noah asked.

"The boss was probably in there with Craigdon for about twenty minutes. Then Beechwood came out and told me he wouldn't be laying any charges. The driver swerved in the dark to miss a kangaroo and had lost control and collided with a tree. It was being ruled an accident."

"Did you ask him about the drug and alcohol tests?"

"Yes, of course. I was almost certain Craigdon would register over the limit."

"What did Beechwood say?" Noah asked.

Bettino's lips tightened. He looked down and shook his head. When he looked up again, his expression was bleak.

"He said I was to provide the samples."

"And did you?" Noah asked, already knowing the answer.

"Yes."

"And of course, they were negative for both alcohol and

drugs and the file was marked accordingly," Noah finished.

"What happened to the samples?" Declan asked.

"They were destroyed to avoid the potential for cross-contamination, as is standard practice."

Noah winced. A shaft of pain ran through him, swift and agonizing. "And just like that, Henry Craigdon walked free while my mother lay in the morgue, her body still cooling."

Though he'd had many years to come to terms with his mother's tragic death, learning his uncle had been responsible and had gotten away with it was a harsh blow. Still, now wasn't the time to fall apart. He had an interview to complete.

He looked at Bettino. With shoulders hunched and head lowered, the sergeant was a broken man.

"Why are you telling us this now?" Noah demanded. "Why not come forward years ago? Or even better, at the time it happened?"

Bettino's face flushed with shame. He stared at the floor. "It was never questioned. My superior told me to forget it happened. If I'd known then how it would affect me going forward, I would have spoken up regardless. You can't imagine how many times I wished I had. Ever since it happened, my life's gone to shit. I've been overridden with guilt. I'm an alcoholic. My wife left and took the kids. I'm not even fit for the job anymore. A job I used to love."

He looked up at them and his eyes shimmered with tears. "I've had a lot of time to think about this. When you came calling the other day, I was taken by surprise. I clammed up. I was frightened. But then I started thinking, to be honest about what happened that night might be my way out. My way to redemption and a better life. So I've told you the truth about what happened that night. I'm prepared to take the consequences. You do with it what you will."

"You'll need to come down to the LECC and make a formal statement," Declan said.

Bettino nodded. "Is tomorrow okay?"

"First thing, got it?" Noah said, his gaze hard.

As they left the house and made their way back to the car, Noah allowed himself a moment of sadness. If only he'd known the truth all those years ago. He could have made sure his uncle paid for his actions. He might have only been eighteen at the time, but Noah would have done whatever he could to make sure his mother got justice. Now it was too late on both scores.

Still, it wasn't too late to make the commissioner pay for his subterfuge. Now that they had the evidence from Bettino, they were well on the way to getting the proof they needed to lay charges. Still, it was Joe's word against another. Beechwood could just as easily deny it or say Bettino acted alone. They needed to pay the commissioner another visit, and this time they wouldn't be quite as amiable.

As he climbed behind the wheel and pulled out into the traffic, Noah's thoughts turned to Ayla. She was the only shining light in this whole sorry investigation. Thank God he had her in his life to talk to. No one understood the job like another cop. It was only Wednesday. He didn't know how he'd get through the hours before he could see her again.

Chapter Eleven

It was Friday. Ayla couldn't believe the day had finally arrived. In a matter of hours, she'd see Noah again. Though he'd called the commissioner's office the day before and again earlier that day requesting an interview with her boss, on both occasions, Beechwood had declined to see him. The commissioner had left it up to her to make his excuses. Ayla couldn't help but wonder if it had anything to do with the Craigdon investigation.

Of course it's about the Craigdon investigation. Why else would Noah be wanting to meet with my boss?

Her heart clenched with dread at the thought that any day Noah might discover she'd been there the night his mother had died.

I need to tell him. Come clean. Explain while he might still be in the mood to listen…

"Ayla."

She jumped at the sound of the commissioner's voice. He stood right in front of her.

"S-sorry, sir. You startled me."

He shot her a snide look. "Clearly. Listen, about those calls from that detective… I'm getting concerned about Bettino— that he might say something to the police."

Ayla gathered her wits and gave her boss a steady look. "I don't think you need to worry about that, sir."

"Why not?"

"He's in pretty bad shape. His marriage has fallen apart. He lost custody of his kids. He's… He's hitting the bottle pretty hard."

The commissioner gave her an assessing look. "You seem to know a lot about him. Have you two kept in contact?"

"No. In fact I hadn't seen him for about six years. It's only recently I reconnected with him."

"Well, while there are LECC investigators sniffing around, I want him silenced. Go and see him and tell him to keep his mouth shut. Understand?"

"Yes, sir."

The commissioner gave her a hard look before turning away and disappearing back into his office. Ayla drew in a shaky breath and made an effort to slow her heart rate. When she felt she was able, she picked up the phone and called Joe. After a few minutes of pleasantries, she told him the reason for her call. He agreed to meet her for coffee in the city.

"Give me a couple of hours," he said.

"Great." She gave him the details of a café that she liked to frequent and then hung up. Though she had no intention of threatening him, like the commissioner seemed to want her to do, she did want to talk to him and check he was doing okay. It was the least she could do.

Christopher Barrington left the offices of Sydney Legal and crossed against the lights. He wove in and out of the traffic, ignoring the blast of angry horns. He'd just come from another frustrating meeting with his lawyers. Though he'd generously agreed to settle his claim against Henry Craigdon's estate for the sum of eighty-five million dollars, none of

Christopher's so-called family were inclined to accept his offer. Worse still, they hadn't come back with a counter-offer. He'd been left hung out to dry. It seemed they were determined to have this dragged through the courts.

So be it... If they want a messy, dirty fight played out in the public eye, then that's exactly what they'll get...

He felt a momentary pang of guilt at the thought of Elizabeth. Henry's long-suffering wife had shown Christopher nothing but kindness over the years. More recently, she'd tried to get him to reconsider his lawsuit and let the family work out some mutually agreeable arrangement. Well, that's what his offer had been. An attempt to work out a settlement. And it had failed miserably. They'd rejected it and him out of hand, failing to consider his peace offering.

Fools!

He strode through the Pitt Street Mall, still fuming. Ten yards away, he spied Ayla Rodriguez. He was surprised she didn't notice him. It was obvious she was even more distracted than he was. He remembered what Aaron had told him about her being stationed in Maitland the same year Janelle Craigdon had come to her sad and untimely end. He also remembered wondering how someone so young had come to hold such a powerful position in the police force. She'd piqued his interest then and he felt the same stirring of curiosity now.

She walked with her head down, her stride long and determined. He kept a few yards back, letting a number of people come between them. In her smart police uniform, she stood out in the crowd and though she wasn't very tall, he had no difficulty following her.

A couple of blocks later, she crossed the street and walked into a café. She placed an order at the counter and then came back outside and sat down at one of the tables. The place was busy, but not completely crowded. It was a perfect place to hide out. He could sit in a far corner and observe her and she'd never be any the wiser. What he hoped to learn, he didn't know, but he had nothing else to do and who knew what he might discover.

Discreetly, he entered the café and ordered a long espresso. He waited a few moments to collect his order. Then he headed back outside and took a seat next to a large potted ficus that would help conceal him from prying eyes. He was close enough to Ayla to watch and listen in to any conversation.

He wondered if she was meeting someone. *Noah, perhaps?* Christopher's half-cousin certainly appeared interested. They'd made quite the stylish couple on the dance floor. A man Christopher didn't recognize slipped into the chair opposite Ayla. She greeted him with a friendly smile, but they didn't touch.

So, not a lover then… Noah might still have a chance… Perhaps a work colleague, or a friend?

Christopher pulled out his phone, flicked over to the video option and pressed "record." He angled it in such a way that Ayla and her companion could be clearly seen. Smiling to himself, he settled in to watch the show…

Ayla thanked the waitress as the young woman set two large coffees down in front of them. A latté for her and a black for Joe. She'd also taken the liberty of ordering a selection of pastries—éclairs, apple turnovers, iced donuts. All of her favorites. She had a terrible sweet tooth she only occasionally indulged. Today she'd decided to throw caution to the wind. She hoped Joe was hungry.

She was relieved to see he looked better. His hair was freshly washed, as were his clothes. He was clean shaven and smelled a lot better than he had the last time she'd seen him. In fact, he looked almost like his old self.

She greeted him with a smile. "You're looking great, Joe."

He took the seat across from her. "Thank you. I took your advice and I'm trying hard to get my life back in order, starting with telling the truth about what happened ten years ago."

Her stomach lurched. "You haven't said anything to anyone, have you?"

"As a matter of fact, I got a visit from two cops the day before yesterday. The same two who'd been there before. From IA." He paused and then added, "I told them everything."

She gasped in alarm. "Joe! What did you say?"

He continued on, unperturbed. "I told them the truth."

He went on to say how he'd related to the investigators the series of events that occurred the night Janelle Craigdon was killed, ending with the demand Beechwood had made that Joe provide the drug and alcohol samples.

"Don't worry, I kept you out of it. I know who the real mastermind was. You were nothing but a probationary constable on your first posting. You did as you were told. You probably didn't even understand what went on. I don't hold you responsible for the cover up."

Ayla breathed out a sigh of relief. "Thank you. I appreciate that. You're right. I knew something was awry, but I wasn't sure what had gone down. I'd seen Henry Craigdon. I thought he was drunk. But then Beechwood told me the results had come back negative and he was being released without charge."

She didn't add that a part of her had remained confused and suspicious. She'd sat beside Craigdon on the backseat of the squad car. She'd smelled the alcohol on the man's breath. Over the years, she'd managed to put the niggling guilt about her lack of questioning aside and had managed to get on with her career.

But now the LECC investigators knew the truth about the drug and alcohol tests conducted on that fateful night. It was only a matter of time before they turned up on the commissioner's doorstep to demand answers—and this time, they wouldn't be put off. No wonder they'd been constantly calling.

And then she thought of how the commissioner might react if the pressure on him was increased. If it came down to saving his own ass, she had no doubt he'd throw her under the bus. She shivered in fear.

To complicate things further, the commissioner would want an accounting of her meeting with Joe. He'd specifically ordered her to meet with him. No doubt he'd badger her with questions, demand to know what Joe knew and if he posed a threat. She could imagine how her boss would react if she told him the truth. An icy trickle of foreboding filled her veins. Her hands went cold.

What am I going to say? What can I do? If I tell the truth, I could put Joe in danger. Still, it's only a matter of time before the investigators make their move. Then the commissioner will be left in no doubt about the extent of Joe as a threat and then he might turn his attention to me...

A ripple of fear gave her pause. What was the best move? As she sipped from her coffee, warming her hands around the mug, she was no closer to knowing what to do.

From his vantage point concealed behind the greenery, Christopher stared at Ayla and her companion in shock. "Joe," she'd called him. It was obvious from their conversation he was a fellow cop. One she'd worked with years earlier—including the night Janelle Craigdon died.

Christopher could hardly believe what he'd heard. That good old Henry had been drunk behind the wheel when his sister-in-law had met her death. It was a shocking discovery. From what Christopher remembered of that time, the family had circled the wagons around Henry, sympathizing with the terrible guilt he felt for causing her death. All the family had rallied around him, consoling him, beseeching him to accept it had been a terrible accident.

It wasn't Henry's fault that a kangaroo stepped out right at that moment in time. He'd swerved instinctively and it had all gone wrong, but that wasn't his fault. He wasn't to blame for Janelle's death. He had to believe that…

And yet he was. It was most definitely his fault.

Christopher didn't know if any of the remaining Craigdons were aware of Henry's lack of sobriety at the moment when their mother and aunt were killed, but he was certain Noah sure as hell had no idea the woman he was so keen on had been in on it from the start. She might not have been guilty of instigating the cover up, but at the very least, she'd looked the other way, and that was just as bad in Christopher's book. He was sure Noah would see it the same way.

Christopher smiled to himself, filled with a malicious kind of satisfaction. Now all he had to do was to wait until the opportune moment presented itself to drop his bombshell. He wasn't quite sure how or when he'd do it, but do it he would. And then he'd sit back and watch the fallout.

When Ayla made it back to her office after meeting Joe in the city, her stomach was twisted with dread. She walked slowly through the automatic doors and over to the lifts. All the way up to her office, she thought about what she was going to say to the commissioner. She still hadn't decided what to do.

The lift *dinged* and the doors slid open and she stepped out on her floor. She greeted the receptionist with a weak smile.

"Hi, Sarah. Is the commissioner in?"

"Oh, Ayla. I'm sorry. You've just missed him."

She came to a halt. "He's gone out?"

"Yes. He decided to get an early start on his weekend. He told me to tell you he'll catch up with you next week."

Ayla breathed a surreptitious sigh of relief. She felt like she'd been given a get-out-of-jail-free card. A reprieve from her execution date. All of a sudden, she felt freer, lighter. She thrust her misgivings aside and embraced the fact it was almost the weekend. Beginning with an evening date with Noah.

A quick stab of guilt and apprehension gave her pause. She still hadn't told him about her involvement. She was a coward, through and through. The problem was, she was scared he wouldn't understand her position, or the reason she'd kept quiet. And she selfishly wanted to savor her time with Noah for as long as it lasted. Once she came clean, their relationship would irrevocably change. She wasn't sure how severely he'd judge her, but there was no doubt he'd be upset and disappointed by her revelations.

She felt helpless. If she told him everything and he didn't believe her, they were doomed. If she didn't tell him, and he found out through other means, they were also doomed. Of course, the right thing to do, the *only* thing to do was to tell him. And she would. She definitely would. But not tonight. Tonight was a night she was determined to enjoy. It would be something to look back on, pull out of memory and reflect upon, hopefully with a smile.

Decision made, she set the guilt aside and relaxed enough to allow anticipation to surge through her veins. In a few short hours, she'd be meeting Noah and dancing the night away. They might even exchange a few more kisses.

She'd chosen a South American club on the edge of the city. It was tucked away on the southern end, away from the hustle and bustle of the more fashionable nightclubs which were closer to the harbor. You were unlikely to stumble across a celebrity at Let's Salsa, but the drinks were cheap and plentiful and the dancing was lively and fun. She hoped Noah approved of her choice.

Hurrying into her office, she shut down her computer and tidied up the papers on her desk. Switching off her desk lamp, she collected her handbag and left. If her boss thought it was time to get the weekend started, who was she to argue?

They'd agreed to meet outside the club. Noah looked gorgeous in form-fitting black pants, shiny black dress boots and a loose, white, long-sleeved button-up shirt. The top three buttons were undone, revealing a slice of firm, tanned skin. His dark-blond hair was messy in an incredibly sexy way. His cheeks were freshly shaven and his cologne smelled delicious. It was all Ayla could do not to throw herself into his arms and kiss him senseless.

Of course she restrained herself. She wasn't sure how he'd react. She was aware of his lack of experience with women. The last thing she wanted to do was to send him running for his life.

"You look amazing," he said. He pecked her on the cheek and then blushed furiously. He pushed his glasses higher up on bridge of his nose.

She grinned. He was so adorable. *And so dangerous…*

"Thanks." She turned for him in a swirl of fabric. Her floaty, bright yellow dress swished around her bare legs. "You look pretty good yourself."

"Ready?" she asked.

He chuckled and offered her his arm. "Absolutely!"

Noah paid their cover charge to enter the club and together they walked inside. There were a scattering of other patrons. Some stood by the bar, drinking. Others were gathered in groups, laughing and talking above the noise of the music. The syncopated salsa music filled the air. Ayla looked over toward the dance floor. This early in the night, it wasn't as crowded as it would be later on.

"Can I get you a drink?" Noah asked.

Ayla shook her head. "No. Let's dance first."

Noah's face lit up. She took his hand and led him over to the dance floor. She stepped into his arms and he drew her in close. He led her into a New York style of salsa. It felt as natural as if they'd been partnering each other for years.

Ayla had danced with a lot of men. None of them had made her feel as safe and secure as Noah did. He danced so well. He led with confidence and signaled each move clearly, giving her plenty of time to accommodate him. He had a natural grace and rhythm that couldn't be taught. He made it seem so easy. Graceful. Elegant. Fun. As they danced back and forth in a straight line, she took a moment to enjoy the sheer exhilaration of dancing with a man like Noah Craigdon.

Finally, the music came to an end and she fell against him, laughing. The crowd of onlookers who'd gathered around the dance floor broke into spontaneous applause. Noah looked down at her and beamed. A fine sheen of sweat was visible on his forehead. Again he pushed his glasses further up on his nose.

"That was great!" she exclaimed.

He winked. "You bet."

Her stomach turned over and desire rushed through her veins. Giving in to a sudden urge to kiss him, she went up on tiptoes and pressed her lips against his. She felt his momentary surprise, but then his arms tightened around her and he pulled her close. At the same time, his lips opened under hers.

Heat enveloped her. What he lacked in experience, he made up for in passion. His lips were firm and supple. They moved over hers, seeking pleasure, giving as much as he received. And then she remembered where they were and reluctantly brought the kiss to an end.

Easing back down off her tiptoes, she reflexively touched her lips. "Whoa!"

Noah flushed, a combination of pleasure and embarrassment coloring his cheeks. "How about that drink?" he asked.

She nodded and hand in hand, they moved over to the bar. She asked for a G&T and he ordered himself a beer. When their drinks arrived, she touched her glass to his.

"Cheers."

He grinned. "Cheers."

They enjoyed their drinks and shared friendly conversation. Noah talked about his brothers—Logan and Flynn. Ayla vaguely recalled seeing them at the ball, though she hadn't spoken to them. She told him more about her family—her parents who'd emigrated from Uruguay when she was eight.

"Brothers and sisters?" Noah asked.

"Nope. I'm an only child."

Noah looked appalled. "No siblings? Poor you. I can't imagine going through life without my brothers around. Sometimes they can be a pain in the neck, but for the most part, I wouldn't trade them for anything."

The sincerity in his voice touched her deep inside. "You care a great deal for them," she said softly.

"I love them."

His simple statement, spoken without embarrassment or artifice affected her. Warmth stole through her, turning her insides to mush.

How can he be so perfect? So wonderful in every way?

And then a familiar voice of caution eased into her consciousness. *Careful, Ayla. You're moving too fast... This man knows nothing of your secret and when he finds out...*

But right now that threat hanging over her head didn't seem to matter. She'd made the decision to enjoy this night for what it was and she was determined to see it through. She could tell from the intensity of Noah's gaze and the warmth in his smile that he was just as into her as she was him. Awareness arced between them. At one point, his hand accidentally brushed against her bare arm. The slight touch left her skin tingling and warmth flooded her core.

As the evening wore on and they once again took to the dance floor, Ayla's heightened awareness of the man pressed close against her was almost more than she could bear. Like before, when the music ended, it seemed inevitable that they'd kiss again. She tilted her head and he bent his and seconds later, their lips touched. Softly at first, and then passion exploded between them.

Noah crushed her to him and plundered her mouth with his tongue. Her arms stole up around his neck. She held him to her and returned his kisses with a passion that matched his. When they finally pulled apart, they were breathing hard.

The crowd erupted into loud clapping and cat calling. There were wolf whistles and shouts for them to get a room. Ayla ducked her head in embarrassment.

"Are you ready to leave?" she asked him.

His eyes were dark with emotion. He stared down at her and nodded. "Yes."

"Come." She took his hand and led the way through the press of bodies that had now swelled to twice their number from an hour before. Breaking free, they stepped outside and breathed deeply of the warm summer air.

She looked up at him and hoped she wasn't being too forward. "My place or yours?"

Chapter Twelve

Noah's heart thumped. He felt like he'd run a marathon. Okay, so they'd gone pretty hard on the dance floor, but that wasn't why his heart felt like it was about to burst right out of his chest. No, that had everything to do with the beautiful woman who stood beside him, her face turned up toward him, her expression filled with anticipation as she waited for his response.

As much as Noah wanted to go home with her and love her until they were exhausted, he was filled with uncertainty.

What if I make a fool of myself? What if I mess it up? I've never been with a woman before…

As if sensing his panic that lay just below the surface, Ayla touched his arm. "It's okay, Noah. We don't have to. I shouldn't have said anything. It's probably way too soon…"

He shook his head back and forth, a little frantically, anxious she didn't get the wrong idea.

"No, no. It's nothing like that. It's not that I don't want to. It's just…" He stopped, feeling helpless. Heat flooded his face.

"It's just what?" she asked.

He hated the uncertainty in her voice. Stepping forward, he framed her face with his hands and kissed her hard on the lips.

"I like you, Ayla. I really like you. I want to go home with you. I want to make love to you."

She frowned. "Then what's the problem?"

He lowered his head and then forced himself to look at her. "I've never done this before. I'm a virgin."

Now his face flamed. He braced himself for her bark of laughter, her stunned disbelief. Instead, she chuckled with good humor.

"So, is that what this is all about? You've decided you're ready to lose your virginity and I just happen to be around?" she teased.

Noah's embarrassment deepened. "No! Of course not!"

"Then what?

Noah closed his eyes and prayed for courage. It was now or never. "The thing is… I… I like you, Ayla. I *really* like you. I might even be in love with you. Does that scare you? I think it scares me."

Her expression sobered. Shadows passed over her face. His heart sank.

Damn it! I shouldn't have said anything! Now I've frightened her off!

She stared up at him. "Of course it scares me, but I just can't stay away from you. I want to—for so many reasons— but I can't." She shrugged helplessly. "I like you too, Noah. I… I might be in love with you, too. Are you okay with that?"

Elation coursed through him. He wanted to whoop with the joy of it. He settled for a wide grin.

She smiled back and lifted her hand to cup his cheek. "Thank you for telling me. That you're a virgin. I can tell you're embarrassed, but there's no need to be. Do you have any idea how incredibly sexy that is? To know you've never been with another woman? Never shared that kind of intimacy?" She followed her words with a soft, slow kiss. "I'd be honored to be your first."

Noah sucked in a breath at the enormity of the moment.

Blood rushed to his cock which hardened in anticipation of what was to come. Once again, they kissed until they were breathless. When they finally pulled apart, Ayla's chest was heaving.

She grinned. "So, what's it going to be? My place or yours?"

He grinned back, unable to help himself. "Yours is closer."

She winked. "Sounds good to me. Are we walking or catching a taxi?"

He pulled her to him once again. This time, he pressed his erection against her stomach.

She groaned. "Let's find a taxi."

Christopher scrubbed a hand through his hair and tried to shake off his bad mood. He'd been irritable all afternoon. Lately, it seemed nothing was going his way. He'd been unforgivably snubbed by his father when he'd been left out of Henry's will. He'd lost his comfortable job at McClintock Properties. His troublemaking schemes against his half-brothers and sisters had come to nothing. Nothing was going right for him and he was sick and tired of it.

He'd come into the city in the hopes of finding a willing woman to cheer him up, if only for the night. The city was crowded with people spilling out of nightclubs and bars. He'd spent the first few hours at his favorite haunt. Harry's Bar wasn't known for its crowds, but sometimes he got lucky. Not tonight. So he'd made his way further uptown to The Pitt.

The last time he'd been there, he'd seen Noah and the cop. Ayla Rodriguez. The dancer. The deceiver. He half-hoped to run into them again. It would be fun to drop vague hints about the video footage he'd captured and now had stored safely in the cloud. Neither of them would have a clue what he was talking about, but it might plant a seed of doubt. Noah would wonder what Ayla had to do with his mother's death. Ayla would be stricken with the knowledge someone knew her secret. It would provide Christopher with hours of entertainment, but alas…it hadn't come to pass. Noah and Ayla weren't at The Pitt.

He'd spent another couple of hours at the bar, surveying the crowd, looking for a potential bedmate. There was no one. Well, not *no one*. The brassy blond with the big tits and bad teeth had made it clear she was his for the taking, but he hadn't gotten that desperate. She had more than a decade on him.

Then there was the cute brunette with the freckles and braces, but she was way too young. She barely looked legal. He had no idea what she was thinking, making moves on him. He was old enough to be her father.

And so, now he found himself outside the nightclub, feeling jaded and contemplating his sad and sorry life.

Where did it all go so wrong?

He didn't have to look far for an answer. Everything came back to his father. *Henry Craigdon.* The man he utterly despised. Henry's death hadn't lessened the anger. If anything, the fact Christopher wouldn't ever be given another opportunity to tell his father exactly how he felt only fed his fury.

Come on. I'm forty years old… I need to let this go…

That was the problem. He couldn't let it go. His anger was now what sustained him, gave him the incentive to keep up the fight. He was no longer able to fight against his father, but he could definitely make it hard for the family members Henry had left behind.

The thought brought a smile of satisfaction to his face. Feeling better, he pulled off his jacket. Even though it was late, it was warmer out there than it had been in the nightclub. Draping the jacket over his arm, he looked around for a taxi. He spied one pulling up right across the street.

The rear taxi door nearest to the footpath came open and as Christopher watched, Noah and Ayla stepped out. They stood there with their arms around each other looking very friendly indeed.

Interesting…

Oblivious to his presence, they turned and headed through the double doors of an apartment building. From his vantage point, Christopher saw them walk over to a set of stairs. A short time later, they disappeared.

Well, well, well…

This was even more proof Noah was besotted. Noah lived in Manly, a few blocks down from Flynn. That left Ayla. She must live in the city. In the apartments across from him. The ones they'd just entered hand in hand.

Christopher was filled with a sharp burst of jealousy, followed quickly by another bout of self-pity. Typical. Even shy Noah was getting laid tonight.

What the hell's wrong with me? Why doesn't anyone love me? Not even my father.

With an effort, Christopher forced the self-pity aside. That would get him nowhere. Far more interesting was the fact Noah and Ayla's relationship had obviously ramped up a notch. They were sleeping together. That little tidbit was significant. It showed how serious they'd become, and how much she meant to Noah. He wasn't like Flynn. Noah didn't go through women like some men changed their clothes. Noah having sex with Ayla, was a big deal.

Christopher smiled. He thought of his footage. This was about to become so much more fun than he'd realized. He'd bet every cent of his contested inheritance that Noah didn't have a clue little Miss Ayla wasn't as innocent as he assumed.

Noah followed Ayla as she walked into her apartment and starting switching on lights. Though she had no views to speak of, the apartment was spacious and stylishly furnished and he could tell from the floor-to-ceiling windows in the open-plan kitchen and living room that in the daytime, the place would be filled with light. Right now, she moved to close the curtains and cocoon them inside. He was immediately filled with a rush of nerves.

"Can I get you a drink?" she asked.

He nodded. "Thanks. A beer sounds good."

She walked over to the fridge and pulled out a Corona. Expertly twisting off the lid, she handed it to him.

"Thanks." He grinned. "That's not the first time you've done that."

She chuckled. "You're right. There's nothing like a cold beer after a hard day at the office."

She twisted off the cap of another beer and took a healthy swallow and then directed him toward the couch. He took a seat beside her.

"Tell me about working for the commissioner. Have you worked for him long?"

She looked momentarily startled and then shook her head and grinned. "It's Friday night. No talk of work. Let's talk about *us*."

She clinked her bottle against his and gave him a cheeky wink. Another surge of nerves rushed through his veins and settled uncomfortably in his gut. He licked his suddenly dry lips and then took another gulp of his beer.

She laughed gently. "Relax, Noah. We're not going to do anything you aren't comfortable with."

He blushed, hating she could read him so easily, but appreciating her efforts to help him relax. Drawing in a deep, restorative breath, he eased it out on a sigh.

She shot him a disarming grin. "Wow. That sounds heavy. Am I that hard to be around?"

He opened his mouth to protest and caught the teasing glint in her eyes just in time. He shrugged self-deprecatingly and grinned. "You got me."

She set down her beer on the coffee table and moved closer. "I'm done talking. Come here."

With that she drew his head down to hers and kissed him. It was a slow, sensual kiss of exploration and it set his blood on fire. Blindly, he set his beer aside and took her in his arms. His nerves dissolved in a rush of excitement. There was nothing and no one but Ayla.

Her tongue pressed against his lips and he willingly opened his mouth. Her tongue swept inside and she set about tasting him, kissing him, loving him with her mouth. And then she moved lower. She kissed her way down his chin and buried her face in his neck. The blood pounded in the pulse where she concentrated her efforts.

Meanwhile, her hands stroked his chest, his stomach, his shoulders through the soft cotton of his shirt. Impatient to have her hands on his skin, he pulled slightly away. Tugging his shirt out of his pants, one by one, he popped the buttons. Ayla joined in, pushing the shirt off his shoulders. It fell to the couch, unheeded.

The feel of her soft palms caressing him drove him wild. Never before had he felt something so exquisite. She stroked her fingernails across his nipples, leaving them hard. She trailed her fingers over his pectorals, squeezing them, filling her palms with their shape. And then she bent her head and her lips followed in the wake of her fingers. When she sucked one of his nipples into her mouth, he almost came off the couch.

His body burned. His cock throbbed painfully. He needed to feel her against him, skin to skin, from head to toe. Frantic now, he reached for her clothes. She turned her back on him and he went straight for the zipper on her dress. He eased it down and she shimmied out of the soft fabric, standing before him in nothing but a black bra and matching panties. He gazed at her in awe.

"You're so beautiful."

She blushed with pleasure and held out her hand toward him, urging him up. He put his hand in hers and she pulled him to a standing position. Her hands went to his belt and moments later, she'd worked it free from his pants. She popped the button on his pants and slid down his zipper.

With his gaze fixed on hers, he stepped out of his pants and kicked them out of the way. Unfortunately the cuffs got caught on his boots. Laughing, he toppled onto the couch and quickly rid himself of the problem. Then he came upright again and stood before her in his underwear.

She gazed at him with such intensity, he began to feel embarrassed. "Is there something wrong?"

She shook her head and immediately stepped forward and tugged his head down to hers. After giving him a fierce kiss, she pulled back. "Absolutely nothing." She raked him from head to toe. "You... You're magnificent."

Her words pleased him and filled him with warmth. Though he'd never considered himself especially good looking, he took pride in his appearance. He worked out regularly in the gym and liked to jog, cycle, and swim. Though he spent most of his working life behind a desk, it was important to him that he maintain his fitness. Now he was happy that he did. Ayla's approval made his heart skip a beat.

Taking his hand, she led him down a short hallway and into her bedroom. The queen-sized bed took up most of the room. Two matching antique bedside tables and a tallboy completed the furniture. And then Ayla reached around behind her and undid the clasp of her bra and all thought of furniture and anything else scattered from his mind.

Her breasts were full and round and perfectly formed. Her nipples were a rosebud pale pink. With her gaze on his, she stepped out of her panties and stood proudly naked before him. He'd never seen anything so beautiful.

Slowly, she walked toward him and came to a halt a breath away. She reached out and trailed her fingernail across his chest and then lower, to hook in the waistband of his underwear. His breath caught in his throat. He stood stock still. With both hands now grasping his waistband, she stared at him and eased his boxers over his hips.

His heart pounded. His cock, thick and hard and throbbing, jutted out. She was the first woman to see him naked. He should have felt embarrassed, but he didn't. In fact, he stood tall and proud before her, letting her look her fill.

Desire flared deeply in her eyes. He stepped out of his boxers and kicked them away. And then he drew her close until she was flush against him. The feel of her soft curves against his heated skin was indescribable. She was tiny. Not even coming up to his shoulder. And yet she fitted perfectly against him, like she'd been made for him.

He bent his head and kissed her softly, learning the shape and texture of her mouth. She tasted faintly of beer. No doubt he tasted the same. And then she opened her mouth under his and changed the angle of her head. His tongue swept out and traced the line of her lips, before seeking refuge inside her mouth. She was hot and moist and delicious. He could kiss her all night.

But then she moved and pressed herself even closer against him. All he could think of was burying himself inside her, losing himself in her heat. With that thought driving him forward, he bent and picked her up in his arms. He carried her the short distance to her bed and gently lowered her to the mattress.

He followed her down, unable to stay away. They kissed with tongues and legs entwined. The fire inside him burned hotter. His heart thumped. His breath came fast. He felt like he might explode.

As if sensing how close he was, Ayla moved out of his arms. She reached into the bedside drawer and pulled out a condom. Now the moment was upon him, he was suddenly filled with nerves. Once again, she seemed to sense his uncertainty.

With gentle hands, she took his cock and sheathed him with the condom. He trembled beneath her touch. Still on her knees, she kissed him deeply and then drew him down on top of her, holding him close.

He nudged her thighs open. She let her legs fall wide. Positioning himself at her opening, he prayed his control held long enough to make it good for her.

"Make love to me Noah," she whispered.

Forgetting his nerves, he acted on instinct. He pressed against her entrance. With the slightest flexing forward of his hips, he slid inside her. He gasped.

"Ayla."

She felt exquisite. Tight. Hot. Amazing. It was like nothing he could have imagined. Her hands tightened around his neck. She murmured quiet words of encouragement. Once again, moving by instinct, he began to thrust in and out.

Despite his best intentions, it was over all too soon. With a cry of triumph, he reached the peak and toppled over the edge. Still joined, he collapsed against her, his breath coming harsh and fast.

"I'm sorry," he managed. "I tried so hard to make it last."

She merely kissed him on the lips and smoothed back his damp hair. "It's all good. The night's still young."

Noah grinned. "You're right. I'm sure I have at least another round in me yet."

True to his word, it didn't take long for Noah to recover. Ayla reached down between them and tightened her hand around his erection. It was long and hard and thick. Renewed desire surged inside her.

Taking the initiative, Noah moved until he straddled her hips. Bending over her, he kissed her softly on the lips. Then he kissed her closed eyelids and then kissed his way down her face. Her nose, her cheeks, her earlobe and then he nuzzled the side of her neck.

Fire trailed in the wake of his heated mouth. Her hands clutched at his shoulders, at the soft warmth of his bare skin. Her heart pounded a rapid staccato in her chest and a pulse beat frantically in her neck. And still he kissed her.

He moved lower and bent to kiss her breasts. He picked one up, testing its weight and then swept his tongue over her nipple. She gasped. The sensation of his hot, wet mouth on her sensitive flesh was indescribable.

"Do you like that?" he asked, his face filled with curiosity.

"Yes," she breathed. "I like that a lot."

He continued his sensual exploration, kissing his way down her chest. His lips skimmed over her ribcage. He paused to dip his tongue into her belly button.

She moved restlessly beneath him, hungry for the feel of him inside her once again. She pulled away and tore open another condom. This time, she showed him how to roll it on.

Now fully sheathed, once again, he took up position between her thighs. This time, he entered her in a single thrust, snatching away her breath. And then he began to move.

Slowly at first and then increasing the pace. She clung to the solidness of his shoulders. Her breath came faster her desire increased and her body grew hot and flushed. And then she was there, at the peak and free-falling. She cried out in triumph and relief, savoring the feelings inside her for as long as she could.

Another few quick thrusts and Noah had joined her in climax. Breathing hard, he collapsed against her momentarily and then rolled onto his side, taking her with him. Kissing her tenderly on the lips, he fell asleep with a smile on his face.

Chapter Thirteen

Monday morning dawned bright and sunny. Noah walked into work with a spring in his step. Ever since he'd spent the night with Ayla, he hadn't been able to wipe the grin off his face. They'd gone out for breakfast Saturday morning and had lingered over bacon and eggs and pancakes so long the waiter asked if they were staying for lunch. Ayla was very easy to talk to. Noah forgot about his shyness. His habitual timidity around women disappeared when he was with her. He hardly recognized himself.

He supposed losing his virginity to her had helped build his confidence. She knew him more intimately than anyone on the planet. Their night together had been magical. She seemed to feel the same way. It was only when she remembered an errand she'd forgotten about that she'd left. Her departure had been a little abrupt, with her only bending to give him a quick kiss before she left, but she'd promised to call him and he had no reason to believe she wouldn't. Although he didn't know her well, he knew enough to be confident she was trustworthy—a woman of honesty and integrity. He couldn't wait to see her again.

"Someone's in a good mood."

Noah spotted Declan coming out of the tearoom, coffee in hand. He set his briefcase on his desk and grinned. "You bet."

"You look like a man who just discovered a couple of million dollars in a long-forgotten bank account. What happened?"

Though the feelings bubbling up inside him were still so fresh and new, Noah found himself telling Declan about his weekend. He didn't go into any detail, but he said enough for Declan to get the picture Noah's date had gone well.

"She sounds pretty special," he agreed. "Do I know her?"

Noah blushed and was immediately irritated by his reaction. So what if Ayla worked for the police commissioner? It wasn't like she was connected to their investigation.

"Actually, you do," Noah responded. "Her name's Ayla Rodriguez. She's Beechwood's chief of staff."

Declan frowned. "Don't you think that's a little too close for comfort?"

Noah held Declan's gaze a little defiantly. "No."

Declan stared at him a moment longer and then shrugged. "If you say so."

Noah felt a surge of defensiveness. "Just because she works for the commissioner doesn't mean she had anything to do with the accident. That happened a decade ago. She would have barely been out of high school. Besides, I met her before we began this investigation."

Once again, Declan shrugged and then changed the subject. "Speaking of the investigation, where are we up to?"

Noah nodded briefly. "Bettino's evidence is damning. We're still waiting for him to come in and make a formal statement. Once we have that, we'll be in a stronger position, but of course, it's all hearsay. We need more proof of Beechwood's involvement in the cover up."

"You're right. We have to tread lightly, here. We're dealing with very sensitive information. Bettino might have made an effort to clean himself up, but there's no guarantee he won't fall off the wagon. If that happens, it'll take a defense lawyer about thirty seconds to discredit him. We need more than Bettino."

"Yes. As soon as Beechwood gets an inkling about the direction of our investigation, he's going to hit the roof. We can't afford to leave the department open to a defamation lawsuit. We need to have a watertight case before we show our hand."

"What do you suggest?"

"We need to get a statement from John Hassad. Though we initially dismissed what he told his daughter, given what Bettino told us, that appears more and more likely."

"Where is he?"

"Thanks to a successful DEA sting, he's currently warming his butt in jail."

"Long Bay?"

"Yes."

"I'll call and set up a meeting," Declan offered.

"Thanks. I also issued a warrant for Henry's bank statements and telephone records." Noah reached for two large yellow envelopes that sat on his desk. "I'm hoping these are them."

"What are you looking for?"

"Nothing in particular. I'm interested to see what he spent his money on in the hours before my mother was killed. Of course, evidence of alcohol purchases won't prove he was the one who consumed it, but it's a start."

Declan nodded. "I'll go and call the jail. Let me know what you find." With that, Declan left Noah's office.

Hanging up his jacket, Noah returned to his desk. He opened the first envelope. Just as he'd hoped, it contained pages of Henry's bank statements. He found the one that covered the month up to and including the fateful night. Using a ruler, he slowly and methodically went through the list of charges made against Henry's credit card.

According to the police report, Noah's mother had died at 2318 hours on Saturday, April 10, 2010. Noah's gaze snagged on several entries for hotel accommodation and meals from the Friday and Saturday. The last charge made that day was from a restaurant at a winery in Pokolbin. If what John Hassad had told his daughter was true, Hassad must have been there, too.

Noah needed to contact the winery and see if they had any CCTV footage of the night. Given it had happened ten years ago, it was a long shot, but one he had to at least inquire about. With that thought in mind, he searched online for the contact details for the winery and picked up the phone. His call was answered on the third ring.

"Pokolbin Winery. This is Shane."

Noah explained who he was and what he was looking for. The man on the other end of the line merely laughed.

"Sorry, mate. We only keep the footage for thirty days. Those tapes are long gone."

Noah swallowed his disappointment and thanked the man for his help. He ended the call. Stacking his hands behind his head, he sighed. He wasn't surprised the footage was gone. It just meant he had to find the evidence somewhere else.

He reached for the second envelope and pulled out Henry's phone records from the same time period. Noah hoped they might shed more light on his uncle's movements that day—and those of his mother. He still couldn't believe his sweet, gentle mother had died with cocaine in her blood. More than likely Henry had supplied the drugs. After all, he had easy access to them. But why would she have taken them? It just didn't fit with the mother he knew.

Okay, so he was only eighteen when it happened, but he was still living at home. Surely he would have had some idea if she was taking drugs. Or maybe he'd been too wrapped up in his own issues to notice.

At the time, there had been a lot going on. He'd never told anyone about his connection to his uncle's drug business, not even his brothers. The shame of it still burned. There had also been decisions to make about going to university to study law or do something else. In the end, he'd completed one year of law school, but discovered it wasn't for him. He'd dropped out and entered the police academy. He hadn't looked back.

He flipped over another page of entries and ran his ruler down the dates. Several calls had been made on the Friday and Saturday in question. Two had been made to his aunt, Henry's wife, Elizabeth. Neither had lasted more than forty seconds. There was also a call to Noah's mother on the Friday morning. This call lasted much longer. Seven minutes, to be exact. There were a few calls made over the course of the two days to Craigdon Enterprises. Noah also highlighted a handful of numbers he didn't recognize. He'd follow those up later.

Included with the log of phone calls were pages of Henry's texts. Once again, Noah went straight to the relevant days. Shortly after the seven-minute phone call Henry had made to Noah's mother on the day before she died, his uncle had sent her a text. Unlike the phone calls, which gave no indication of what had been said, the texts were there in plain black writing for all to see.

Meet me @ Northbridge
I'll pick u up from Harriet's
@ 12pm

Noah frowned. Harriet Young was his late mother's closest friend. She lived in Northbridge. Janelle had told Noah's father she was staying with Harriet for that weekend. And yet, according to the text, she'd planned all along to go somewhere with Henry.

I need to speak with Harriet... I need to know what she knows... Whether she was complicit in this, or whether she was as oblivious as the rest of us as to what had been going on...whatever that was.

If the puzzle pieces were to be believed, it was highly likely his mother and uncle had been involved in an affair. What other reasonable explanation was there? Noah scanned through more of their text messages, many of which suggested an intimacy that couldn't be denied.

Miss u xxx

Thinking of u xxx

Can't stop thinking about last night. Ur so sexy

How long b4 u can leave? I need 2 c u

I love u 2 xxx

There were endless entries. Not all of them so intimate, but many of them were. Noah shook his head, stunned by the evidence. He couldn't believe the double life his mother had led. Right under their noses. Just like his father with Aunt Elizabeth. All this time, everyone thought they were playing happy families when that couldn't be further from the truth.

And then another unwelcome thought intruded. His parents weren't the only ones who'd led secret lives.

Perhaps that's why I feel so angry? I'm guilty of the same thing myself.

And then that thought was quickly followed by another far more frightening one.

What if Ayla finds out….?

Ayla stared at her computer screen and tried to focus. It was already mid-morning and apart from the usual meeting first thing with her boss as they went over the day's schedule, she'd achieved nothing. The problem was Noah. They'd had a wonderful Friday night together that had stretched into Saturday. It might have been his first time, but he was a quick learner. She blushed at the thought of some of the things they'd done.

They'd still been basking in the afterglow on Saturday morning. They'd gone out for breakfast. He'd been sweet and attentive and funny. But then she'd thought about what she'd been keeping from him, and just like that, the comfortable air between them had dissolved and Ayla hadn't been able to get away from him quickly enough. She'd given him some excuse about needing to tend to some errands and she could tell from the surprise on his face he'd been taken aback, but she hadn't been able to help it.

Now, a day and a half later, she was still struggling with what to do. It wasn't fair to Noah to keep what she knew about Beechwood from him, and her knowledge would likely help his case, but she was terrified about how he'd react.

Will he blame me? Will he think I was involved?

Once again, thoughts of their night together flooded her mind. He was an unselfish and considerate lover. After that first time, he'd taken the time to explore every inch of her body and ensure she received as much pleasure as he did. He cared about her in a way no man had ever cared for her before. She wanted to see him again. But she also needed to do the right thing.

Oh, God, Don't tell me I'm falling in love with him? How can I be? It's way too soon…

All she knew for certain was that he'd suddenly become the most important thing in her life. She hadn't planned on that happening, but there it was. Because of the secret she concealed, the knowledge of how much he meant to her was more terrifying than anything she'd ever faced. Then there was the very real threat to her career…

Oh, God! What am I going to do?

Noah drove the unmarked squad car out to Long Bay Correctional Center. Declan kept him company in the passenger seat.

"So," Declan said. "Tell me what you know about John Hassad."

Noah glanced at his partner and then returned his attention to the road. "Not much. I've never had any direct dealings with the guy. My older brother dates Hassad's daughter."

Declan whistled. "How does that work?"

Noah explained how Jayde was an undercover DEA operative. "Her father was oblivious to her profession. She'd told him she worked in admin. He had no reason not to believe her."

Declan frowned. "How could she be a cop and her father not know anything about it?"

"It's a long story. Jayde's father walked out on her and her mother when she was seven. She hadn't seen him for more than twenty years. She was aware of the DEA's interest in him. She offered to go undercover to find enough evidence against him to put him away."

Declan's eyes widened in surprise. "Wow. She must have some balls and a lot of hate to go undercover in order to entrap her father. It could have gone terribly wrong if he'd discovered what she was up to."

"Yes. Lucky for her, and for Flynn, she managed to get what the DEA needed before the truth came out. Hassad's been charged with a whole list of drug offenses. If he's convicted, he's looking at twenty to twenty-five years."

"Is that why he offered up the information about Henry Craigdon?"

"No. That came before. Jayde was aware the DEA had also been looking at my uncle. At the time I met her, she was actively investigating my family." He gave a brief laugh. "We just didn't know it."

"Wow. I'm impressed. I'd like to meet this Jayde Hassad."

Noah shrugged. "That can be arranged. If you can ever drag yourself away from your kids and attend a social function with me."

Declan grinned and gave Noah the finger. Noah laughed.

Swinging the car into the entryway, he drove up the paved driveway to the huge steel gates. He gave his credentials to the security guard and moments later, they were heading inside the jail.

After going through another security checkpoint, including a metal detector and scanner, Noah and Declan were shown into an interview room. It was the standard décor of plain wood-and-steel furniture and pale olive-green walls. A camera was fixed to a steel bracket in one corner and directed downwards. They waited for ten minutes before the door opened. A corrections officer walked in and behind him followed the man Noah assumed was John Hassad.

Noah could see the resemblance to Jayde. Both had striking blue eyes, olive skin and black hair, although John's was peppered with gray. Noah sensed a keen intelligence as Hassad assessed Noah and Declan with wariness. The corrections officer undid the handcuffs around Hassad's wrists and indicated he take a seat. The guard then left to stand outside the closed door.

"Are you John Hassad?" Noah asked, seated opposite, alongside Declan.

"Who wants to know?"

"I'm Detective Noah Craigdon and this is my partner, Detective Declan Munro."

Hassad tilted his head to one side, curiosity sparking in his gaze. "Craigdon? Any relation to Henry?"

"He was my uncle. He and my father were brothers."

"I see."

Noah leaned slightly forward. "In fact, my uncle's the reason we've come to see you."

"Oh, yeah? How come? The poor bastard's been dead for nearly a year."

"You're right," Noah replied. He told Hassad about the investigation he and Declan were involved in.

"Janelle Craigdon was my mother," he added, his voice flat.

Hassad nodded, his expression filled with understanding. "Ah. I see."

Noah watched him carefully. "You told Jayde you were with my mother and my uncle the night my mother died. Was that true?"

"Of course it was true. What do you think, I'm a liar?"

"No one's calling you a liar," Declan stated calmly. "We're just trying to get to the truth. Did you tell your daughter you were with Henry and Janelle the night Janelle Craigdon was killed in a motor vehicle accident?"

"Yes. And I was."

"Where were you?" Noah asked.

"In the Hunter Valley."

"Whereabouts?"

"Pokolbin."

"Why were you there?" Noah demanded.

Hassad gave Noah a sly look. "Well, Detective, I can't rightly say. I'm not going to rat anyone out."

Noah made an impatient sound in his throat. "Listen, Hassad. I'm not from the DEA. Whatever drug charges you're facing, that's between them and you. All I want to know is where you met my uncle the night my mother died."

Hassad eyed him steadily, a smirk on his face. Noah's hands tightened into fists. It was all he could do not to punch the man. Then Hassad spoke.

"What kind of deal are you offering?"

Noah glared at him. "No deal. We just want the truth."

Once again, Hassad took his time in replying. Noah sat with his fists clenched, trying to hold on to his patience. Just when he thought their mission was hopeless, Hassad spoke.

"I met your uncle in a restaurant at the Pokolbin Winery. Your mother was there. We had dinner, a few drinks. Okay, lots of drinks. Your uncle was plastered by the end of the night. Your mother was in pretty bad shape, too. She hadn't been drinking as much, but she'd been snorting coke. It was her first time. She had it all over her nose. It was funny."

Noah stared at him in disbelief. "She snorted cocaine right there in the restaurant?"

"Yeah. What can I say? The place was nearly empty. We were in a corner booth. The lighting was dim."

Noah shook his head in disgust. He was still coming to terms with his mother's secrets. He wasn't sure he'd ever be able to reconcile them with the woman he'd known and loved.

"What time of night was this?" he asked.

Hassad shrugged. "I don't know. It was late. Maybe eleven."

The police report indicated the accident had occurred at 2318 hours. If Hassad's timeline was true, the accident occurred not long after Henry and Noah's mother left the restaurant. There was no way his uncle would have passed the breath test. It was as Bettino had said. The sample had been provided by him.

Noah closed his eyes briefly against a wave of pain. It was difficult to accept his uncle had been at fault. For ten long years, Noah and everyone else in his family had lived with the knowledge his mother's death had been a tragic accident. They'd supported his uncle through his guilt. Had encouraged him to let it go. Now Noah knew the truth. He could hardly contain his anger.

Sometimes, life just isn't fair...

Chapter Fourteen

oah sat in silence, his mind in turmoil, as he pulled away from the jail and joined the traffic headed back toward the city. Declan appeared equally consumed by his own thoughts. Coming to stop at a set of lights, Noah finally spoke.

"Remember when you asked what my mother was doing with my uncle when she died?"

"Yeah."

"You wondered if they worked together."

"Yeah. You said they didn't."

Noah grimaced. "Right. They didn't." He paused and then went on. After all, as soon as Declan got a look at the text messages, he'd know right away why Noah's mother had been with his uncle that night.

"The thing is… They were having an affair. My mother and Uncle Henry."

"Shit." Declan turned to look at him. "I kind of guessed as much."

Noah bit his lip. "Yeah."

"That's hard to take."

"Yeah. I'm not sure if it's harder to find out now, when she's dead and I can't talk to her about it, or whether it would have been easier to find out while she was still alive."

"It's not worth worrying about, mate. What's done is done. You can't change the past."

"You're right. But there's someone I need to talk to. Harriet Young. She was my mom's best friend. I've been able to gather from the text messages Harriet knew what was going on."

Declan shot him a dubious look. "Do you think it'll make a difference? Talking to her?"

"I don't know," Noah admitted, "but I've got to do it. I thought I might take the rest of the afternoon off. Will you cover for me if something comes up?"

"Of course. You do what you have to do."

Noah smiled gratefully. "Thanks, mate. I owe you one."

"Not at all. That's what friends are for."

It was mid-afternoon when Noah pulled up outside the two-story sand-colored brick house in Northbridge that had been owned by Harriet Young for as long as Noah could remember. He'd gotten her number off an old phone he found in the bottom drawer of his office and had called ahead. She'd been surprised to hear from him, but thankfully had agreed to see him.

The house backed up to a council reserve filled with native gums, Moreton Bay figs and other lush greenery. The established trees and shrubs not only were nice to look at, they also provided privacy. He pressed the doorbell and stood back to wait. A few minutes later, Harriet met him at the front door.

She looked well. Dressed in a pale blue, short-sleeved pants suit, she was as trim and toned as she'd always been. Her graying hair had been artfully touched up with blond highlights. Her skin was barely wrinkled. Though it had been more than ten years since he'd seen her, it was obvious time had treated her favorably. He wondered if his mother would look as good if she'd lived that long.

He pushed the useless thought aside. The fact was, his mother had died at the age of fifty. There were no what-ifs.

"Noah! How wonderful to see you! My, haven't you grown into a strapping lad."

Harriet opened the door and greeted him with a brief hug and a peck on the cheek. He smiled.

"It's nice to see you, too. It's been a long time."

"Far too long," she agreed and then stood back and allowed him to enter.

He walked into a wide entryway that opened up into a large and airy living room that boasted great views of the parklike reserve. He could still remember coming over to the house as a kid. When they were children, his mother had often collected them from school and gone over to visit with her friend. Harriet's two sons were a bit older than Flynn, but they got on well enough and they all played together while their mothers chatted over coffee. Noah had fond memories of PlayStations, Minecraft and just hanging out with the boys.

"How have you been? You look well," Harriet said. She walked past him and headed into the kitchen. Noah followed.

"Yes, I've been great. Busy at work. The usual."

"I heard you worked for Internal Affairs," she said.

"Yes. It's called the LECC now. The Law Enforcement Conduct Commission. A long name for what is essentially still Internal Affairs."

She laughed. "Well, whatever it's called, I'm sure your mother would have been proud."

At the mention of his mother, Noah's chest tightened. After all these years, it was at times like this he missed her most. Harriet had been her best friend. She known his mother as well, if not better, than anyone. He'd forever associate Harriet and this house with his mother.

"Can I get you a coffee?"

Setting his thoughts aside, he nodded. "Thanks. That would be great."

They took their coffee and sat outside at the round wooden table Noah remembered from years ago. The wood had weathered to a dull brown and had cracked in a few places, but the serenity that surrounded them in the garden was both familiar and therapeutic. He could barely hear the traffic from the street. Occasionally the sound of birdsong filled the air.

"It's lovely out here, Harriet. I bet you use it a lot."

She smiled. "Yes. I do."

They swapped small talk over her sons and Noah's brothers. She asked after Archie.

"He's fine," Noah replied. "We've had a few surprises since Uncle Henry died, but nothing we can't handle."

Harriet regarded him with cautious curiosity. "Such as?"

Noah drew in a breath. When he'd called her, he'd made no mention of the reason for his visit. He'd let her believe he wanted to catch up for old times' sake. While he'd come there specifically to ask Harriet about his mother's affair with Henry, it was a delicate subject. He had no idea how much Harriet knew, nor how she might react. Though she looked sturdy and well, he didn't want to be the cause of a heart attack. So he took refuge in something that didn't involve her.

"We recently discovered my father and my Aunt Elizabeth had an affair that produced a daughter. Sophia. Up until now, I thought she was my cousin. It turns out she's my half-sister."

Harriet's eyes widened. "Wow. That's huge."

Though she sounded surprised, the shock he'd expected wasn't there. His gut told him she'd already known something about it. He shot her a sideways glance.

"You don't sound too surprised."

To her credit, she didn't deny it. She lowered her gaze to her lap and sat in silence for a moment, as if weighing her options. Then she looked at him and nodded.

"No wonder you went into policing. You're too perceptive by half, Noah Craigdon."

"So you did know?"

"Yes."

"About Dad's affair?"

"About all of it."

"You knew Sophia wasn't Uncle Henry's daughter?"

"Not conclusively, but there was certainly a question about it in my mind."

The information had to have come from his mother. There was no other way Harriet could have known about it. When he put the question to her, she confirmed it.

"Janelle suspected your father was having an affair. She wasn't sure when it had started, but she was sure it was going on. She wasn't certain Archie was Sophia's father, but she couldn't help but wonder."

"So that made two of them. They were both as bad as each other."

There. He'd said it. The words hung heavy between them. His stomach clenched with nerves as he waited for her answer. She remained silent for a long time. He snuck a glance at her to check she was okay. Her color was high and her chest rose and fell rather rapidly, but she appeared otherwise fine.

"Harriet?" he asked gently.

And then her narrow shoulders slumped on a weary sigh. "How did you find out?"

"Does it matter?"

"It does to me. She swore to me secrecy. She told me I was the only person, apart from Henry, who knew. All these years I've kept her secret. So, yes, it matters how you found out."

This time it was Noah who took refuge in a sigh. "We've opened an investigation into my mother's death. During the course of the investigation, I went through my uncle's phone records, his texts. It was obvious they were having an affair."

She nodded in acknowledgement. "Why are you looking into Janelle's death? It happened so long ago."

"You're right. Let's just say there were questions that had gone unanswered for far too long. I wasn't the only one in my family who's wondered why my mother was with Uncle Henry that night, so late and so far from home. She'd told my father she was staying with you that fateful weekend."

Sadness filled Harriet's wrinkled face. "I want you to know I didn't approve of the affair and I told your mother that. But she and Henry really loved each other. It was plain for me to see. Who was I to judge, or to step in the way of true love?"

"Do you know when it started?" he asked as calmly as he could.

"A long time ago. You were only two or three, as far as I can recall."

Noah tensed in shock. He was eighteen when his mother was killed.

The affair had been going on for fifteen or sixteen years… I imagined it began much later than that…

He filed the information away to take out later and examine from all angles when he wasn't feeling so blindsided. Right now, it was too much to deal with. Besides, he had to get to the bottom of his investigation. Put to bed those unanswered questions once and for all, including holding responsible the person who'd allowed Uncle Henry to walk away from his mother's death without so much as a traffic ticket. That was his priority.

"My father's adamant my mother never cheated on him. Even now. How did they get away with it for so long without anyone knowing?"

A look of resignation flooded Harriet's face. "I guess that was my fault."

"How do you mean?"

She sighed wearily. All of a sudden, she looked every bit of her sixty years. "I used to cover for them. They often met here. Sometimes just for drinks and conversation. Other times your mother would leave her car here and go somewhere with your uncle. I never asked any questions. On the odd occasion when your father would phone here looking for her, I'd tell him she was in the bathroom and offered to give her a message. He always declined. I was careful to send Janelle a text warning her she needed to call him."

Noah looked at her, aghast. "So you actively took part in the deception?"

Harriet regarded him sadly. "I like to think I was doing my bit to support a dear friend. I might not have agreed with what they were doing, but I could see how much they were in love. Who was I to come between that? To judge them for their decision? That was between them and God."

Noah stared at her, his feelings in turmoil. He wanted to rant against what she'd done. Without her help, the affair might not have gone on for so long. She'd enabled the deception, even lying to his father. It was too much.

"Have you ever been in love, Noah?"

The question was asked so softly, for a moment he didn't think he'd heard right. Then Harriet repeated it. Noah bit his lip and then slowly shook his head.

"No. At least, not until recently. I've met someone. I don't know if it's love or not, but I've never felt this way before. She's all I can think about."

Harriet nodded sagely. "And how would it feel if you were told you couldn't have her? That she belonged to someone else?"

A flash of pain went through him. He opened his mouth to protest against the suggestion and then closed it again.

"It's not the same Harriet," he said weakly. "They could have divorced. That's not illegal. They could have come to their families and told them everything, explained how much they loved each other and how they needed to be with each other."

Harriet continued to regard him somberly. "Could you see that happening? Could you ever imagine your uncle breaking up his family like that? Your father? You've already told me he's still denying Janelle could have been unfaithful to him. Do you think she could have hurt him like that?"

"But she was having an affair!" Noah exploded. "Didn't she consider how much that might hurt him?"

"And so was he. Why are you judging her harsher than your father?"

Pain and anger surged through him. Noah opened his mouth to protest, but Harriet cut him off.

"I'm sorry, Noah. That wasn't fair. I have no idea how you feel about your father's actions." She drew in a deep breath and eased it out quietly. "The thing is, I don't think Janelle was thinking at all. She was consumed by Henry. He made her so happy. As for the rest, I truly think they both agreed to ignore it, pretend it wasn't there. When it was just the two of them, nothing else mattered."

Unable to sit there a moment longer, Noah stood and mumbled a hasty goodbye. His suspicions about his mother and his uncle had been confirmed, but that didn't mean he was happy about it, or able to understand. And now it was too late to talk to either of them. He needed to speak to Ayla, take comfort from her, hold her in his arms. She was the only thing in his life right now that made sense.

Ayla switched off the lights in her living room and padded barefoot into her bedroom. She was immediately reminded of Noah. Memories bombarded her of the night they'd spent together, wrapped in each other's arms. Though it had been three nights since he'd been there, his scent was still on the sheets.

Pulling back the covers, she crawled into bed and lay down against the coolness of the soft cotton. She wanted to call him. She wanted to see him again. But she was scared to reveal her secret. On the other hand, there couldn't be anything serious between them until he knew the truth.

Every time she was with him, it would be front and center of her mind. A secret like that would taint everything they did together, every moment they spent growing closer. And she wanted to grow closer. Noah was special. He ticked all her boxes. If she really wanted this to go somewhere, she needed to find the courage to tell him.

The phone rang, startling her from her thoughts. She checked the screen. Her heart skipped a beat.

Noah.

She stared at the screen with indecision. The phone continued to ring. Her pulse rate galloped. Her finger hovered over the green button, but she couldn't bring herself to answer it. Finally the ringing stopped and the call diverted to voicemail.

She cursed herself for her cowardice. The problem was, what they had together was so new, so fragile. It might not be strong enough to withstand the truth. Especially when it concerned the death of his mother. What Ayla knew, what she'd been involved in... Then there was her career to consider.

Maybe I should wait until we know each other better? Wait until our relationship's on firmer ground?

She sighed and lay back against the pillows, hating herself for her lack of courage. A moment later, her phone beeped, indicating a new text. She assumed it was from Noah, but when she looked at the screen she frowned. It was a message from an unfamiliar number. There was a video attached. With a growing sense of foreboding, she tapped the screen and waited for the video to load.

The footage was a little unfocused, but there was no denying it was her and Joe Bettino on the screen. They were seated at the café where they'd met last week. While the video wasn't so clear, the audio was perfect. She listened in shock to the sound of her voice discussing with Joe details of the night Janelle Craigdon was killed in a car accident.

With her heart pounding, Ayla replayed the footage two more times, growing increasingly furious. It was obvious someone had illegally recorded their conversation. Someone who knew who she was. Mixed with her anger was a fast growing fear.

Who did this? And how did they get my number?

A moment later her phone rang. It was from the same number. Once again, her fingers hovered over the green button, but this time she tapped it. She was more furious than scared. She was ready to give the caller a piece of her mind.

"Who the hell is this?" she demanded, grateful her voice sounded sure and strong.

"*Tut, tut, tut.* That's no way to greet a friend. It's Christopher Barrington."

Ayla wracked her brain to put a face to the name. And then she remembered. *Christopher Barrington.* Noah's half-cousin. She'd met him at the first responder's ball. Even back then, he'd made her feel uncomfortable.

"How did you get my number?" she asked, her tone still fierce and commanding.

"That's none of your business," he replied smoothly. "Let's just say you're not the only one who has friends in high places."

She gritted her teeth and held on to her anger by sheer force of will. Right now he had footage of her that might destroy anything she and Noah had together, if it fell into the wrong hands.

"What do you want?" she asked, modifying her tone.

"Why does everyone assume I want something? Never mind. This isn't about me. I'm doing this for Noah. He deserves to know the truth. He thinks he's in love with you."

Ayla frowned in confusion. How could Christopher know something like that? Her relationship with Noah was still so new…

She decided to call his bluff. "I don't believe you. You're making that up."

Christopher's answering chuckle was devoid of humor. "Think what you like. Believe me, I know the signs. Noah falls in love at the slightest encouragement. You're just the latest in a long line."

Ayla's frown deepened. She was sure Noah hadn't lied about his inexperience with women and he certainly hadn't acted like a man who knew his way around a woman's body. At the time, she'd thought it adorable, his eagerness, his self-consciousness, his blushes—

"The thing is," Christopher continued, "he's my half-cousin and I care about him. I especially care about you breaking his heart. He's clueless about who you really are and what involvement you had in the death of his mother."

A flash of fear went through her. "I had nothing to do with—"

"Either you tell him the truth, or I will. If you care for him at all, I suggest you come clean."

Fury arced through her. "How *dare* you threaten me! I don't know how you got my number, but don't ever call me again!"

With that, she ended the call and tossed her phone on the bed. She was trembling all over with a combination of adrenaline, anger and fear. She couldn't believe Christopher had been there, in the café where she'd met with Joe. She wondered what had given him the idea to record them. Had someone tipped him off? Was there someone else with knowledge of the decade-old investigation who had a grudge to bear?

She tried to think of a name, but kept coming up blank. There was no way it was the commissioner. He had more to lose than anyone. And apart from Joe Bettino and the two paramedics who she'd barely spoken to, there hadn't been anyone else there that night.

Panic mounting, she sprang out of bed and began to pace the carpet. There was no way she could sleep now. She was in an impossible position. It didn't matter if she told Noah the truth or if she left it up to Christopher. Either way, Noah would hate her.

She pulled at her hair and let out an anguished groan. "*Ahhhh.*"

It was way past late when she finally came to a decision. The only thing she could do was gather her courage and tell Noah the truth before someone else did. She could hope that he listened to what she had to say and accepted her explanation and that ultimately, he'd understand. If breaking her silence meant losing her job, then so be it.

Chapter Fifteen

It was late the next afternoon when Noah and Declan paid the police commissioner another visit. Their delay had been caused by Bettino's continued no-show. Though he'd promised to come in and make a formal statement the very day after they'd spoken to him, they were now several days past that time and he still hadn't shown. Noah had managed to track him down over the phone and he'd promised to come in that day. They'd waited over an hour past the agreed appointment time for him to arrive, but he hadn't materialized. That was concerning.

Though he'd given them a verbal account of what had happened, that wasn't enough to take to court. They needed a sworn statement. Noah had phoned Bettino again, but the call had gone through to voicemail. In the end, they'd had no choice but to leave for their appointment with Beechwood. If the traffic was heavier than usual, they'd be late. Not the best way to kick off a meeting with the most senior representative of the police force that no doubt would prove tense.

"We just have to hope Bettino calls when he gets your message," Declan said as they pulled away from the curb and headed toward Parramatta. "There's always a chance he's stuck in traffic. Or maybe he's ill."

"Yeah, maybe. Let's hope he hasn't fallen off the wagon."

They traveled in silence, each lost in their own thoughts. Though traffic was slow, they arrived at police headquarters only a few minutes late. Noah found a parking space within walking distance. The two of them strode into the building and after clearing security, headed for the bank of lifts.

They were whisked up to the commissioner's floor. Noah gave their names to the receptionist. Like the time before, they were taken into an inner sanctum where Ayla sat behind a desk. Noah's heart skipped a beat. She looked as gorgeous as ever. Instead of her uniform, she wore a tailored lime-green skirt and ruffled, long-sleeved white blouse. The skirt fell just above her knees and emphasized her slim, muscular legs. He was immediately reminded of how elegantly she moved around the dance floor and later… He smiled.

To his surprise and consternation, she barely met his gaze and offered him only the semblance of a smile. There was a definite strain around her eyes. His smile of greeting faded.

What the hell…? He frowned in confusion. His earlier doubts came rushing back.

Four days before, they'd spent the night together. Had an amazing time. They'd been as close as two people could get physically. He thought they were also on the same page emotionally. And yet last night, she hadn't returned his call. He was filled with a renewed surge of insecurity.

Why isn't she looking at me? What's going on? Did I misread the situation entirely? Misread her?

He glanced at Declan, who seemed oblivious to the tension in the air. Ayla sat calmly behind her desk.

Perhaps I'm imagining her standoffishness? Maybe she's acting so cool because she's at work. She doesn't want anyone to know we're in a relationship… If that's what this was. To be honest, he didn't know.

And then he again wondered why she hadn't returned his call. His stomach sank. *Why not?* He swallowed a sigh. Now wasn't the time. He'd call her later and hopefully get to the bottom of it. In the meantime, they were there for more important matters.

"We're here to see the commissioner," Noah said.

"I'll let him know you've arrived. Take a seat."

Though her demeanor and tone remained perfectly polite, Noah was still ill at ease. He'd expected more from her than treating him like any other stranger who might pay a visit to her boss. Still, there was nothing to be done about it now.

He took a seat next to Declan and picked up a glossy magazine on boating. He tried to concentrate on the first story, evaluating the various pros and cons of the latest *Sea Ray* offering, but it was difficult. Even when he found an article on the newly released design out of Craigdon Super Yachts, he couldn't stay focused. Ayla sat a few yards away. Though she kept her gaze steadfastly fixed to her screen, he was sure she was as aware of him as he was of her.

The phone near her elbow buzzed. She picked up the receiver and listened a moment before setting it back down again. She looked up at them. Her gaze collided with his before skittering away.

"The commissioner will see you now."

Grateful to make his escape, Noah set the magazine aside and stood. Declan followed suit. Ayla came around the side of her desk and led them down a short corridor. She knocked on a closed wooden door.

"Come in."

Noah was acutely aware of her presence. She opened the door and gestured for them to step inside. Her perfume wafted toward him. He closed his eyes briefly against a surge of erotic memories.

Declan shot him a knowing grin and then preceded him into the commissioner's office. Fighting back a blush, Noah made a concerted effort to clear his thoughts of all things Ayla and focus on the job at hand.

"Commissioner Beechwood. Thank you for seeing us," Declan said, offering the man his hand.

The commissioner looked at him with distaste. "Do you people have any idea how busy I am? I hope this isn't going to take long."

"That depends," Noah replied in a steady voice.

"On what?" The commissioner's tone was filled with impatience.

"On what you have to say," Declan said smoothly.

"About what?"

Suddenly tired of the games, Noah glared at him. "Joseph Bettino."

The commissioner's expression turned wary. "I've told you everything I know about him."

"We don't think so," Noah said. "All you told us was that Bettino was on duty with you the night Janelle Craigdon was killed."

"What you didn't say," Declan continued, "was that you ordered Bettino to provide a sample when the alcohol breath test submitted by Henry Craigdon came back positive."

The commissioner's face turned puce with anger. "How dare you!"

Noah stared back at him, unmoved. "Cut the histrionics, Commissioner. We've spoken to Bettino. He told us everything. And he's willing to testify."

The commissioner's lip curled up in disgust. "Ha! Bettino! A down-and-out drunk and drug user with zero credibility. Why do you think he's on stress leave? He's incapable of doing his job. He's damn lucky he hasn't been fired. That's what I would have done if it were up to me." He sneered. "Good luck prosecuting me with *him* as your star witness."

Noah glared at him, his patience at an end. "I didn't say he was our *only* witness. We also have a statement from John Hassad. He's willing to testify he was with Henry and Janelle

Craigdon in the hours before she died. They were drinking heavily."

The commissioner shook his head and laughed. "Oh, Detective. Is that the best you can do? John Hassad? Really? Another star witness. A drug lord, no less. Sitting on remand out at Long Bay, if I recall. A lowlife criminal with a record as long as your arm. Scum." Once again, the commissioner looked at them in disgust. "What kind of a deal did you offer him?"

Noah's anger rose. The smug conceit on the commissioner's face—as if he thought he was untouchable—incensed Noah. The arrogance of the man! Well, Noah had a surprise for him. There was no way he'd let his mother's death go unavenged. Someone must pay. His uncle had escaped censure and punishment for Noah's mother's death because of the actions of the man who stood before him.

As if aware of his thoughts, the commissioner's expression suddenly changed. His gaze drilled into Noah's, cold and calculating and mean.

"I'm sure I don't have to remind you, Detective. I'm a very powerful man. I have friends in high places. Friends who'd do anything I say."

Noah saw Declan tense. Shock and anger filled his face. Declan's reaction set Noah off. He wasn't the only one feeling outraged.

Noah's fury ignited and almost overwhelmed him. He clenched his fists together in an effort to restrain himself from punching the commissioner in the face. When he had himself under control enough to speak, his voice was low and guttural.

"Are you threatening me, Commissioner?"

The two of them exchanged a hard glare. The commissioner was the first to look away. He followed it with a strained laugh.

"Threatening you? Of course not!" His chuckle sounded forced. "My, what an active imagination you have!"

Noah continued to glare at the man. His chest was tight. His breath came fast. He wanted to wipe the smirk off the man's face, but that wouldn't be wise. As if sensing how close he was to losing control, Declan put a restraining hold on his arm.

"I'm sure the Commissioner didn't mean what he said." Declan shot a hard look toward Beechwood. "We'll be talking to you later, Commissioner. Thanks for your time."

Noah merely narrowed his eyes at the man. "Don't go leaving town."

From beneath her lashes, Ayla surreptitiously watched Noah and his partner leave. She was so riddled with guilt she could barely bring herself to look at him. Not that it mattered. Neither man as much as glanced in her direction. She felt Noah's rejection like a physical pain. It cut like a knife. Not that it came as a surprise. They both knew she hadn't returned his call. It had been a gutless thing to do, but at the time, she couldn't bring herself to do it.

The sound of the commissioner's door slamming made her jump. Whatever the investigators had said to him, he was far from happy. Even through the closed wooden panel, she heard him hurling obscenities. A moment later there was the sound of breaking glass. Alarmed, she went to his door and hesitantly knocked.

"Sir? Are you all right?"

"I'm fine."

"Are you sure?"

The door between them came open. The commissioner stood there, looking slightly disheveled, but otherwise all right.

"Of course I'm sure. I accidentally knocked over a glass on my desk. That's all."

"Would you like me to clean up the mess?"

"No, it's fine. I'll see to it." He glanced at his watch. "It's already half-past four. Why don't you finish early? Go shopping. Or whatever."

She blinked in surprise, but didn't argue. It was obvious he was done with her for the day.

"Thank you, sir. If you're sure you're going to be okay?"

"Good-afternoon, Superintendent. I'll see you in the morning." With that, he closed the door in her face.

Hours later, Noah was still fuming about his confrontation with the police commissioner. The galling thing was, the commissioner was right. Bettino was a drunk and though Noah hadn't seen any evidence of drug use, that could also be true. Bettino still hadn't made it to the office to make a formal statement. Without him, they had squat.

Then there was John Hassad. Though they hadn't offered him a deal as incentive, most jurors had watched enough cop shows on TV to make that assumption, no matter what the prosecutor said. Once again, the commissioner was right. Hassad would be a crap witness.

The fact was, they needed more and Noah was determined to find it. There was no way Beechwood was going to walk away from this unscathed. Noah was determined to get justice for his mother and he was going to nail the bastard who orchestrated the cover up if it took everything he had.

There was no doubt in Noah's mind Beechwood was the one responsible. He'd been in charge of the investigation. It wasn't conceivable Bettino, a junior officer, had volunteered to provide the sample when Henry's had turned up positive. Noah still hadn't worked out Beechwood's motive, but his uncle had been a powerful man. It was possible he'd pressured Beechwood in some way, promised to further his career if he made the DUI disappear. After all, Beechwood's career had scaled heights most cops only dreamed of. He'd made it all the way to the top.

Is it possible Uncle Henry had a hand in that?

Noah didn't know and with his uncle now gone, it was unlikely he'd ever uncover the truth. That didn't mean he'd give up on prosecuting Beechwood. The man was going down. All Noah had to do was prove the case that was coming together.

Unfortunately, it wasn't a simple matter of digging out the sample used for the negative result. His witnesses were all they had; and they were dubious at best. Right now, he didn't even have Bettino on record.

Noah thumped his desk in frustration and then winced. Thank God the day was over. He needed to get out of there and clear his head. He needed to kick back somewhere over a couple of drinks and relax, blow off some steam.

Logan immediately came to mind. His brother had a spiffy bachelor pad in Balmoral, overlooking the ocean. It was on the way to Noah's apartment in Manly and was the perfect place to unwind.

With that thought in mind, he bid farewell to Declan and headed for the lifts. He pulled out his phone and called Logan who readily agreed to Noah's suggestion.

"You must be psychic," Logan laughed.

"Why's that?"

"Flynn called me an hour ago, asking the same thing. He's already here."

Noah grinned. "Good. Make sure you've got plenty of cold beer. I'll see you in a bit."

It would be good to shoot the breeze with his brothers. It had been a long time since they'd done that. Just the three of them hanging out, drinking, talking, laughing. It would be good to talk to someone unrelated to his investigation. It also meant he could tell both brothers at the same time about what he'd discovered and what had been validated by Harriet Young. He sure as hell wasn't looking forward to that, but it had to be done. They had a right to know.

The traffic was heavy across the bridge and it took Noah longer than usual to get to Balmoral. Logan met him at the door to his apartment carrying a beer. He greeted him with a friendly hug.

"How's it hanging, Noah?"

"Not too bad, mate. Yourself?"

Logan shrugged and chugged down half of his beer. "Nothing's changed. My life's shit."

Noah shook his head. "Let's not get into that right now. I came over here to have some fun! To take my mind of my troubles!"

"What kind of troubles would you have, Noah?" Flynn called from his position on Logan's massive leather couch. He also had a beer in hand.

Noah followed Logan inside. He looked across at Flynn and sighed. "You wouldn't believe."

Flynn winked. "Don't tell me you have women problems again."

Noah gave him the finger. Flynn merely laughed.

"Where *is* Jayde, by the way?" Noah asked. "I thought you two were joined at the hip."

"Now, now," Flynn chided good naturedly. "Haven't you heard? Jealousy's a curse."

Noah merely grunted and threw himself down on the couch. Logan handed him a beer.

"Thanks," he said and screwed off the cap. After a couple of mouthfuls he sighed. "Ah. That tastes good."

Logan sat down beside him, still looking morose. Noah nudged him in the side with his elbow.

"Come on. Cheer up. Things could be worse."

"You think?" Logan asked, his expression glum.

"Of course. What's worse than being dumped by the woman you love?"

Logan glared at him. "Are you deliberately trying to be a smart-ass?"

Noah threw his hands up in a sign of surrender. "No, mate. I'm serious. I'm in trouble."

Both Logan and Flynn sat forward, their expressions somber. "What is it?" Flynn asked.

"Don't look so worried, boys. I'm not dying, or anything."

The obvious relief on their faces was heartening. It warmed Noah to know how much his brothers cared. He felt the same way about them.

"The thing is, I've met someone. A woman. I need advice."

Logan merely rolled his eyes and leaned back against the couch. "So it *is* a woman problem."

Flynn chuckled. "Don't tell me you're in love again?"

Noah blushed. He pushed his glasses further up his nose. "I don't know. I've never felt like this before. It scares me."

"What's her name?" Flynn asked.

"Ayla. Ayla Rodriguez. She's a cop."

"Just what we need. Another cop in the family. What is it with you guys and cops?" Logan complained.

"Shut up Logan," Flynn said. "You're not helping."

Noah scrubbed at his hair. "How do you know it's for real? I mean, not so long ago I thought I was in love with Jayde. That felt real. And yet, it wasn't. I know that now, but at the time, I was head over heels."

Flynn looked at him. "Were you really? Or did you want to be in love so desperately, you talked yourself into thinking you were?"

Noah sighed. "You're right. When Jayde and I talked about it, I realized she wasn't meant for me. And I was fine with that. See, that's the thing. Ayla has me twisted up in knots. I can't stop thinking about her. I want to be with her all the time. Last weekend, we spent the night together." He smiled at the memory. "It was amazing. But we haven't spent any time together since. I called her, but she didn't call me back. This afternoon I was at her workplace and she pretty much ignored me. What the hell does that mean?"

Logan shook his head. "Get away as quick as you can, bro, before she gets her claws into you. Women are all the same. They'll smile and laugh and tell you they love you and all the time they're planning to run off with your best friend—or theirs. They can't be trusted. Take what they're willing to offer, but keep your heart out of it. They'll stomp all over it the first chance they get. Besides, look how tortured you are over her?" Logan's lips twisted. "She's not worth it, bro. Trust me."

Noah glanced at Flynn, who gave a slight shake of his head. They both heard the bitterness in their brother's voice and were equally aware of its cause.

Flynn cleared his throat. "Don't pay any attention to Logan. He had a bad experience. None of us wish that on anyone. But not every woman's a traitor and not every woman's standing by waiting for the opportunity to trample all over your heart." He glanced at Logan and then returned his attention to Noah. "Though I never had my heart broken like Logan, I didn't particularly believe in love. Then I met Jayde. Everything changed. When you're with the right one, it's not torture at all. It's bliss. That's what it is. Pure bliss."

"Yes," Noah agreed. "I might look tortured, but that's because I'm scared. I love Ayla. I want to be with her for the rest of my life. Knowing you've found the one is…indescribable. Liberating. Exciting. Heart thumpingly amazing. I wouldn't change it for anything."

Logan shot him a skeptical look. "Not even for a billion dollars?"

Chapter Sixteen

*N*oah looked at Logan. "Are you talking about Craigdon Enterprises?"

Logan nodded. "Yeah. What if someone offered you a billion dollars, or the love of your life? What would you choose?"

Noah grinned. "Why can't I have both?"

Logan waggled his finger back and forth. "Uh uh. That's not how it works. Love or money. Which do you choose?"

"Love."

Flynn and Noah spoke simultaneously and then broke into bemused laughter. Logan shook his head, a rueful smile turning up his lips.

"You guys are done for. There's no help for you. None at all. Those women have you by the balls and you both love every minute of it. Shame on you, boys. Where's your pride?"

Flynn grinned. "Who cares? Jayde's the love of my life, my soul mate. In fact, you might as well know, I've asked her to marry me and she's said yes. She's a keeper. I wouldn't trade her for all the money in the world."

"I feel the same way about Ayla, even though we're hardly past the introduction stage," Noah quietly agreed, a little astonished at the depth of his feelings. He hoped she felt the same way.

Logan merely rolled his eyes and changed the subject. "Do you have any idea why Uncle Henry left me his company? It felt weird from the very beginning. It's still playing on my mind."

Flynn shrugged. "I guess it was because of the accident. Perhaps the guilt of being behind the wheel when Mom was killed finally got to him."

"But you and Flynn only got a million and she was your mother, too."

Noah's gaze went involuntarily toward Logan's right leg. Though the scars were covered in denim, they all knew what lay beneath. "Maybe he thought you deserved more because of *your* accident."

"Why would he feel responsible for that?" Logan asked, a perplexed expression on his face.

Noah shrugged. "I don't know, but he was pretty upset when it happened and it became obvious your shot at a professional sailing career was over."

Logan nodded thoughtfully. "Yeah, he was. He came and gave me a pep talk about how it didn't matter. That just because my dream had been shattered along with my leg, I still had a life to live. It was a surprisingly thoughtful gesture and I was grateful at the time." Logan paused and then added, "But I think leaving me his company had to do with something else."

Noah started in surprise. Flynn looked equally startled. "You do?" Noah asked.

"Yeah."

"So what's your theory?" Noah asked.

Logan looked so glum, Noah felt a frisson of concern. "Logan? What's going on? Are you all right?"

"Yeah. This… This isn't easy."

"You don't have to tell us," Flynn said.

Logan's expression turned resolute. "No. I want to. It's been eating me up inside."

Noah's gut clenched with nerves. He couldn't help but think Logan was about to reveal something about their mother's affair. Something told him after Logan finished speaking, their lives would never be the same again. He tried again to distract his brother from whatever confession, or otherwise, he was about to make.

Noah forced a grin. "Hey, bro. Whatever your theory, it doesn't matter. Would I have liked my uncle to gift me a company worth a billion dollars? Of course I would. But it doesn't cut me up that he gave it to you. As far as I'm concerned, he left it to you and good on you. Make the most of it."

Flynn chimed in. "Yeah, I'm with Noah. We don't give a shit that we only got a million dollars."

Logan looked pained. His chin tilted to a stubborn angle. It looked like he was determined to say his piece, no matter what.

He shook his head. "Guys, stop. I know what you're trying to do and I appreciate it, but I've been living with this secret for far too long. You don't understand. The only reason Uncle Henry left the company to me was because I was involved in his illegal drug business."

Noah reeled back in shock. It was the last thing he'd expected. "What the hell are you talking about?"

Logan stared at the floor. Color heightened his cheeks. "The drug dealing. I was a part of it."

Noah shook his head in confusion. "Like, how?"

Logan sighed. "Like, everything. It started when I was just a kid, maybe six or seven. Uncle Henry asked me if I was interested in earning some pocket money. Of course I said yes. It was my job to keep a lookout when a load was coming in. Mostly it came in by boat. Remember the boatshed at the back of the house Uncle Henry had in Maroubra?"

"Of course," Noah replied. "I loved that house. It was right on the beach."

"Exactly. A very convenient location for someone running a covert drug operation." Logan grimaced. "Fortunately we lived close enough that I could come and go between our house and theirs as I pleased. No one was the wiser. Of course, as I got older, my responsibilities increased. Whenever Uncle Henry was short of dealers, he asked me to step in."

Flynn's eyes flared wide. His expression was grim. "How old were you by then?"

Logan shrugged. "Eleven, maybe twelve. He encouraged me to deal to my friends. I didn't want to, but hell, you didn't say no to Uncle Henry. You remember what he was like."

"Oh, yeah, I remember," Noah said dryly. "I once saw him smash a man's kneecaps with a baseball bat. He was as calm and cool as you please. Didn't even seem to hear the man's screams."

Logan gaped. "How awful. How old were you?"

"Seventeen."

"Where did it happen?" Logan asked.

"In a warehouse out in the suburbs."

"How did you come to be there?" This was from Flynn.

Noah averted his gaze. "I can't remember," he lied. "The fact is, I know exactly how brutal our uncle could be if you crossed him. I understand more than you think how you couldn't say no to him."

Logan smiled with relief. "Thanks, Noah. That means a lot to me. Ever since I found out he left me his company, I can't help thinking it was because of everything I'd done for him when I was a kid. Oh, he gave me a handful of hundred dollar bills every now and then, but it was a pittance compared to what he was making.

"I think I was about thirteen when, I told him I was through. Not because of the money, but I was sick of feeling guilty about what I did. I wanted to live a normal life, earn money the right way. We argued about it. He called me ungrateful and all sorts of other things. In the end it didn't make any difference. I walked."

Noah tamped down a surge of guilt. "Did you ever tell Dad?"

"No."

"Why not?" Flynn asked.

Logan shrugged. "I was ashamed."

"So you think leaving you Craigdon Enterprises was Uncle Henry's way of saying thank you?" Flynn asked.

"Yes."

Noah stared at Logan. No one knew of Noah's involvement in their uncle's drug business. Until now. "I think you're wrong," he said.

Logan grimaced. "You're only saying that to make me feel better."

"No, I'm not. I'm saying it because it's the truth."

Logan managed a half-smile. "You're such a liar."

Noah sighed. "I know because I also worked for Uncle Henry. In his drug business."

"What?" The shock in Logan's voice was reflected on Flynn's face. Both of them stared wordlessly at Noah.

Noah stared down at his lap, his cheeks burning. All these years later and he still felt the shame.

"Yeah," he muttered. "Like Logan, it started out innocently enough. I stumbled across Uncle Henry by accident unloading a shipment of drugs—cocaine to be precise. He told me to stop staring and start helping. So I did."

"How old were you?" Flynn asked softly.

Noah ducked his head. Shame threatened to overwhelm him. "I wish I could tell you I was just a kid who didn't know any better, like Logan. But I was fifteen. And I knew darn well what we were doing was illegal. I went to Uncle Henry once and told him I was out. That's when he threatened me."

Logan gaped. "What the hell did he say?"

Noah compressed his lips. "He told me he knew a dirty cop who'd be only too willing to put me in jail. He made it clear he'd load me up with gear right before he made the call. 'You'll probably only get five or six years for a first offense,' he said. 'Not a lifetime, but definitely long enough. I've heard pretty boys like you are very popular among the inmates.'"

Logan and Flynn sported equal expressions of shock and fury.

"The bastard!" Flynn cursed.

"Fuck! I can't believe he threatened you like that! Why didn't you tell us?"

Noah stared down at his hands. "I was ashamed. I still feel ashamed. After all, no one forced me to start dealing. I did that all on my own."

He blew out his breath on a heavy sigh. "I always used to think Uncle Henry was so much smarter than Dad," Noah continued. "That's why he was wealthier than us. There obviously was more money in construction than building yachts. Then I learned the truth. I asked Uncle Henry if Dad knew about his sideline operation. Uncle Henry laughed so hard, I thought he'd burst. I can still hear his response.

'Of course not. Your father would probably turn me in to the police. Archie was always a stickler for the rules. Lucky for me, his son isn't so particular when it comes to making money.'

"I felt grubby after that. I didn't want to deal drugs, but Uncle Henry's threat was always hanging over me and I'm ashamed to admit I enjoyed the money. I was at the age where I thought the girls would be impressed if I wore the latest clothes and drove a car that cost more than their father's. I thought it could buy me confidence."

"And did it?" Flynn asked.

Embarrassment heated Noah's face. "You know the

answer to that. I'm twenty-eight years old and I've only just lost my virginity."

"That's nothing to be ashamed of," Flynn said quietly.

"Of course and I'm not. In fact, I'm glad I waited until I found a woman I'm head over heels for. I don't think it would be the same with just anyone."

"You're right," Logan agreed a little wistfully. "I've lost count of the number of women I've slept with, but none of them have even come close to what I used to feel with Virginia. She was my first."

His voice had thickened with emotion. Moisture glimmered in his eyes. Noah's gut clenched with sympathy.

"Fuck," Logan muttered, his voice filled with anger and pain. "Why the hell did she have to fuck it all up? And with another woman! For fuck's sake!"

An uncomfortable silence fell between them. Neither brother knew what to say. In fact, there was nothing they could say. Logan spoke the truth. Virginia had messed up everything when she'd run off with her best friend.

As if by silent agreement, they all took refuge in their beers. Then Flynn sighed.

"Since we're in the mood for confessions, you might as well know. Uncle Henry approached me when I was in high school. He wanted me to sell E's to my friends."

Noah and Logan were startled. "What did you say?" Noah asked.

"I told him where to shove it."

Logan grinned. "You always had more balls than I did."

Flynn shrugged. "I'm not sure about that. I was a lot older than you when he approached me. I had a bit more experience standing up for myself."

Noah grinned. "No wonder you've gone on to have such a successful career in the law. Even as a teenager, you were incorruptible."

"I'm not sure what that says about me," Noah mumbled. "But I remember feeling outraged at how easily Uncle Henry got away with it. Dealing in drugs. I think it ignited a fire inside me to do my best to bring those kind of criminals to justice."

"So that's why you became a cop?" Flynn mused.

"Yes. I think it was. Of course, I ended up going in a slightly different direction…"

Logan snorted. "You can say that again. You investigate other cops."

"Bad cops," Noah retorted. "Not all cops."

Silence fell between them. Once again, they busied themselves with their drinks. Then Logan's shoulders slumped on a sigh.

"So you really think Uncle Henry left me Craigdon Enterprises for some other reason? That it wasn't because of the drug dealing?"

Noah nodded. "Yes. Otherwise, why wouldn't he have left it to all of us?"

"I told him to shove it, remember?" Flynn chuckled. "I think that disqualified me from any extra inheritance."

"Maybe," Noah replied. "I wasn't involved from such a young age as Logan and I was paid rather well, but still… I was a good and loyal employee for a long time." He shook his head. "No, it can't be the drugs. There must be some other reason."

Logan sighed again. "It's doing my head in."

Noah's conscience pricked him. He thought about what Harriet had revealed about their mother. Then there was the offhand comment made by Aunt Elizabeth about Logan's parentage. Noah had been thinking about it non-stop. He kept coming back time and time again to the same conclusion, but he wasn't sure he was ready to voice his suspicions. After all, what good would it do now? So much time had passed. Some things were better left alone. Still, his brothers had the right to know about the affair. That much at least he could share.

"There's something else you need to know."

He didn't know if it were his words or the somberness of his expression, but both of his brothers tensed. Noah felt their stares.

"What is it?" Flynn asked.

Noah bit his lip. Now the moment was upon him, he wasn't sure where to start. "It's about Mom. As you both know, the LECC opened an investigation into the accident that killed her. Several things have come to light."

"Such as?" Flynn asked. His voice was steady, but the gaze he fixed on Noah was intense.

"Just spit it out, mate!" Logan exclaimed impatiently.

Noah drew in a deep breath. "Remember when you told us about John Hassad telling Jayde that Uncle Henry was drunk behind the wheel?"

Flynn's reply was cautious. "Yes."

"Well, it's true. I found someone else who corroborates that story. A cop who was at the scene."

"Then why the hell wasn't Uncle Henry charged?" Logan exploded.

"Someone else provided the sample," Noah said.

Flynn looked shocked. "Fuck."

Noah nodded grimly. "Yeah."

"So Uncle Henry used his influence to get the samples switched?" Flynn said.

Noah compressed his lips. He understood the shock that flooded his brothers' faces. "Yep."

"The bastard!" Logan cried.

"Who was it? Who was in charge that night?" Flynn asked.

Noah braced himself. "The current police commissioner. Kevin Beechwood."

Flynn looked aghast. "You're fucking kidding?"

"No. I'm afraid not. That's why we need to tread carefully. This is all highly confidential. Neither of you can breathe a word. We need to have all our ducks in a row before we can go public. Understand?"

There were mumbled murmurs of assent. Noah took another deep breath. "I'm afraid there's more."

Logan groaned. "I don't know if I can take any more."

"What is it?" Flynn asked.

"This is also going to come as a shock, but according to the autopsy report, Mom had drugs in her system when she died. Cocaine, to be specific."

"What the hell?" Logan shouted. He jumped up off the couch and started pacing. "Mom didn't do drugs!"

Noah shrugged. "Apparently she did. At least this once. I have a witness who saw her snorting coke that night. He did say he thought it was her first time."

"Fuck." Flynn looked as dazed as Noah had felt when he'd discovered his mother had taken illegal drugs.

"How come we didn't know?" Flynn asked.

"I've asked myself the same question," Noah replied. "I guess it wasn't on our radar. We weren't looking for signs Mom was a user. I know I wasn't. And of course, there's every possibility it was her first time."

"She wasn't a user! There's no way I'll believe that!' Logan cried, looking distressed.

"No one's saying Mom was a user," Flynn soothed. "But the autopsy doesn't lie. She had cocaine in her system. We'll never know for sure if it was her first try."

"There's something else," Noah said quietly. Before he could lose his courage, he told them about the affair.

"Are you sure?" Flynn asked.

"Yes. I always wondered why Uncle Henry and Mom were together that night. I obtained copies of Uncle Henry's phone records around the time of the accident. The texts he sent to Mom make it quite clear."

"Hell," Flynn muttered. He'd once raised the question of

their mother's fidelity, but no one had actually believed it, including Flynn.

"I can't believe they were having an affair!" Logan cried. "Do you think *that's* the reason Uncle Henry left me his company? Because I'm his *son?*"

Flynn was quick to respond. "No one's saying that, Logan. You were fifteen when this happened. It's ridiculous to think it had been going on for years beforehand. Put that out of your mind."

Recalling Harriet's words about the length of the affair, Noah battled a wave of guilt. He was pretty sure Logan was Henry's son, but he didn't want to be the one to tell Logan. What would anyone gain from it? Look how hurt and upset Sophia had been when she found out the man she thought was her father wasn't her father at all. No, it was best to keep quiet and leave that minefield alone.

Logan continued to look uncertain. He glanced from one brother to the other, as if trying to find the answers. In an effort to distract him, Noah stood and gave Logan a reassuring hug.

"Don't sweat it, bro. Does the reason Uncle Henry left you his company really matter? You're richer than you ever dreamed possible." Noah chuckled. "Embrace it, bro."

Flynn stood, too. "Yeah, mate. Noah's right. Put this shit aside and just go for it. You're rich enough to live whatever life you want. Some people would rush at the chance for that kind of freedom."

Logan's shoulders slumped. He threw himself back down on the couch. "I wish it was that easy. I don't *want* to own a property development company and I sure as hell don't want the responsibility. I don't know the first thing about building or property. I'm happy Nicholas is running it. And I'm happy designing my boats."

"I guess you could always sell it," Flynn mused. "I'm sure Nicholas would jump at the chance to own it."

Logan brightened. "You're right. He's been doing such a good job as managing director. And with Harper by his side, they're a force to be reckoned with. Now that we've managed to identify the illicit income portion of the business and separate it from the legitimate operations, it's been easier to get a true picture. I don't know why Uncle Henry felt the need to expand his income opportunities. The property development business does very well all on its own."

"Uncle Henry was dealing drugs long before he took over Craigdon Enterprises from his father," Noah reminded him. "It was happening back when he was an accountant in Maroubra, remember?"

Logan nodded. "Yeah. Maybe it was for the thrill of it, then?"

Noah shrugged. "Who knows? I'm just glad I got out of it unscathed and that it hasn't followed me into the police service. It would kill me if something I did when I was younger destroyed my career."

"Didn't you do a year of law school? What gives?" Logan asked.

Noah gave a self-deprecating smile. "You're right. A complete contradiction. Like I said, I was secretly angry at how easy it was for Uncle Henry to get away with drug dealing. I mean, we weren't just talking about a traffic ticket. This was serious law breaking. Not only did he get away with it, he didn't seem to give a toss that what he was doing was illegal. I might have been reaping the benefits, but I wasn't without guilt. I eventually got to the point where I couldn't do it any longer."

Logan's expression sobered. "Yeah, me too. The guilt ate into my gut night and day. It was giving me an ulcer. I was no longer a kid who tried to provide acceptable reasons for my behavior. It was wrong and there was no justification for it. That's why I quit."

"I'm so pleased I didn't take him up on his offer," Flynn mused. "I've managed to avoid all sorts of angst."

Logan suddenly sat bolt upright. "What about Uncle Henry's books?"

"Shit," Noah swore.

"What books?" Flynn asked.

"Uncle Henry kept records of his drug dealers in the Craigdon Enterprise books," Noah explained. "They were recorded as if they were legitimate employees of the company. It was only when Nicholas found that secret stash of entries that we discovered the truth, remember?"

"Right. Yes, I remember," Flynn replied.

Logan suddenly looked fearful. "What if our names are in them?"

Noah's gut churned with dread. That was the last thing he needed. It was one thing for his brothers to know about his shameful past. There was no way he wanted the whole world to know, and that included his cousins. To say nothing of how it might affect his career…

"Didn't you say Uncle Henry paid you in cash? Besides, surely Nick would have said something," Flynn said. "He's been over those entries, after all."

Logan continued to look concerned. "But what if they're there and he merely overlooked them?"

"I'll call Nicholas in the morning," Noah said. "I'll give him some excuse as to why I need to go through the books. Tell him it's something to do with the LECC investigation. I'll check and see if our names appear."

"You think he'll buy it?" Logan asked hopefully.

"Yeah. Leave it with me."

Logan offered to get everyone another round of drinks. Upon his return, silence fell between them as they became lost in their thoughts. They'd all but finished their fresh beers when Flynn spoke again.

"So, what are you going to do about Miss Ayla?"

Noah looked at him. "I think I'm going to ask her to marry me."

"Don't you think you're being a bit hasty? You've only just met her," Logan protested. "Have you forgotten Virginia? I'd known her for most of our lives and yet, in the end, I realized I didn't know her at all."

Noah nodded. "I understand what you're saying, bro, and I appreciate where you're coming from, but I'm twenty-eight. Old enough to know when I've met the right woman. I want to hold on tight and never let go. I feel like my life's been on hold for so long and everything I've ever wanted is right within my grasp."

"You said she's a cop. Does she know about your dealing?" Flynn asked quietly.

"No. And she never will," Noah said firmly. "That was a long time ago. I wasn't even an adult. It has nothing to do with the person I am today."

"You're right," Flynn agreed.

"Your secret's safe with me, bro," Logan assured him.

Noah shot him a grateful look. "As yours is with me."

"I love you, bro." Logan raised his gaze to encompass Flynn. "You too, Flynn."

Flynn chuckled. "I love you, too."

As one, they clinked their empty beer bottles together and smiled.

Chapter Seventeen

After another fitful night of tossing and turning, Ayla wasn't surprised to see the shadows under her eyes as she stared at her reflection in the bathroom mirror the next morning. She'd spent the night thinking about Noah and how badly she'd treated him. They'd made love for the first time—for heaven's sake, she'd taken his virginity—and she hadn't bothered to call him, ask him out, reassure him everything was all right.

She thought about how she'd feel if it had been her making love for the first time. How distressed she'd be if the guy she'd been so intimate with had failed to follow up afterward with a phone call, a text…anything. It got even worse. When Noah had turned up at her office, she'd all but ignored him. How confused and hurt he must have been!

The guilt of her actions almost overwhelmed her. She had to tell him. She had to come clean with what she knew. Whether it changed things between them, or not, she had no way of knowing, but she couldn't hide behind her cowardice any longer.

Decision made, she padded back into her bedroom and picked up her phone from the bedside table. Before she could lose her nerve, she dialed Noah's number. The call rang out and eventually went through to voicemail. She felt a tiny bit relieved and was immediately disappointed in herself. Telling Noah the truth was the right thing to do. He deserved no less.

When the phone beeped, she left him a message. "Hi, Noah. It's me. Ayla. Um… Could you call me back? It's important. There's something I need to tell you."

Noah was on his way to see Nicholas when his phone rang. He pulled it out of his pocket and glanced at the screen.

Ayla.

His heart skipped a beat. He'd been hoping she'd call; confused when she didn't. Now he was in the car without Bluetooth, or any other kind of hands-free option. There were too many cameras around to risk getting caught on the phone while he was driving. Besides, he didn't want to have their first private conversation while negotiating his car through heavy peak-hour traffic. Ayla would have to wait.

To his relief, he heard a beep indicating she'd left a message. A part of him wanted to pull over to the shoulder right there and then and listen to it, but then he came to his senses. He was in the middle of three lanes of traffic. There was nowhere he could safely pull over. After his business at Craigdon Enterprises was done would be the first opportunity he could shift his attention to Ayla. If he could wait that long.

Nick met him in the impressive foyer of the Craigdon Enterprises building. They passed through security and headed toward the bank of lifts.

"So, what brings you here?" Nick asked.

"I was wondering if you could let me take a look at that list of entries you found in your father's safe. The ones detailing amounts owed to those laborers who were actually drug runners."

Nick nodded. "Sure. I take it this has something to do with your investigation?"

Noah kept his response deliberately vague. "Yeah. Something like that."

"How's it going, anyway? Are you any closer to finding some answers?"

"We're certainly making progress. At this stage, I'm not at liberty to say too much."

Nick nodded. "Of course."

The lift arrived and whisked them to the top floor. Noah had been there only a few times in his life. The last time he'd been there was when he'd told his uncle he wanted out of the drug business. His uncle hadn't taken the news well. He pushed the uncomfortable memories aside and focused on Nick's conversation.

"The police have the right to confiscate the proceeds of crime, right?"

Noah nodded. "Yes. Why do you ask?"

A worried expression flooded Nick's face. Noah tensed, unsure what was coming.

Nick blew his breath out on a sigh. "Well, from what I can tell, at least half of Dad's money came from the sale of illegal drugs. Money we've now inherited."

Noah hid his relief. "Rest easy, cuz. Unless you were aware of your father's illegal activities, there's no need to worry. The police aren't interested in seizing your inheritance."

"Whew. That's a relief. Some of us have actually already spent a fair chunk of it. But it still leaves a bad taste in my mouth. To think Dad was a drug dealer… We had no idea. It's absolutely unbelievable."

"Yeah. I know what you mean."

Nicholas led the way into his office, stopping to kiss his fiancée, Harper, on the way. Noah gave her a wave of greeting.

Nick went to the wall safe and dialed the combination. He pulled out a sheaf of papers and handed them to Noah.

"Here you go."

"Thanks." Noah accepted the papers.

"You can sit in there, if you like." Nick indicated a small interview room off to the side of the main part of the office.

Once again, Noah murmured his thanks.

"Can I get you a coffee, or something?" Nick asked.

"No, thanks. I'm fine. This shouldn't take long."

"Am I allowed to know what it is you're looking for?"

Noah gave him an apologetic look and ignored the stab of guilt. "Sorry, mate. Confidential."

"Of course. Well, I guess I'll leave you to it. Let me know if you need anything."

With that, Nick left him alone. Noah walked into the adjoining room and closed the door behind him. Pulling a chair up to the boardroom-style table, he started going through the ledgers. The name "Petrov" showed up over and over again, along with a few other constants. He was more than halfway through and he still hadn't found any reference to either his name or Logan's. He kept going. Right at the bottom of the page, his gaze snagged on another name. His gut took a nosedive.

Kevin Beechwood.

Surely it couldn't be the same one. But what if it were? The name was listed many times over the next dozen or so pages and each time for large amounts. Noah did a quick calculation. If Beechwood was another fake company employee like the others Nick had investigated on the list and sold drugs for Henry, it seemed at one point Beechwood was owed more than half a million dollars.

Was Beechwood one of Henry's dealers? Was he selling drugs on the side for Henry? Is that what this was about? Had Henry threatened to expose him? Is that why Beechwood falsified the breath test? Or was it Henry who'd owed the money? Had Henry been paying Beechwood to look the other way and cover his tracks?

Though relieved he hadn't found his or Logan's name in the ledgers, Noah's head was still consumed with questions about Beechwood. Packing up the papers into a neat pile, he took them back to Nicholas.

"Finished?" Nick asked.

"Yes, thanks."

"I hope you found what you're looking for."

"Maybe," Noah replied. "I saw entries for a Kevin Beechwood. Do you know anything about him?"

"No. I checked him out, along with all the other entries. All I can tell you is he wasn't an employee. He didn't have a personnel file. HR had no record of him."

"So you don't think the amounts listed beside each entry for him was for money owed to Beechwood for drugs he'd sold, like the others?"

"It's impossible to tell for sure. After all, he's on the list. But all the others were on our books. That's why they went unnoticed for so long. Beechwood was never employed here, legitimately or otherwise. Knowing what I do now, my guess is that he's a small-time dealer who got his supply from Dad. Or maybe he was a user. The monetary amounts noted on each entry are more likely amounts Beechwood owed. The entries go back a long time. It wouldn't be hard to rack up a debt like that if he used regularly. It seems Beechwood had an open line of credit which appeared to be paid off every now and then. The total owing by Beechwood when Dad died was just under three hundred thousand dollars."

"Did you track him down?"

"No. I don't know who he is. I was able to contact the others through their personnel files. Regarding Beechwood, I have nothing. I wouldn't know where to start. As far as the money owed to those fake employees goes, somehow I can't see them fronting up to Craigdon Enterprises and demanding payment. They must know Dad's dead and that there's someone else in charge. I can't imagine they'd be so stupid as to out themselves as drug dealers."

"What are you going to do about them?"

"I'm going to pretend they don't exist."

Noah nodded. "Fair enough. Listen, do you mind if I get a copy of this list? It might come in handy in my investigation."

"Sure," Nick said. "Give me a few minutes. I'll ask Harper to copy it for you."

In no time at all, Noah held a copy of Henry's list in his hand. Having got what he'd come for, plus a bit more, Noah thanked Nicholas for his time and access to the papers, and left.

Ayla tried her best to concentrate on the work in front of her, but inside she was on tenterhooks. It was a couple of hours since she'd left the message for Noah and she still hadn't heard from him. No doubt he was at work and it was possible he was in the middle of an important interview. He might even be interviewing a witness related to his uncle's accident.

On the other hand, he might simply be paying her back. After all, she'd pretty much ignored him the day before. Maybe he was regretting their night together, regretting that she'd been his first. No, she refused to believe that. It had been amazing between them. Sweet and gentle and sensuous. The memory of their lovemaking made her feel even more ashamed of how she'd kept him at a distance ever since, but it also reminded her of why she'd distanced herself.

She might have gathered her courage and made the decision to be tell him, but she was still anxious about how he was going to react. But there was no use thinking about a future for them until he knew. He was special. Someone she might very well be in love with. She didn't want there to be any secrets between them if they were moving forward. A relationship built on secrets didn't stand a chance.

Her phone rang, interrupting her heavy thoughts. *Noah!* She dived into her handbag, grabbed her phone and checked the screen. The number was vaguely familiar, but she couldn't place it. She was flooded with disappointment.

"Hello?"

"Ayla. It's Christopher."

Her stomach flip-flopped with dread. *Oh, God.* Though his threat had prompted her soul searching, she'd almost forgotten about the part he'd played while she'd been agonizing back and forth about her decision.

"Have you told him?" he asked.

Panic raced through her. "N-not yet. B-but I will. I need more time."

"You've had plenty of time."

"I've left a message for him to call me. I can't do any more than that."

"Sounds like an excuse to me. Not good enough."

Her panic ratcheted up a notch. "Please! Christopher! I'll tell him. I promise."

"Sorry, Ayla. You had your chance. I have to look out for my cousin. Time's up."

Noah made it all the way back to his office and had sat down to go through his emails before he remembered Ayla's call. He dug out his phone and dialed into his voicemail. Before Ayla's message came through, the phone started buzzing in his ear. He checked the screen.

Christopher.

Ending the voicemail call, he pressed the green button.

"Christopher. What's up?"

"Noah, we need to talk."

"Fire away," Noah replied, only mildly interested.

"I'm outside your building. Can you meet me downstairs?"

Noah started in surprise. He couldn't remember the last time Christopher had visited him at work. In fact, he couldn't remember if it had ever happened. He was curious about what had brought his half-cousin there now. "Sure," he agreed. "I'll come down."

On his way down in the lift, Noah's thoughts once again returned to Ayla's message. He still hadn't listened to it. Now that he was on his way to meet Christopher, her message would have to wait.

Christopher stood a few feet away from the front entrance of the building. Spying Noah coming toward him, Christopher held out his hand. Noah shook it.

"Thanks for taking the time to see me," Christopher said.

Noah shrugged. "No problem. What can I do for you?"

Christopher grimaced. "Hell, I wish I didn't have to show you this."

Noah frowned. A trickle of foreboding filled his veins. "What are you talking about?"

"It's Ayla. Ayla Rodriguez. I know how much you like her. I… I think you need to see this."

Christopher held out his phone toward Noah. The dread in Noah's gut increased. "What is it?"

"Just watch."

Christopher shoved the phone in Noah's hand. He took it grudgingly and stared at the screen. It was a video. Noah hit PLAY. The screen filled with the noise of conversation and traffic. He immediately recognized Ayla. It took him a bit longer to recognize the man who sat across from her.

Joe Bettino?

What the hell was Ayla doing with Joe Bettino?

And then as Noah began to pay attention to their conversation an iciness filled his veins. The longer it went on, the colder he got until he felt like his feet were weighted with concrete.

"Where did you get this?" he rasped.

"I happened to be at the same café. Seated nearby. Mere coincidence. I recognized Ayla from the ball. I knew how much you liked her. When that bloke came along, I wondered if she was cheating on you. That's why I started recording. Then she started talking about Henry. I knew you were investigating the accident that took your mother's life. I thought she might have some information you were unaware of. Something that might help fill in the gaps."

Noah's head was filled with so much noise, he could barely focus on what Christopher was saying. His words sounded like they were coming out of a long tunnel—echoing, distorted, indistinguishable.

"I'm really sorry, cuz," Christopher said. "I always thought it odd that someone so young was promoted to such a lofty position. Chief of staff to the police commissioner and she's not even thirty. Now it makes sense. It was a reward for keeping her mouth shut. I wish it didn't have to be this way. I know how much you like her. That's why I couldn't stay silent. You deserve to know the truth."

With that, Christopher took back his phone and after giving Noah a reassuring pat on his shoulder, he turned and walked away. Noah stared after him, shocked, devastated, furious. And underneath all of that was a hurt so deep he didn't know how he'd ever get over it.

Over the course of the day, Noah lost count of the number of times he reached for his phone with the intention of calling Ayla—and every time, he pulled up just short of dialing her number. He was still so furious, so hurt, so filled with shock and disbelief he didn't trust himself to remain civil. No wonder she'd been so interested in his investigation. She'd plied him with questions at the ball. He'd merely dismissed them as curiosity. Now he knew better. She'd been trying to find out what he knew. In particular, if he knew about *her.*

And then his thoughts escalated to where he began to wonder if she'd only befriended him, gone out with him, hell—*slept* with him, in order to keep him off-balance. To keep his mind focused on her and not the investigation.

No! Everything inside him wanted to rebel against that idea, but once the insidious thought snuck inside his brain, it was impossible to ignore. He'd never been a winner with women and yet this beautiful, charismatic woman had fallen into his arms.

Looking back, it seemed so effortless and he'd been too blown away by his good fortune to question her motives. He didn't want to believe Ayla could be that cold and calculating, but what did he really know about her?

By the end of the day, he was no closer to cooling down, but one thing was for sure. He was going to have to face her and have it out. For his own self-preservation, he needed to know the truth. It was after six when he found himself riding his motorbike toward her apartment, determined to get to the bottom of all this. He hadn't phoned ahead. He was taking the gamble that she'd be home.

He pressed on her buzzer and waited impatiently for her to answer. Less than a minute later, she did.

"Noah. Hi. Come up."

With that, she buzzed open the entry door and he made his way up the three flights of stairs to her apartment. With a conscious effort, he tried not to think about the last time he'd been there. As the memories bombarded him, he was filled with a fresh wave of anger. By the time he knocked brusquely on her door, he was spoiling for a fight.

Ayla opened the door. She took one look at him and her eyes went wide. A moment later, wariness filled her face.

"Noah? Are you all right?"

He stared at her coldly. "No, Ayla. I'm not all right."

She paled. "I take it you got my message. Is that why you're here? To talk?"

"I didn't get your message. It was Christopher who filled me in."

With that, he pushed past her and walked down the short hallway that led into her open-plan kitchen and living room. On his way, he noticed a small framed photo on the wall of her and Joe Bettino and Kevin Beechwood. She looked very young. He wasn't sure why he hadn't seen it before. Probably because the last time he was there he'd been far more intent on more pleasurable things than gazing at pictures.

"Where was this taken?" he demanded, spinning around to face her.

"Maitland," she said quietly. "It's where I was posted during my probationary year."

"Let me guess. In 2010, right?"

She held his gaze. "Yes."

"All this time, you knew. You knew about the accident."

To her credit, she didn't look away. "Yes."

And then another thought occurred to him. His eyes widened in shock. "Oh, God. Don't tell me you also attended the scene?"

"Yes."

"Fuck! You have to be kidding! Why didn't you *say* anything?"

She shook her head, helpless tears gathering in her eyes. "I'm sorry."

"You're *sorry*?"

"I… I didn't know what to say. The truth is, I've fallen in love with you and I knew that the moment you found out I was there that night… That I was complicit in the cover up…you'd hate me. I'm right, aren't I?"

He couldn't meet her gaze, too filled with shock and anger and disbelief. "You betrayed me!"

"No!"

"Well that's how it feels! All this time you knew what happened and you said nothing!" He strode toward the door, intent on leaving.

"Noah! Please!"

He was so angry he could punch something. He glared at her. "All this time, you *knew*. You attended the accident that killed my mother and kept silent about the fact the alcohol sample came from Joe Bettino. All this time, you let my uncle get away with murder, or at the very least, manslaughter. Now Henry's dead. He'll never be punished for what he did; not once did you say anything to me about the facts you were privy to."

His laughter was completely devoid of humor. He glared at her, hurt and anger still raging through him. "But wait, there's more. Not only did you keep silent, you *benefited* from it. Now it all makes sense. Your superfast rise to chief of staff and all before you turned thirty." He turned away before he did something stupid like put his fist through the wall. He headed toward the door.

"Noah, please! Come back! Please let me explain."

"No. The time for explanations is well past. I need to get away from here," he muttered.

Letting himself out, he slammed the door behind him.

Chapter Eighteen

oah's face felt so hot he thought he might combust. He was fuming as he climbed on his Fireblade and roared out of the street. He couldn't believe it! All this time, Ayla had lied to him. She knew he was investigating the accident. She knew there were dirty cops. And now he'd discovered she was one of them.

Okay, so she hadn't been the officer in charge, or even the second in charge, but she was just as culpable. She'd been there that night. She'd known all about the false sample and she'd stood by and said nothing. Not then. Not now. She'd even used the word 'cover up.' The extent of her deceit was unbelievable. She was just like his mother. A woman with many secrets. A woman he'd loved and lived with for eighteen years and had never really known.

To top it all off, Ayla had declared her love for him. A day earlier, he would have been filled with joy at the thought she felt the same way he did. Now it filled him with disgust. After all that had happened, how could he believe her? She'd proven how deceitful she was. How could he put any faith in a declaration of love? He couldn't. It was as simple and as devastating as that.

Noah made a sound of disgust in the back of his throat. His chest was tight with hurt and anger. Checking over his shoulder for oncoming traffic, he turned onto the street that would take him out to the Pacific Motorway. He needed to blow off some steam. Opening the throttle on his powerful Honda was just the way to do it.

Noah was still seething when he walked into his office the next morning. While his wild ride along the motorway the night before had helped ease the tightness in his chest, every time he thought of Ayla's betrayal he got angry all over again. There had been so many opportunities when she could have said something. The very first moment he'd turned up at the commissioner's office and told her the reason for his visit, for starters. She could have told him she was there. That she had knowledge of the event. And yet she hadn't. The only logical conclusion he could draw was that she'd remained silent to protect herself, to prevent him from discovering her involvement.

She would have known there was no mention of her in the police statements made that night by Beechwood and Bettino. After all, there was no reason to include the observations of a probationary constable. If Christopher hadn't videoed that conversation and Noah hadn't seen her in that telling photo, he would never have known.

Perhaps that's exactly what she'd been hoping…?

Noah made an agonized sound in the back of his throat. Perhaps he should call in sick, leave before someone saw him. He was in no state to be at work. With that thought in mind, he collected his briefcase and headed back out the door. Before he even cleared the entryway, he ran into Declan.

"Hey, Noah. What's happening?"

Too late…

Noah turned around to face Declan. His partner's eyes widened in surprise.

"You look like shit. Craigdon. Did you write yourself off last night?"

Noah glared at Declan. "I'm not in the mood, Munro."

Declan held his hands up in a sign of surrender. "Whoa! Just saying it how it is." Declan paused and then added, "Anything I can do?"

"Nope. Just shut up about me and start concentrating on catching Kevin Beechwood. We both know the prick's guilty of a cover up. Last night I discovered there was someone else there that night. A probationary constable. Ayla Rodriguez."

Declan's eyes flared wide with surprise. "Beechwood's chief of staff?"

Noah blew out his breath. "Yeah."

"The woman you…?"

"Yeah."

"Shit."

"Yeah."

Declan shook his head. "Did she know about the swapped sample?"

Noah compressed his lips. "I don't know," he replied honestly. "She admitted she was there that night and that she attended the scene. It's impossible to believe she wasn't also in on the cover up… Or at least had knowledge of it."

"Do you think that's why she's risen up the ranks so fast? Quid pro quo?"

"We have to consider that as a possibility."

"Wow." Declan scrubbed his hand through his hair. "Is she willing to come in for an interview?"

"I don't know. I left before the conversation went that far."

"So, what do we do now?"

"Has Bettino come in and given us a sworn statement yet?"

"No."

"Get on that. We need him in here, pronto. Once we have him on tape, we can bring Beechwood in for a formal interview, see if we can rattle his tree. Arrogant prick."

"What about Ayla?" Declan asked.

For reasons he couldn't explain, Noah paused. "At this stage, I'll try and keep Ayla out of it. She might have been aware of what went down that night but so far there's no evidence she instigated it or even participated in it. Bettino only mentioned Beechwood. It's my bet he's the mastermind."

Declan nodded his agreement. "No worries. I'll call Bettino right away. Make darn sure he's going to show this time, even if we have to go and get him."

"Good."

Declan left Noah's office and closed the door behind him. With a curse, Noah threw himself down in his chair. God knows why he felt the need to protect Ayla. She didn't deserve his consideration, but he couldn't bring himself to willingly tarnish her name. At least, not until he knew without a shadow of a doubt that she not only knew, but actively participated in the cover up.

Despite everything, he clung to the slim hope that she was innocent. He didn't want to think about the kind of sorry sap that made him.

Ayla felt sick to her stomach. Her head ached. Her eyes were gritty. Nerves kept her on edge. She hadn't slept a wink since Noah's unexpected visit and now she had to show up at work. She'd seriously considered calling in sick, but had then reconsidered. The work piled high on her desk wasn't going away and there would be double that by tomorrow.

So, she'd dragged herself out of bed, showered and did what she could with makeup to repair the damage of yet another sleepless night. Now every time the phone rang, she jumped, thinking it might be Noah.

Don't be ridiculous. He's done with me. He believes I betrayed him.

He's never going to speak to me again…

What hurt the most was that Noah was right. No matter how hard she tried to believe she'd been promoted on her work record alone, there had always been the tiniest suspicion that it had also had something to do with what had happened that night ten years ago. She'd never had the courage to question it before, especially not out loud. Recently the commissioner had implied her role as his chief of staff relied entirely on her staying silent. It was only a matter of time before he learned about what she'd done.

As if privy to her thoughts, the door to Beechwood's office opened and her boss came striding out. He gave her a smarmy grin. "What's in the diary this morning, Superintendent?"

Anger surged through her. She'd done the right thing by telling Noah the truth about that night. Her only regret was that she hadn't come forward earlier. If it cost her the job she loved, so be it. She was done with working for the likes of Beechwood.

Squaring her shoulders, she stared him in the face. "Why was I promoted to chief of staff?"

Beechwood's expression registered his surprise. It was almost as if he'd forgotten his earlier, thinly veiled threat.

"Wow. Where did that come from?"

Ayla held her ground. "Please, just answer me."

The commissioner shrugged. "Okay. Well, because you earned it, of course. Have you forgotten you once held the highest solve rate in your local command? You impressed a lot of people on your way up the ladder. Or maybe I should say you impressed the *right* people." He winked. "And of course, one good turn deserves another, doesn't it?" he added with a smirk.

Ayla stared at him, incensed. "Don't you *dare* tell me my positon as chief of staff has anything to do with that night!"

Beechwood brushed away her words as if they were of no

consequence. "I don't know what you're getting so worked up about. Henry Craigdon dropped dead of a heart attack, so I heard. So neither of us have to worry about that asshole anymore."

"Except, we both know the LECC is investigating the accident and from what I hear, they're getting close to discovering the truth."

Beechwood's gaze sharpened. "How the hell do you know that?"

Ayla thought fast. "Bettino. You ordered me to go and see him. He told me what happened. What you forced him to do."

"Ha! Forced him! I didn't force him to do anything!"

"That's not what he says and from what I understand, he's told everything to the LECC."

Anger glinted in the commissioner's eyes. "The bastard! Who the hell does he think he is?" Then Beechwood shook his head dismissively. "It doesn't matter. He's a drug addict and a drunk. Hardly a credible witness."

"You're wrong. The last time I saw him, he was sober and I didn't see any evidence of drugs. In fact he denied—"

"Of course he's an addict. Has been for years." Beechwood's eyes narrowed menacingly. "Just you make sure you keep your mouth shut. Otherwise you'll not only find yourself out of a job, you'll find yourself on the wrong end of an IA investigation." He moved closer, until they were mere inches apart. "Mark my words. It would be very easy to drop a word here or there. It wouldn't be at all difficult to inculpate you in what happened that night. After all, who's going to believe you over the police commissioner?"

With that, he turned on his heel and stalked away in the direction of his office. Ayla collapsed in her seat. She was trembling all over. Fear weighed heavily in her stomach. Ice poured through her veins. She started shivering in delayed shock and wished Noah was there.

Blindly searching for her phone in her handbag, her fingers closed around the device with relief. She unlocked the screen and started searching for Noah's number. And then she remembered the way he'd looked at her right before he'd left her apartment. The shock, the anger, the devastation… She dropped her phone back into her handbag.

Kevin Beechwood strode back to his office, glad for the reprieve. His head was buzzing, filled with what Ayla had said about Bettino. He'd already been told by the LECC detectives that Bettino had spilled his guts. He hadn't paid it too much heed at the time because he knew Joe would never stand up to cross examination. Just like that criminal, John Hassad.

But according to Ayla, Bettino had cleaned up his act. If he came across as a credible witness, Beechwood was fucked. No, he wouldn't stand for that. There was no way he was going to let some no-good, lily-livered fuckup destroy his career. Not when he'd worked so hard to get to the top. He had to get busy. There was much to plan.

Noah gunned the engine of his Fireblade and peeled out of the LECC staff parking lot. Thank God the day was finally over. The hours had dragged by until he thought it would never end. His head had been full of tortuous thoughts of Ayla.

Thankfully Declan had made contact with Bettino. The man had been out of town, visiting with his wife and children. Apparently, things were looking up for him in that department. Declan had convinced him to come to the LECC offices and give a statement. He was expected there first thing in the morning.

Noah had finally taken the time to listen to Ayla's voicemail, asking him to call her. Apparently she had something to tell him. Something important. He could hear the fear and hesitancy in her voice. He was left to wonder if she'd left the message with the intention of coming clean about her involvement with Beechwood and Bettino that fateful night in Maitland, or if something else entirely had prompted the call. He guessed he'd never know.

And even if that had been her intention, to tell him about Beechwood, that didn't make up for the fact she'd kept it secret all this time or that she'd no doubt used her leverage from that night to elevate her in the ranks of the police force. Either way he looked at it, he was left with a sour taste.

As he headed over the Harbour Bridge toward home, he thought about dropping by Flynn's apartment. They only lived a few blocks away from each other. But then he remembered that Jayde was probably there. He'd heard she'd moved in with his brother. He was happy for the two of them. He was glad it had worked out for someone. There was no need for all of them to be miserable in love.

Still, he didn't want to be alone right then.

I could always drop by Logan's place… It's also on my way home…

Decision made, he opened the throttle and began to weave in and out of the heavy peak-hour traffic. It was the best part of forty-five minutes before he arrived at Logan's apartment. Parking the bike, he pulled off his helmet and headed for the gate that led to Logan's building. He gave a perfunctory knock on the front door and turned the handle. The door opened and he walked inside.

Logan was seated on the couch with a pretty blond close beside him. Logan was bare chested. The buttons on the blond's blouse were undone. They each held a glass of wine. Logan looked up at him in surprise. Noah's face flamed with embarrassment.

What the hell… Am I the only Craigdon who can't make it work with a woman?

Noah immediately averted his face and turned to leave. Logan stood and set his glass on the coffee table before going to him.

"Hey, Noah. What are you doing here?"

"Sorry. I knocked, but you mustn't have heard me. The door was unlocked. I… I…" He ducked his head. "Sorry. I'll get going."

"Don't be silly," Logan replied. He moved closer and lowered his voice. "Don't worry about Melanie. She's no one important."

With that he moved back to the blond and had a quiet word with her. She stood and did up the buttons on her blouse before reaching for her handbag. She threw a sulky look in Logan's direction and then let herself out.

"You didn't have to do that," Noah said.

"Sure I did. You didn't drop by here unannounced for idle chit chat. You look like hell. What's going on?"

With a heavy sigh, Noah threw himself down on the couch. He buried his face in his hands and gave an indistinguishable groan.

Logan cocked an eyebrow. "That bad, huh? Don't tell me you're still having woman problems?"

Noah groaned again and scrubbed his hands through his hair. "Are there any other kind?"

"Sounds like you need a drink before we get into this. Can I get you a beer?"

Noah shot him a grateful look. "Thanks, mate. A beer would be great."

"Heineken okay?'

"Sure."

Logan returned with two beers and handed one to his brother. Noah opened it and took a long gulp.

Logan settled himself on the other end of the couch. "Righto, bro. Hit me with it. I assume this has something to do with the girl you were moaning about the other night."

Noah nodded grimly. "Yes. Ayla."

"Ayla. Well, start from the beginning."

Noah thought it would be hard to spill his guts, but the moment he opened his mouth, his hurt and anger and disappointment poured out. Logan let him speak without interruption and Noah was grateful for his brother's consideration. Eventually he came to a stop.

Logan whistled low. "Wow. No wonder she's made it to Beechwood's chief of staff at such a young age!"

Noah's stomach sunk. "You think her rapid rise had something to do with keeping quiet?"

Logan looked uncomfortable. "Hey, I'm not a detective and I don't know anything about this woman or her achievements, but it sure as hell sounds like staying silent didn't do her any harm."

Noah nodded grimly. "You're right. I should have known from the beginning something was off. I actually thought she'd gotten there on merit. I mean, she's smart, articulate, hardworking, loyal." Then he scoffed, "Ha! Loyal! Yeah, loyal all right. Loyal to the boss who appears at the very root of the corruption."

"Hey, you don't know all the facts about her involvement or lack thereof. You admitted that yourself. Besides, no one's perfect. You really like this woman. Last time we were together, you told us you were in love with her. You're not a fool. She must have some redeeming qualities. We all have our reasons for keeping secrets."

"It's a hell of a big secret to sit on all these years," Noah said bitterly.

"How did you find out about it?"

Noah grimaced. "Christopher. He's a pain in the ass, but this time he actually did some good, even if his motive's likely to cause trouble. He said he overheard Ayla in conversation with the cop she used to work with in Maitland. He recorded it on his phone."

"Gee, that must have been tough, finding out like that. Do you know why she kept quiet?"

"No."

"Maybe you should ask her. Surely you owe her that much." He paused. "She isn't the only one with secrets."

Noah's cheeks heated with shame. Logan was right. Noah had lived a lie all these years too, hiding the fact he used to sell drugs for his uncle. He could have gone to the police at any time and turned his uncle in, blown apart a multi-million dollar drug business and yet he'd said nothing.

Okay, so Uncle Henry had taken him aside at one point and made it clear he was to keep his mouth shut, or else. The threat had made it clear his uncle had the power to get him arrested and sent to jail. But still…

With guilt flooding his pores, he drew in a deep breath and let out a weary sigh. "You're right."

In two more gulps, he finished his beer and then got to his feet.

Logan looked at him in surprise. "You're leaving already?"

Noah nodded. "Yeah. Thank you, bro. Thanks for listening. Sorry about ruining your evening. I gotta go."

Logan stood. "Don't think anything of it. I'm here for you. Anytime." He gave Noah a hug.

Noah muttered something about catching up later and took his leave.

Chapter Nineteen

Ayla sat curled up on the couch, a glass of wine in her hand. She'd opened the bottle of Merlot upon her return home and was more than halfway through it. In between bouts of self-pity that she'd ruined her chance at a relationship with a good and decent man, she was intermittently filled with spurts of anger over Beechwood's insinuation her failure to speak up against what had happened that night in Maitland had helped her rise more quickly through the ranks.

She'd always refused to give serious consideration to the fact her actions, or more aptly, her *inaction* had contributed to her success, but after what Kevin implied, she'd begun to doubt herself. Then there had been his express threat to frame her. That frightened her more than anything. He certainly had the power to carry it out. She'd finally found the courage to speak out, but at what cost? Her career? Her freedom? Most definitely her relationship with Noah. Fresh tears streamed down her face.

Sodden tissues were wadded up in piles on the couch beside her. Her eyes felt swollen from crying. She'd taken a shower in an effort to rid herself of the sadness and disappointment that threatened to overwhelm her, but it hadn't helped. She pulled on the pale pink oversize T-shirt with the teddy bear imprint that fell just above her knees. It was so old, the print had faded and the fabric was worn. But it was her favorite nightshirt. Her go-to whenever she felt down and when she wore it, somehow it brought her comfort. She was still waiting for it to lift her mood.

I should go to bed. Sleep on it. Things will look better in the light of day…

At least, that's what her mom always said and her mom was usually right.

With a sigh, she stood and collected the pile of soggy tissues. There was nothing she could do about Noah right now and as for the other… There was no way she was letting someone like Beechwood destroy her self-esteem—or her career. She had Joe on her side. He'd back her over Beechwood. She was sure of it. Kevin could go and shove his insinuations and threats. She was made of stronger stuff.

She was almost at the kitchen when the front doorbell rang. She frowned. It was getting late. Past nine o'clock. She didn't normally get visitors that time of night. Not even from her neighbor across the hall who sometimes called in for a chat.

Determined to ignore it, she tossed the tissues into the garbage bin under the sink and washed her hands. The doorbell rang again. She sighed. Tucking her loose hair behind her ears and tugging down her pajama top, she padded barefoot to the front door. She looked through the peephole and her heart skipped a beat.

Noah.

For a brief moment, she considered telling him to go away. They hadn't parted on the best of terms and besides, she looked a mess. Then he rang the doorbell a third time and accompanied it with a loud knock.

"Ayla? It's Noah. We need to talk. Please, let me in."

Her hand wavered above the door knob and then her shoulders slumped in defeat. As much as she wasn't up for this confrontation, it would be cowardly to tell him to go away. She owed him an explanation. Might as well get it over with. Then perhaps she'd be able to sleep.

She opened the door and stood back to allow him to enter. His eyes flared wide with surprise at her appearance. The swollen eyes, the faded nightshirt… Ayla lifted her head and glared at him, daring him to comment. Wisely, he remained silent.

"Thank you for seeing me," he said quietly.

She merely shrugged and turned away, heading back to the living room. She took a seat on the couch. His gaze fell on the half-empty wine bottle and the glass that stood beside it on the coffee table. Once again, he didn't comment.

"Can I get you a drink?" she asked, belatedly remembering her manners.

He shook his head. "No. I'm fine." He took the armchair opposite her and then leaned forward with his elbows resting on his thighs. The fact he looked so unsure of himself made her feel a little better.

"We need to talk," he said again.

She nodded. "Yes."

He sighed wearily and rubbed his hand over his stubble. Though she was an emotional wreck, she was still aware of how good he looked with a five o'clock shadow.

"I'm sorry for the way I left here the last time. I was angry and hurt and disappointed. To be honest, I was in shock. But I should never have shouted at you like that. I should have given you the chance to explain. So here I am. Calm. Kind of. Collected. Maybe." He gave a half-smile and then his expression turned earnest. "I want to hear your side of the story."

Her chest tightened with emotion. When she spoke, her voice trembled. "Thank you, Noah. I appreciate that. And I'm sorry, too. I should have told you earlier about my involvement. I shouldn't have let you find out like that. Believe me, even before Christopher showed me the video I wanted to and it was on my mind all the time."

Noah started in surprise. "So you knew he'd taped you?"

She shook her head. "No. I had no idea. He did that in secret and then sent the video to my phone."

Noah looked like he wanted to say more, but then he slowly let out his breath. "We've both made mistakes. Let's not dwell on that. Since our fight, I've had some time to think. I was very quick to judge you. That wasn't fair. None of us are perfect and you're not the only one with secrets."

Surprise surged through her. She wondered what he meant. She shot him an expectant look.

He sighed again. "I'm not sure how much you know about Henry Craigdon, but for years my uncle was a big-time drug dealer. I was a teenager when my uncle approached me and asked me to work for him selling drugs."

Ayla gasped. Though she'd heard rumors Henry wasn't the upstanding citizen he appeared to be, Noah's revelation that he'd been involved in his uncle's illegal drug business was the last thing she expected to hear. She wondered if he still was.

No, that's ridiculous! He's a good and honest cop. There's no way…

As if aware of the tumultuous emotions coursing through her, Noah continued to explain.

"In case you're wondering, I stopped my involvement a long time ago. Long before I went to the Academy. That doesn't mean I'm not ashamed of what I did. I knew the harm drugs were doing and though my uncle threatened to turn me into the police if I quit, I always felt I should have tried harder to walk away from it earlier."

He looked so distressed, Ayla took pity on him. "Talk to me, Noah."

"My father had never managed to acquire the kind of wealth his brother enjoyed. Though we lived a comfortable life, it wasn't even close to the opulent lifestyle my uncle provided for his family. I was young and stupid and hungry for attention. I thought about all the things I could buy with the extra money. I thought it would improve my chances with the girls if I wore designer clothes and drove a flashy sports car."

"And did it?" Ayla asked softly.

Noah bowed his head. "No. See, what I didn't take into consideration was the *me* factor."

Ayla frowned in confusion. "What do you mean?"

Noah sighed again. "See, I was wrong. No matter how much money I had, or what clothes I wore, or what kind of car I drove, it didn't change who I was. I was still the shy, dorky teenager who stumbled and stammered over his words and blushed like crazy whenever a girl I liked happened to walk by. No amount of money could make a difference to that."

She felt a stab of sympathy for him. "I'm sorry. That must have been lonely at times."

He compressed his lips. "It was. I used to wonder why I couldn't be more like Flynn or Logan, or even some of my cousins. Life seemed to come so much easier to them. Well, when I say life, what I really mean is, girls. That was the most important thing for any guy back when we were teens."

"Some would say finding the perfect soul mate, someone to love and who loves us back is still the most important thing," she said quietly.

Noah looked up. Their eyes met and held. The silence stretched between them as they searched for answers in each other's faces. Ayla finally looked away.

"I owe you an explanation," she said.

Noah looked like he was about to protest, but Ayla waved it away. "Please, Noah. You've confessed your secrets. It's time for me to do the same."

Noah reluctantly nodded. He sat back against the chair. Ayla drew in a deep breath and released it slowly, gathering the courage she needed to see this through. She nervously cleared her throat.

"Okay. Here goes. I was nineteen, fresh out of the Academy and eager as a new puppy. I was a first generation Australian. My parents were so proud of me. A police officer! I was so excited! I couldn't wait to start serving my community. My first posting was out in the country. Maitland, in the Hunter Valley. Kevin Beechwood was my superior. Joe Bettino was also stationed there."

She paused and drew in another breath as the memories of that night came back to her. Her fists clenched.

"It was Saturday, tenth of April 2010. It had been a quiet night up until then. There was only a skeleton staff. Kevin, Joe and I were on duty. Joe took the call about the MVA. He relayed the information to Kevin and they made preparations to attend the scene of the accident. As a newly minted police officer, I was keen to experience all I could and I asked if I could ride along."

She glanced at Noah. He watched her in silence, his expression unreadable. She kept going.

"We arrived at the scene. Kevin took command. It was a single-vehicle crash. A silver Mercedes sedan had collided head-on with a tree. There was extensive damage to the front of the car, particularly the passenger side. There were skid marks on the road where the driver had attempted to brake. Your uncle told Kevin he'd swerved to miss a kangaroo."

Noah nodded. "That's what we were told, too."

"Being a probationary constable, there wasn't much I was

allowed to do. Joe got busy directing traffic and keeping bystanders out of the way. An ambulance was already there and the paramedics were attending to Henry. They'd already covered your mother with a blue tarpaulin. She was several yards away from the vehicle. It was obvious she'd gone through the windscreen. The usual procedures were followed under Kevin's command. Eventually, Henry was taken back to the station for mandatory drug and alcohol tests and a formal interview."

"Were you there when they brought him in?"

"Yes. And so was Joe, but Kevin was in charge and he conducted the interview in private."

"Was Henry breath tested?"

"Yes."

Noah started in surprise. "You saw him take the test?"

"Yes."

"I don't understand. Bettino said this was done behind closed doors. That he didn't see anything. The first he knew of it was when Beechwood ordered him to provide the samples."

Ayla nodded. "He was telling the truth. Kevin ordered Bettino from the room. I'm not sure why, but I was allowed to stay. Perhaps Kevin didn't see me as a threat of any kind. Anyway, he followed procedure and after he'd concluded the interview, he tested Henry for alcohol and drugs. While the drug test came back negative, it was a different story for the breath test. Henry exploded. He asked to speak to Kevin in private. Kevin looked like he wanted to argue, but eventually asked me to leave the room. I did."

"What happened then?"

"I sat outside in the squad room with Joe. We could hear Kevin and Henry arguing, but their words were indistinct. A short time later, Kevin ordered Joe into the adjoining room. I didn't see what happened then, but as you're aware, I spoke to Joe only recently about that night. He told me Kevin forced him to provide more samples. Given the mess Joe's life has become since, I believe him."

Ayla sighed and rubbed the back of her neck where an ache had developed. "I didn't actually see them do it, but all of a sudden, Henry was being released. When I questioned Joe about it later that night, he told me the samples were negative. I was confused, because I was sure Kevin had told Henry his breath test had come back positive. That was the reason they'd argued. But Joe insisted that wasn't the case. What could I do about it? I was a probationary constable. Who was I to argue? I didn't want to start my career off on the wrong foot. Though it left me with a bad feeling, I let it go."

"And Henry wasn't taken to the hospital at all?"

"No. He was treated at the scene by the paramedics for minor scratches and a graze on his forehead, but they said he was fine to leave. As for the drug and alcohol tests, I'm sure you know, it's not necessary to attend hospital for blood tests if the tests at the station are negative and even though his actions had resulted in someone's death, there were no charges laid."

Silence fell between them as they were both caught up in their own thoughts. Noah looked sad and thoughtful. Ayla felt a lingering sense of guilt. After a while, she voiced the one thought that had continued to trouble her for so long.

"What I don't understand is what Henry had over Kevin?"

Noah sighed wearily and scrubbed at his hair. "I might be able to shed some light on that."

Ayla listened in shock as he told her about what he'd discovered among Henry Craigdon's papers and how Kevin's name had shown up several times.

"He owed my uncle hundreds of thousands of dollars. Three hundred thousand at Henry's death. I'm guessing they were drug debts."

Ayla's eyes wide with shock. "Kevin was a dealer? I don't believe it."

"Either that, or he was using himself. Maybe both. It's my guess the night of Henry's accident, he knew he was over the limit and he threatened to call in Beechwood's line of credit or destroy his career, or both, if Beechwood didn't falsify the test. I think that's what they argued about. We both know what happened after that."

Noah paused, but his face bore lingering tension. While guilt still lay heavy in Ayla's stomach, she needed to hear everything he had to say. If there was ever going to be a chance for something between them, they had to lay everything bare.

"What is it, Noah?"

His gaze remained steady on hers. His expression was dark and somber. "You said you didn't see anything, but it's odd that you've been promoted to such a lofty position at such a young age. I can't help but think you saw more than you've admitted."

A flash of anger burned inside her, but she forcefully pushed it away. Noah was within his rights to think like that. After all, there had been others before him. In a quiet but firm voice, she spoke again.

"I worked my guts out over the years since then. There wasn't a case I wouldn't do. At one stage, I had the highest solve rate in the whole of my local area command. I've had to prove my worth every step of the way and no one cut me any slack."

She paused to drag in a ragged breath. "Still, there were colleagues who thought I'd slept my way to the top or was promoted for reasons other than merit. No doubt there are some people out there who still think that. There's nothing I can do about that. I've learned to let that go. The other night, Beechwood insinuated the same thing, but even he knows the truth. I got where I am through sheer hard work. Nothing else."

Once again, their gazes caught and held.

"I believe you," Noah said. "I have one final question. Will you attend my office and provide a formal statement evidencing what you told me about that night?"

Ayla stared at him. This was a no-brainer. This time, she'd do what was right. She nodded decisively. "Yes."

"You understand there might be professional consequences for you? You might be censured, demoted… I have no control over any of that."

She continued to hold his gaze. She'd take whatever punishment was necessary. "I understand." She paused and then added, "Beechwood threatened to frame me for the cover up if I talked to you."

Noah's eyes widened in shock. "He did *what?*"

Feeling a renewed sense of fear, she relayed the commissioner's threat.

Noah stared at her in disbelief. "Are you absolutely certain that's what he said?"

She held his gaze. "Yes."

"That bastard! How dare he think he can get away with something like that!"

Ayla's mouth twisted in a grimace. "He's the most powerful member of the New South Wales Police Force. I can see how he might think he has the authority to make it happen." Her chest tightened on a wave of fear. She looked at Noah. "I'm scared, Noah."

Noah's eyes flared with emotion. In one swift movement, he stood and came toward her. He sat down beside her and took her in his arms. The moment their lips touched, she was gone. The kiss was warm and sweet and tender. Noah pulled slightly away and stared at her.

"There's no need to be afraid. No one's going to hurt you. Ever. Not while I'm around. Especially Beechwood. That prick's going down."

Ayla was filled with a wave of gratitude and relief that quickly turned to desire. She moved and brushed her lips against his. Fire ignited inside her. They kissed like they couldn't get enough. And it was true. She couldn't get enough. Their mouths opened, their tongues danced. Their kisses were filled with longing, but there was also possessiveness—he was hers and she was his and nothing and no one could change that.

Gasping for breath, Ayla broke off the kiss and then pressed her lips against his eyelids, his cheeks, his nose. She kissed him all over his face and then returned to his lips. Once again, they kissed deeply, more deeply than she'd ever kissed or been kissed before. There was an urgency inside Noah and she felt it too. As one, they tore at each other's clothes.

When they were finally naked and lying skin to skin on the couch, Noah pressed his forehead against hers. He stared into her eyes. His gaze was hot and intense.

"I'm going to keep you safe forever. No harm will ever come to you. I give you my word."

His words filled her with warmth. Her heart swelled with an overwhelming feeling of love and contentment.

"Thank you. That means so much to me. Knowing how much you care… For so long I wanted to tell you everything, but I was scared about how you'd react. I was a coward. But now, I'm so glad you know. When all this is over, let's wipe the slate clean and start again. Deal?"

He kissed her soundly on the lips and grinned. "Deal."

Just like that, passion reignited and they kissed deeply. Noah's cock felt huge and hard against her belly. She longed to feel him inside her, filling her, assuaging her need. Restless, she stirred against him.

He shot her an apologetic look. "As much as I'd like to ravish your body, I don't think the couch is quite up to the task. How about we relocate to the bedroom?"

She didn't need to be asked twice. Scooting out from under him, she padded naked down the hallway. She felt Noah's gaze upon her and wiggled her ass. He gave a throaty laugh that rumbled with appreciation. Catching up to her, he lifted her in his arms and strode into her bedroom. He lowered her onto the bed and immediately followed her down.

They rolled naked across the coverlet, their lips fused together. Need burned through Ayla and centered in her core. She pressed against him, her hips, her breasts, but Noah wouldn't be rushed. It was as though this time he wanted to slow things down, take his time, explore.

He kissed his way across her breasts, taking time to suck her nipples. She arched her back, giving him greater access, silently encouraging him. He used his tongue and his hands and his lips in a way that drove her wild. Squeezing her sensitive flesh, flicking at her nipples. And then he kissed his way down her belly and buried his face between her legs.

As if the torment couldn't get worse, he began laving her most sensitive flesh with his tongue. Long, slow strokes meant to drive her wild. And it worked.

"Do you like that?" he rasped.

She made a sound of contentment and murmured "yes." She buried her fingers in his hair, holding his head in place. "That feels wonderful," she managed.

Desire continued to build in her core and she whimpered in desperate need. Noah continued his sensual onslaught in a slow and rhythmic way. Before she knew it, she was at the peak and her inner muscles were contracting around his tongue. She cried out and clenched her fists as the waves of pleasure washed over her.

When it was over, she looked at Noah and sighed. "That was amazing."

His answering smile was filled with tenderness. There was also shyness. It endeared him to her even more.

"Your turn," she said.

Noah made as if to protest, but she was having none of it. Taking charge, she forced him to lie down on his back and then started kissing him all over. She started at his face and then moved lower. She sucked at his neck, she flicked at his ears, she kissed her way across his sternum. She teased at his nipples with her tongue and ran her fingers through the light sprinkling of dark brown hair that covered his chest. All the time, Noah's eyes were closed. He murmured indistinguishable words of pleasure.

She kissed her way down his flat belly and finally reached her goal. His cock lay thick and heavy against his stomach. Reaching for it, she encircled its width in her hand and squeezed.

"Ayla!"

"Did I hurt you?" she asked, feigning innocence.

"God, no. It feels…amazing."

She smiled to herself and started stroking him, slowly, rhythmically—just the way he'd stroked her. A tiny pearl of moisture appeared at the tip. She bent her head and swiped her tongue over his engorged head. He groaned again and his breath caught. When she took him fully in her mouth, he gasped.

"Ayla…"

Increasing the pressure, she sucked him hard, as much as she could take. He moved restlessly against her, thrusting his hips upward, encouraging her not to stop. With her lips and tongue and fingers, she kept up the relentless pressure until suddenly he was there.

With a cry, he tensed against her. Moments later, her mouth filled with his hot seed. She continued to make love to him with her mouth until she'd swallowed every last drop. When it was over, she crawled up beside him and rested her head on his chest.

He turned his head and smiled. "Wow. I don't know what to say. I'm beyond words."

She grinned, filled with contentment. This was how it was supposed to be. She was so glad they'd bared their souls and come out the other side. No matter what happened with Beechwood and the investigation, they could at least move forward. Together.

Chapter Twenty

Kevin Beechwood had a headache and it wasn't only because of the number of generously poured glasses of scotch he'd consumed over the past few hours, or the line of coke he'd snorted. No, the main reason his head thumped was because of a single LECC investigation that had become a serious pain in his ass.

Ever since the very first visit from the two detectives, his life had been going off the rails. He thought he'd gotten himself into a pretty good position—he was the police commissioner, no less. The lofty position came with numerous perks, including a decent salary, a staff car and an office with a view, but it hadn't come without sacrifice. Now it appeared his house of cards was about to come crashing down. And all because of Joe Bettino.

Bettino had spilled his guts. The detectives had said it and so had Ayla. He'd taken it as a bluff from the detectives, but Ayla was a different matter. She had nothing to gain by telling him anything but the truth and he was glad she had. For a decade, she'd kept her mouth shut about what had happened and he was sure she'd keep her silence now. After all, what did she have to gain by coming forward? Her career was flying. She held a prestigious position within the police force, with a generous salary to match. She was much too smart to put all that in jeopardy.

No, the reason he'd reminded her of how much she had at stake was merely insurance. With Bettino now a real threat, he had to make sure there were no other potential leaks. He'd put the fear of God into her, but he was sure he could rely on her to continue to keep her mouth shut.

So that only left Bettino. The simple matter was, he couldn't allow Joe to testify. It would be the end of Beechwood's career. The man knew too much about what had gone on that night and if he'd truly cleaned himself up and gotten his life back on track, he might just be believed. Kevin couldn't let that happen.

His gaze drifted to his service revolver that sat on top of his desk. He should have locked it away already. It was a breach of protocol to leave it out. Not that he cared much about protocol. Rules and regulations were for the weak.

His gaze remained fixed on the revolver. Bit by bit, a plan slowly formed. He smiled. It wasn't as easy to get hold of gear since Henry Craigdon's untimely demise, but Beechwood still had his contacts. After all, he'd needed someone who could continue to supply him with his own needs. It wasn't like he'd given up his drug habit just because Henry had died. Too bad he'd just snorted the last of his supply.

Sometimes he wondered in passing if Henry's beneficiaries would ever catch on about the money Kevin owed him. It was a pretty penny, too. Up round three hundred thousand dollars. Henry had supplied him with cocaine for more years than he could remember. His habit didn't come cheap. It was fortunate Henry had been willing to extend him a line of credit. Actually, that probably had more to do with the fact Kevin had given in to Henry's threats to expose him the night Janelle Craigdon died. Kevin could still hear the argument.

"You'd better do something about that breath test or your career is over, Beechwood," Henry had hissed.

"What do you expect me to do? I have two other officers

outside who've already witnessed how drunk you are! You stink like a brewery! How am I expected to pass you off as sober?"

Henry had eyed him with a steely glare. "That's up to you. All I know is, I'm not going to jail. There's nothing I can do about Janelle now. All I can do is save my own ass. And you sure as hell are going to help me do it."

Kevin had tried to buy time. "What the hell were you doing out there, anyway?"

Henry had merely smiled. "We were headed back to our hotel. It was only another mile up the road. We were both looking forward to a night of hot sex. That's the reason she was there in the first place."

"And why were *you* there?"

Henry chuckled. "I'd been contacted by a…colleague. John Hassad. He wanted me to check out the quality of a shipment before he offered it for sale. I invited Janelle to come with me." He winked lewdly. "Thought we could make a weekend out of it."

"Why the fuck wasn't she wearing a seatbelt?"

Henry grinned. "Let's just say Janelle was keen to get her hands on me. Or more accurately, her mouth."

Kevin frowned in confusion.

Henry gave an exaggerated sigh. "Do I have to spell it out for you? She was giving me a blow job."

Kevin looked at him in shock. "She was sucking you off when you hit the kangaroo?"

"How the hell was I supposed to know that was going to happen? The fucking thing came from nowhere. I hit the brakes. It was a pure reflex. There was nothing I could do."

"And now Janelle's dead."

Henry looked momentarily upset and defeated, but soon after his expression changed to one of fierce determination.

"You're going to get me out of this, Beechwood. I'm not going to go to jail!"

When Kevin continued to vacillate, Henry had played his final card. The look that had gone along with it chilled Kevin to the bone.

"You do something about that breath test, Beechwood, or I'll make sure everyone knows you're a coke addict. It won't be hard for me to have a word in the right ear, maybe leave some incriminating evidence in a drawer of your desk… It will be the finish of you. Then it will be *you* facing jail. I've heard ex-cops have it particularly tough in the can."

In the end, Kevin had been given no choice, but he'd made it clear to Henry they were even. Henry had merely laughed and added a final request.

"Make sure the autopsy report is buried. I don't want it to appear in the police file. I need to protect Janelle's memory. The last thing I want is for the sordid details of our last night together getting out." Henry had given him another hard look.

"Okay. I'll make sure the report disappears. It won't ever make it to the police file."

A short while later, Kevin had ordered Joe Bettini into the adjoining room and had forced him to do a breath test. Though the young sergeant had protested, Kevin had reminded him of the money Bettini had stolen and the consequences the young sergeant would face if that ever got out. Bettini had provided the breath test.

But now it seemed Joe had developed a conscience. After all these years, he wanted to get things off his chest. It was a damned inconvenience, but one Kevin could deal with. There was always someone willing to sell him gear. It was just a matter of finding them. Filled with a sudden surge of determination, he finished his glass, pushed back his chair and left.

It was late. Christopher should have been home sleeping, but instead he found himself in his car, cruising the streets. He was tired and irritable, but he didn't want to go home. There was nothing for him there.

He headed in a westerly direction. An hour later, he found himself outside police headquarters. Pulling over and parking, he switched off the ignition and contemplated his sad life.

He was forty years of age, no wife, no kids and currently unemployed. He was also embroiled in a fight with his family over his late father's will. Yep, life didn't get any better. The truth was, he couldn't think of a single person who gave a shit about him. Apart from his mother, but that was her job.

The thing was, he'd never felt like he belonged anywhere. He'd been born a Craigdon, but Henry had never felt the urge to recognize him as kin. He was adopted by Frank Barrington when Christopher was twelve, but he didn't feel like a Barrington, either. He was a no one.

Then there was the lawsuit that continued to drag on. He was asking for eighty-five million. Okay, it was a decent lump of cash, but it was chickenfeed compared to what the estate was worth. The truth was, he was Henry's first born. He deserved his fair share. That's all he was asking for. Nothing extravagant. Nothing over the top. Nothing they couldn't afford. And yet they were playing hard ball. Refusing to negotiate. Letting it play out in the courts.

Fuck them.

A man appeared from the shadows, coming from the direction of the police building. Christopher watched him approach. He was average height, average build. Nothing remarkable. He wore a trench coat and carried a briefcase. He walked with purpose and an air of authority.

Christopher frowned. The man looked vaguely familiar. Then he passed beneath a streetlight. It illuminated his face. Christopher blinked in surprise.

Kevin Beechwood.

Christopher recognized the police commissioner from interviews he'd given in the past on the six o'clock news. It seemed strange for the man to be working so late. As he watched, Beechwood climbed into a car and pulled away from the curb.

Curious, and with nothing else to do, Christopher switched on the ignition and began to follow him. They headed in a westerly direction. The streets were quiet, with only the occasional vehicle passing by. The further they went, the rougher the neighborhoods grew. The well-kept, fifties-style bungalows gave way to cheap government housing and ramshackle homes that had seen better days. Then Beechwood turned into a cul de sac and pulled up at the curb.

The house that stood opposite looked as bedraggled and disheveled as its neighbors. Overgrown lawn was scattered with the detritus of life—broken toys, a lounge chair that was missing all its foam, the springs clearly visible in the moonlight. Bags of garbage were piled high along the front fence. To Christopher's surprise, Beechwood climbed out of his car and walked up the cracked front pavement that led to an equally rundown front verandah.

He knocked once on the weathered front door. A few moments later, it opened. An equally disheveled-looking man stepped outside and quickly scanned the street in both directions. Christopher saw the man's gaze pause on Christopher's vehicle, but it didn't seem to give rise to any suspicion. The man returned his attention to the commissioner.

Acting on instinct, Christopher pulled out his phone and started recording. While he watched, Beechwood handed over a wad of cash. At the same time, the man thrust a bag of white powder in Beechwood's direction.

Well, well, well… What do we have here? The police commissioner doing a drug deal? How utterly fascinating…

As the thoughts filled Christopher's head, another part of his brain was already working on how that information might be of benefit to him. It would be incredible to have someone with the power of the commissioner under his control… Laughter bubbled up inside him. Perhaps his luck was about to change…

Beechwood climbed back into his Range Rover. The man didn't even glance in Christopher's direction. The arrogance of him… There was a car parked less than ten yards away from him and yet he didn't even bother to check out who it was. It could have been an over-eager reporter recording everything for all Beechwood knew. It just went to show how untouchable he thought he was. It was obvious this was a well-rehearsed scene.

Beechwood made a turn at the traffic lights and started heading northeast. Openly curious now, Christopher kept on his tail. This time, he put less distance between them. It was obvious the commissioner had no inkling he was being followed, or if he did, he didn't care.

The Range Rover kept up a steady pace in front of him. More than once, Christopher almost turned around. It was well after midnight. He was tired. It had been a long day. Hell, it had been a long year. A wave of self-pity surged through him.

This is stupid. What the hell am I doing tailing a cop around Sydney in the middle of the night? So what if he's using? He wouldn't be the first cop to take drugs. I ought to go home and call it a night. Get some sleep. And he would if it wasn't for the fact that the cop was the highest ranked cop in the state.

They were now in the inner west suburb of Concord, about six miles from the city. The houses in this part of town were mainly post-war bungalows. Some of them had been gentrified, but there were plenty that still sported the original red brick and tile construction so popular in Sydney during the fifties and sixties.

Christopher let out a huge yawn. His eyes were sore. It was time to go home. He looked over his shoulder to check for oncoming traffic, intent on doing a U-turn, but before he could put his blinker on, Beechwood pulled up at one of the red brick and tile houses in front of him.

I've stayed this long… I might as well hang around and find out what he's up to…

The house was still and dark, with not a single light visible from the street. The dilapidated front yard was reflected in the neglected façade. This certainly didn't look like it belonged to the police commissioner.

So he's paying someone a house visit… Interesting…

As Beechwood climbed out his vehicle, Christopher saw him tuck the bag of white powder into his coat pocket, along with a syringe. Sitting up straighter in his seat, Christopher frowned.

What the hell's Beechwood up to? Has he stopped by at a friend's house to get high?

It seemed inconceivable, and yet what other conclusion could Christopher draw? Once again, he pulled out his phone and tapped on "RECORD." He kept the video running while Beechwood opened the low wrought iron gate and walked up the path. As Christopher watched, the commissioner knocked hard on the front door. It took awhile, but finally a light came on somewhere in the house and a few moments later, a man came to the door.

"What the fuck do you want?"

Beechwood held up his hands in a sign of surrender. "Now, now, now. That's no way to greet an old friend. I'm here to help you."

From his vantage point across the street, Christopher heard the derision in Beechwood's tone. The recipient of the comment seemed to hear it, too.

"You're no friend of mine, Beechwood. Where were you

when I was struggling? Fighting demons you knew about all too well? Well, I overcame them all on my own. I don't need your help. Now get the fuck off my property."

The commissioner remained unperturbed. "Or you'll what, Joe? Call the cops?" He chuckled at his joke.

The man stepped forward, his face now fully illuminated. Christopher gasped in recognition.

It's the cop who worked with Ayla in Maitland the night Janelle Craigdon died. Ayla had met him at that café. She'd called him Joe…

Christopher was certain it was the same man. The man he'd recorded as saying he'd told the detectives from the LECC the truth about what had happened that awful night…

All of a sudden, comprehension dawned. *Fuck!* Joe had mentioned the name Kevin Beechwood. At the time, Christopher didn't think much of it. He definitely didn't connect it to the police commissioner. But here he was, standing outside Joe's house… It was far too much of a coincidence.

In response to the commissioner's goading, Christopher saw Joe tense. Anger glinted in his eyes. He grabbed hold of Beechwood's shirtfront.

"How *dare* you come here, pretending to care! It's been ten years, Kevin. Ten years! And you haven't said a word. Haven't given me as much as a call to check if I was okay. You knew I was on stress leave and you darn well knew why and yet you said nothing. I've lost everything! My wife, my kids, my career. Don't come here now pretending you want to help. I don't buy it. Now piss off. I won't tell you again."

Something about the commissioner's demeanor changed. His fists clenched. His face turned ugly. It was like he was done pretending to be nice. While Christopher continued to record the scene playing out in front of him, Beechwood pushed his way past the man he'd called Joe and disappeared inside.

There was an initial shout of anger and then the place fell

silent. Curious, Christopher climbed out of his car and stealthily made his way up to the house. The front door remained open. He crept across the weathered verandah and hoped the sagging boards wouldn't announce his arrival. And then it happened. A board creaked loudly under his foot. He stopped short, his heart pounding.

Silence continued to envelope him. After a few moments, he risked another step. He made it all the way to the front door without further incident and breathed a sigh of relief and then stood there in indecision.

Do I go inside? What if they see me? What excuse am I going to give for being there in a stranger's house in the middle of the night? What if they think I'm a burglar? What if they call the police?

No, Beechwood wasn't going to call the police. Not with a bag of coke and a syringe in his pocket. There's no way he'd take the risk of having to explain that…

Mind made up, Christopher crept down the hallway. A faint light still shone in a room at the far end of the corridor. He could hear the muted sound of conversation and then a shout of alarm. Picking up his pace and with his phone still recording, Christopher eased himself through an open doorway and came up short.

Joe sat slumped over the kitchen table. Beechwood stood over him, an empty syringe in his hand. A teaspoon sat on the table not far away. The bag of white powder was next to it.

Christopher's heart leaped with fear. He slunk back along the wall into the hallway, out of sight.

Oh, God! Did Beechwood see me? Oh, God! I hope not! What the hell just happened? Are they shooting up together? It sure didn't sound like they were on friendly terms. What the hell's going on?

Before he could get a hold of his tumultuous thoughts, the sound of footsteps coming toward him registered. Just in time, he dived into an adjoining room and pulled the door shut behind him, leaving it open the barest crack. He watched the commissioner stride past him, his steps quick and sure. A few moments later, he heard the sound of a car engine starting and then the sound faded away.

With his heart still pounding, Christopher pulled the door open and rushed down the hallway toward the kitchen. Joe was still slumped over the table. Christopher looked around. The drugs and other paraphernalia were gone.

Beechwood must have taken them with him... The teaspoon, the coke, the syringe...

Christopher had a bad feeling about this. He looked at Joe. The man was ashen. His lips had a bluish color about them that didn't bode well. With trembling fingers, Christopher checked the man's pulse. It took him a moment to find it. When he did, he was alarmed at how slow and weak it was.

Frantic now, Christopher grabbed his phone and dialed 000. As soon as the operator answered, he shouted for an ambulance. When the operator asked for his address, he came up blank and then he recalled seeing the name on a sign when he'd turned into it the street.

Walker Street.

He gave the details to the operator.

"What number in Walker Street?"

"Hell. I don't know. Hang on a minute."

He raced out of the house. A cracked and faded number was affixed to the front of the house.

Eighty-one.

Once again, he gave the details to the operator. She assured him an ambulance was on its way. He ended the call. Breathing hard, he sank to the floor beside Joe. As the adrenaline began to subside, Christopher thought about what he'd witnessed. He had an awful suspicion Beechwood hadn't come there to get high with a friend. It looked like he'd come to murder him.

Murder? Hell! That's ridiculous! We're talking about the

commissioner of police. I must be mistaken. So what if there was bad blood between them. There's no way the commissioner would murder someone…

And yet, Christopher couldn't deny what he'd seen and though every ounce of logic inside him argued against it, the deep sense of dread that filled him at the memory of seeing Beechwood standing over the man with a syringe in hand wouldn't go away.

"Fuck."

The expletive fell from Christopher's lips.

What have I gotten myself into? All I was doing was filling some endless hours by following the police commissioner. It was meant to be a bit of fun, a distraction from the boredom and my sorry excuse for a life…

Now it appeared he was in the middle of something he didn't want to know about. Then again…

It was obvious Beechwood was up to no good. How good would it be to have the police commissioner in his pocket? No more traffic tickets. No more having to worry about anything. All he'd have to do is send Beechwood the video and remind him of how much he had to lose if he didn't do Christopher's bidding. It was a dream come true.

But somehow, Christopher didn't feel the elation he thought he would at the thought of having the police commissioner at his beck and call. Playing stupid tricks on Christopher's family was one thing. But this was an altogether different matter. He'd just witnessed what could very well end up in a murder. Was he really prepared to let the perpetrator get away with it, for his own gain? The thought sickened him.

No, he might enjoy manipulating people for his own pleasure, but that was mostly harmless fun. He hadn't stooped so low as to condone murder. Somewhere he had to draw the line. And this was where it ended. He looked at Joe and his stomach swirled with dread. The sound of sirens in the distance snagged his attention. His heart thumped as he scrambled to his feet.

I have to get out of here…

No sooner had the thought formed and he was running down the corridor toward the front door. Wrenching it open, he raced toward his car. With white and blue and red flashing lights illuminating the night sky, he put his car into gear and took off.

He was halfway back to the city before his heart rate slowed down. Taking his foot off the accelerator, he flicked on his indicator and pulled over to the side of the road. His hands were still trembling. Fear and disbelief swirled in his gut. He rested his head on the steering wheel and drew in some fortifying breaths.

The shock of what he'd witnessed was gradually wearing off. He was more and more convinced Beechwood, along with Joe, had been involved the night Janelle was killed and now Beechwood had made an attempt on Joe's life.

For the first time in my life, I need to do the right thing. I need to call Noah…

When Christopher's pulse rate was almost back to normal, he reached for his phone.

Chapter Twenty One

The sound of Noah's phone ringing startled him from a deep sleep. He and Ayla had spent the night loving each other until they'd fallen asleep, exhausted. It felt like Noah had barely closed his eyes when he forced them open again. He picked up his phone and checked the screen.

Christopher.

Great. Just what he needed. The last time he'd answered a call from Christopher, he'd been told about Ayla's involvement in the cover up surrounding his mother's death. Though the two of them had since worked through that, it hadn't been easy. The last person he wanted to talk to at nearly two in the morning was Christopher. With a groan, he switched his phone to silent and pulling Ayla close against him, he tried to get back to sleep.

If he thought that was the end of it, he was sadly mistaken. The phone vibrated again and again as Christopher continued to call him. The fourth time, Noah cursed and sat up. He reached for the phone and answered it at the same time he climbed out of bed and left the room, closing the door behind him.

"Christopher," he said, pitching his voice low so as not to wake Ayla. "What the hell are you doing? Do you know what time it is?"

"Noah! Thank God you answered!"

The fear in Christopher's voice gave Noah pause as he made his way through the darkness into Ayla's living room. He'd never heard his half-cousin sound so rattled. Christopher sounded like he was on the verge of panic.

"What's going on? Where are you?" Noah asked.

"I-I don't know. I've been driving from Concord. I'm pulled up on the side of the road about halfway to the city."

Noah scrubbed at his eyes. "What are you doing out at Concord?"

"It's about Ayla. I—"

"I don't want to hear any more," Noah cut him off. "Ayla and I have worked things out. I don't need you to interfere. Now if you don't mind, I'm going back to bed."

"No! Wait! Please, Noah! Don't hang up! I didn't know who else to call."

The desperation in Christopher's voice made Noah frown. *What the hell's going on with him?*

"What's the matter with you? Are you drunk?"

"No! Of course not! It's not just about Ayla. It's about Beechwood and that cop she met with. Joe. I-I just saw them. Beechwood and Joe."

Noah's heart skipped a beat. Christopher sounded so scared. "Where were they? What happened?"

"Beechwood went to Joe's house in Concord. "I think… I think Beechwood might have given Joe a hotshot."

"*What?*"

Adrenaline surged through him. Noah was now wide awake. His gut swirled with dread.

"I saw him. I saw him with the needle in his hand. I have it all on my phone."

Coldness settled in Noah's stomach. "You were there when Beechwood did that?"

"Yes."

"And you recorded it?"

"Yes."

"Fuck." Noah scrubbed a hand through his hair. "Do you have any idea the danger you put yourself in?"

"I didn't think about that. I acted on instinct."

"Did he see you?"

"No. I don't think so."

"Where's Bettino now?"

"At the hospital. I called an ambulance and then got the hell out of there. I didn't want to have to answer any questions."

Noah blew his breath out on a heavy sigh, trying to take it all in. If what Christopher had witnessed was true, the commissioner was now up for attempted murder. If Bettino didn't make it, that charge would be upgraded.

A fresh wave of shock went through him. And then he remembered Christopher was still on the phone.

"Are you okay?" he asked.

Christopher's voice was subdued. "Yeah. I'm okay. Still a little shaky, but you know…" There was a poor attempt at a laugh.

"Do you want me to come and get you?"

"No. I should be okay. Now I've had time to stop and process what happened… I'll leave it up to you guys."

"Send me what you have on your phone," Noah said.

"No worries. I'll gladly let you take over from this point. I've done my bit. If ever I needed convincing the world of policing isn't for me, this has done it."

"You've done well, Christopher. You might just have the proof we need to put Beechwood away—for this and for the cover up surrounding the death of my mother." He paused and then added, "Thank you."

"No thanks are needed," Christopher responded, his voice rough with emotion.

"I disagree. What you did tonight was brave. Maybe also stupid, but brave nonetheless. You ought to be proud of yourself. I am."

There was a moment of silence. When Christopher spoke again, his voice was rough with emotion. "I'm sure anyone in the same circumstances would have done it. There's nothing special about me."

"That's where you're wrong, Christopher. Dead wrong."

Despite the lateness of the hour, after ending the call with Christopher, Noah immediately went into cop mode. He put in a call to his superior. After apologizing for the lateness of the hour, Noah filled him in on the details. His boss plied him with questions and then promised to do what needed to be done to arrest the commissioner as soon as possible. Though the allegations were gravely serious and there was a need to tread carefully, they both agreed time was of the essence. Noah's boss thanked him for the call.

His phone had beeped halfway through the call and now he took the time to open the attachment Christopher had sent him. There were two videos. The first one showed Beechwood buying cocaine. The second was even more shocking. Shaking his head with disbelief, Noah forwarded the videos to his boss.

Afterwards, Noah stood in Ayla's living room, staring silently out at the night. He slowly shook his head in shock and disbelief. What Christopher had told him was still sinking in. Though Noah had been convinced the commissioner had been behind the cover up, discovering he was capable of attempted murder took things to a completely different level. He still couldn't believe it.

He wanted to call the hospital and get an update on Bettino's condition, but he knew from experience for privacy reasons the hospital staff wouldn't give out any information over the phone. That would have to wait for an in-person visit in the morning. For now, there was nothing else he could do.

With a sigh, he retraced his steps back down the hallway and climbed back into bed. Ayla stirred beside him.

"Is everything all right?" she murmured, her voice thick with sleep.

"Yes," he whispered. "Go back to sleep." With that, he drew her close against him and tried his best to do the same.

Later that morning, Noah sought and was granted permission to interview Kevin Beechwood. Declan accompanied him. Their boss watched the interview through a one-way mirror. Unsurprisingly, Beechwood lawyered up.

While they waited for the commissioner's lawyer to make an appearance and consult with his client, Noah and Declan called on Bettino at the Sydney Harbour Hospital. A woman Bettino introduced as his wife sat in a chair beside the bed. Fortunately, Joe had survived the hot shot and though he felt like crap, he was grateful to be alive.

"You have my half-cousin to thank for that," Noah told him. "Christopher Barrington. He just happened to be in your neighborhood. He found you unconscious and called the ambulance."

Bettino shook his head in disbelief. "Wow. My lucky day, hey? Please give him my sincere gratitude. I wouldn't be here if it wasn't for him."

"That's for sure," Noah agreed. "Can you tell us who gave you the hotshot?"

Bettino closed his eyes briefly. When he opened them again, they burned with fury. "It was Beechwood."

"Kevin Beechwood? The police commissioner?" Declan asked.

"Yes. One and the same."

"Are you sure?" Noah asked. Though they had Christopher's video footage, there was always a chance the judge might not allow it to go in as evidence. It was important to have a backup.

"Of course I'm sure. I'd recognize that prick anywhere."

"Why did he do it?" Declan asked.

Bettino eyed them with resignation. "Because of what happened in Maitland. The night Janelle Craigdon died. He found out I'd spoken to you guys. He knew I'd told you the truth about everything."

"You think he was trying to silence you?" Noah asked, needing Bettino to say the words.

"That would be my guess," Bettino replied dryly.

"As soon as you're well enough, we'll need you to attend our office again and provide us with another formal statement. Same drill as before," Noah said.

"Sure. I'll be there. Soon as I can. I want to put that prick away forever."

"Thanks to the evidence obtained by Christopher, and with your help, there's a good chance that will happen," Declan assured him.

"Take it easy, Joe. Get well," Noah added.

Bettino lifted his hand in a slight wave. "Thanks."

By the time Noah and Declan returned to the station, Beechwood's lawyer had arrived. After filling the woman in on the mountain of evidence against her client and allowing her time to consult with him, Beechwood finally agreed to co-operate. Noah walked back into the interview room feeling pumped. Declan followed him inside.

If Noah was hoping for a fight from the commissioner, he was severely disappointed. The man who'd treated him with so much scorn and arrogance the last time they'd spoken now looked scared. Though Noah addressed his comments to the commissioner, it was his lawyer who did all the talking.

"What kind of a deal are you talking?" the woman asked without preamble.

Noah and Declan shared a look. Both of them registered their surprise. Then Noah shook his head. "There won't be any deal."

The lawyer frowned. "Don't you think you're being too hasty? A conviction is far from certain, Detective."

Noah set his jaw at a stubborn angle. "I disagree. You've seen the evidence. I'm confident your client's going down. If you want to gamble with his liberty, that's between you and him."

With a glance toward Declan, Noah deliberately turned his back and headed for the exit. Declan followed suit. Noah was nearly out the door before the commissioner broke his silence.

"Wait up, Craigdon. Let's talk."

Once again, Noah shared a look with Declan. The two of them knew each other well enough that they shared a quick grin of satisfaction. Beechwood had taken the bait.

Noah and Declan sat across from the man who only a few short hours earlier was the most senior serving police officer in the state.

"Talk," Noah ordered.

It was slow and painful going, but gradually Beechwood told them about what had happened that fateful night in Maitland. The longer he talked, the more he seemed to relax into the storytelling, as if he'd wanted to get it off his chest for a long time, as if it were cathartic. And maybe it was.

Though it was difficult for Noah to hear, he gained a sense of satisfaction and closure as Beechwood confirmed everything Noah had uncovered, ending with the commissioner's visit to Bettino's house in the early hours of that morning. When Noah pressed him about the threat he'd made against Ayla, he admitted to that, too. When he was finished, Beechwood slumped over the table, his head in his hands, broken and defeated.

It was done.

In short order, Noah charged the commissioner with a string of offenses, including attempted murder. Though it was early days, thanks to the commissioner's confession, Joe Bettino, Ayla Rodriguez and Christopher's courage and quick thinking, they had all they needed to secure a conviction. It had been a good day's work.

Chapter Twenty Two

Noah flicked his indicator on and turned the Fireblade into his father's driveway. Ayla sat behind him, her arms wrapped around his waist. It felt so good to have her there, pressed up close against him, providing him support. It was a foreign feeling, having a woman by his side, but one he wouldn't give up for the world. No wonder guys went a little crazy when they fell in love.

He'd seen it with his cousins, even his brother, Flynn. Something instinctive and irreversible shifted inside them. A protectiveness, a tenderness that hadn't existed before. He was overwhelmed with the strength of his feelings for Ayla and was jubilant she felt the same.

It felt like a lifetime ago since he'd laid charges against the commissioner. With a bit of luck, the man would plead guilty and save them all the hassle of a trial. For now, he was happy to set the whole sorry episode aside and concentrate on the woman who sat behind him.

Noah brought the bike to a halt outside his father's home and killed the engine. The sudden silence was deafening. He held the bike steady while Ayla dismounted. She tugged off her helmet and shook her hair free. The shiny black strands caught the light from a nearby lamppost. She looked beautiful.

Staring at her, Noah was filled with a rush of nerves. This was the first time he'd brought her home to his father. Though she'd attended his aunt's emergency responder's ball earlier in the month, he wasn't sure if she'd met his father. Even if she had, it hadn't been in the capacity of Noah's girlfriend. A girlfriend he was crazy about.

He pulled off his helmet and climbed off the bike. Ayla handed him her helmet and he left both of them on the seat. He ran a hand through his hair and looked around him. The garden was neatly tended. The lawn was green and freshly mown. The house, though not on the same grand scale as Craigdon Manor, was decent just the same.

"Welcome to my family home," he said and then ducked his head, feeling a sudden bout of shyness.

Ayla stepped forward and draped her arms around his neck and kissed him. "It looks lovely."

Hand in hand, they walked up to the front door. Noah gave a brief knock and opened the wooden panel, stepping back to let Ayla enter ahead of him. Archie called out to them from the living room.

"Is that you, Noah?"

"Yes, Dad. I've brought Ayla."

"Come on in."

Giving Ayla's hand a reassuring squeeze, Noah led the way across the front entry, past the formal dining room and into the living room. His father was seated in his usual place in an armchair in front of the TV. Aunt Elizabeth was seated in the matching chair beside him.

Noah started in surprise, feeling slightly taken aback. It was after eight at night. He hadn't expected his aunt to be there. Okay, the two of them had been involved in an affair many years earlier that had produced his half-sister, Sophia. But Sophia was nearly twenty-two.

Surely they aren't still involved?

Before he could think on it further, his father and Elizabeth came to their feet and moved toward them. Noah pushed the unsettling thought out of his mind and introduced Ayla.

"I was a guest at your summer ball," Ayla said to his aunt.

Elizabeth smiled. "Yes, I understand you were there. I'm sorry we didn't get to meet then."

Ayla laughed. "Don't think anything of it. There were a lot of people there. It's a really lovely way of acknowledging first responders and all that we do, Mrs Craigdon."

"Please, call me Elizabeth. And thank you. Two of my sons are police officers and Noah, too, of course. And one of my daughters is a doctor. I see how hard they work and the challenges they face every day. Throwing a little party every year to raise some money and celebrate them and their colleagues is the least I can do."

Ayla smiled in agreement. Archie suggested they sit down. Noah led Ayla to the couch and sat down close beside her. Once again, he reached for her hand. The action wasn't lost on his father. He saw a look of surprise and pleasure pass between Archie and his aunt. Their unspoken approval filled him with warmth.

"Can I get you a drink?" Elizabeth asked.

Noah frowned. It seemed strange to see his aunt acting as hostess. He looked at his father, but Archie seemed unperturbed by Elizabeth's offer. In fact, he held up his empty scotch glass.

"Yes, thank you. Another scotch would be lovely. And don't forget the ice."

His aunt merely nodded and looked in Noah's direction. "What about you, Noah? Would you like a drink?"

"I'll just have a light beer," he said. "I'm driving."

"And you, Ayla? Can I get you something?"

"Thank you, Elizabeth. I'll have a G&T, if you have it."

"Of course. Archie's always kept a well-stocked bar. Haven't you, Archie?"

Noah saw the tender look his aunt sent in his father's direction. Once again he frowned.

This feels weird. Something's off… Something I can't put my finger on…

Or maybe he was imagining the whole thing. After all, his father and Aunt Elizabeth had known each other for years. Okay, so at some point they'd had an illicit liaison, but that didn't mean it was still going on.

"So, what brings you here this evening?" Archie asked, interrupting Noah's thoughts.

Noah glanced at Ayla. She gave him an imperceptive nod. They'd talked earlier about how they'd approach what he was about to tell his father. They'd both agreed it would be best for Noah to come right out and say it. They didn't know how the news would be received, but there was no doubt it had to be said. Of course, that was before they knew his aunt would be in residence. Now Noah wasn't quite sure what to say.

Before he could respond, Elizabeth returned carrying a tray of drinks. She distributed them around the group among murmurs of thanks. Then she sat back in the chair next to his father and regarded Noah expectantly.

"Noah was just about to tell us why they're here," Archie said.

His aunt nodded and sat forward in anticipation. Her eyes twinkled. "Does this have anything to do with the fact I've never seen you looking so happy?"

He blushed and looked at Ayla. She smiled at him tenderly.

"Um, no. Yes. Not really. Ayla and I have started dating and we're in a really good place right now, but that's not the reason we came tonight."

"No? What is it then?" his father asked.

Noah glanced at his aunt and then looked away again. Archie seemed to sense his unspoken question.

"Whatever you have to say, you can say it in front of Elizabeth," Archie said quietly. "We have no secrets from each other. Not anymore."

Noah nodded. He assumed his father had referred to the fact his aunt had kept secret for many years that Archie was Sophia's biological father. For a while, it had caused a rift. On some level, Noah was glad the two of them had made their peace.

He drew in a deep breath and eased it out between suddenly taut lips. What he was about to reveal was going to come as a shock. Ayla squeezed his hand in a show of silent reassurance. Not for the first time, he was grateful for her support. He opened his mouth to speak but his courage abruptly deserted him.

"We've charged the police commissioner with attempted murder and corruption," he blurted.

Ayla shot him a curious look. His father and his aunt looked mildly amused.

"Yes. We saw it on TV," his father replied. "Job well done, Noah. The way I heard it, you were instrumental in making the arrest."

Noah blushed under his father's praise. "Thanks, Dad. But I couldn't have done it without Christopher. He's the one who provided evidence of wrongdoing even the commissioner couldn't refute."

"It's such a shame Christopher's wasting so much of his time and effort on this lawsuit," his aunt said quietly.

"How are the negotiations coming along?" Noah asked. With so much on his plate lately, he'd lost touch.

Elizabeth sighed. "We rejected his offer to settle for eighty-five million dollars. He's yet to come back with a more reasonable one. I think most of the family is in agreement that we best leave it up to the courts. Christopher needs to be heard. It's the main force driving him. I understand, I really do. He was treated abominably by Henry. Still, I have an obligation to my children…and to my nephews. Any settlement with Christopher will come out of the estate."

"For what it's worth, I'm happy to give him a cut," Noah said. "Apart from anything else, we all owe him for the Beechwood matter."

Elizabeth cocked her head. "How so? I understand it's always good to get a bad guy off the streets, but how does it affect us personally?"

Once again, Noah was filled with a rush of nerves. The moment of truth was upon him again. This time, he had to find the courage to see it through. Taking strength from the reassuring look Ayla sent his way, he directed his attention toward his father.

"There's something you need to know, Dad."

Archie sipped at his scotch. He looked only mildly concerned. "What is it?"

"It's about Mom."

That got Archie's attention. He shifted uncomfortably and glanced at Elizabeth before his gaze returned to Noah. "What about your mother?"

Noah closed his eyes briefly and then told them about the affair.

"How dare you say that about your mother! You have no proof!" Archie cried.

Noah held his gaze. "Yes, Dad. I do. You already know the LECC opened an investigation into Mom's death. As part of the investigation, I got hold of Uncle Henry's phone records. There were a lot of calls and texts between him and Mom. It was obvious what was going on. I also spoke to Harriet Young. She confirmed it."

Archie gaped at him in shock. His face had paled. His eyes

were wide. He shook his head from side to side, muttering under his breath.

"No… No…. Won't believe it. Never! Gotta get out of here…"

He stood and stumbled from the room, still muttering. Noah sighed. It gave him no pleasure to see his father like that, but there had been no other way. His father deserved the truth.

Noah glanced at Elizabeth. She also looked shocked.

"I take it you didn't know, either?" Noah asked quietly.

Elizabeth shook her head, her expression dazed. "No. I didn't. I mean, I knew Henry had slept with other women, despite the wholesome family man he liked people to see. And there have been times when I've wondered if there was something more behind his generosity with Logan, but I never knew about the affair."

Noah pushed aside her comment about Logan for further contemplation at another time. Instead, he said, "Mom knew about you and my father."

Elizabeth's face lost all color. "How do you know?"

"Harriet told me. Mom didn't know when it had started, but she was certainly aware of it."

Elizabeth stared at the floor, twisting her hands in her lap. "I asked your father about it once. He was certain she couldn't have. We were…discreet.

"She also knew about Sophia."

Elizabeth gasped. "No! I can't believe Henry told her! We'd agreed not to tell anyone. It wasn't fair to Sophia." She paused and then added, "When did your mother find out?"

"I don't know. But Harriet knew about all of it. That information could only have come from my mother."

"Do you think she knew all along? Oh, God. I feel so awful. I can't believe Janelle knew all that time. Maybe from the beginning. No. Surely not from the beginning. That would mean…" Her voice faded away. She looked distraught. Noah finished the sentence.

"Their affair was going on back then," Noah said quietly.

Elizabeth vehemently shook her head. "No! I won't believe it. And your father will back me up. There's no way your mother was unfaithful to him for so long. He's shocked she was unfaithful to him at all."

"How do you know it wasn't happening back then?" Noah persisted, feeling churlish. "You're not exactly in a position to judge. There have been many secrets kept by members of the Craigdon family. Yours included."

Elizabeth's expression closed. Her lips thinned. "You need to leave, Noah. This has all been a bit too much. I… I need to rest."

Noah frowned. "Surely you mean *you* need to leave. This is my father's house."

A rush of crimson stained Elizabeth's cheeks. "Yes, yes of course." She stood and quickly turned her back on him. "I'm sorry about all this, Ayla. It was nice meeting you," she mumbled. "Please excuse me. You'll have to show yourselves out." With that, she left the room. A few minutes later, Noah heard the front door open and close. He turned to Ayla.

"So. That went well."

Chapter Twenty Three

Noah was quiet on the way back to Ayla's apartment. After all that had gone down over the past few weeks, she could understand his need for solitude. Wrapping her arms tightly around his waist, she tried to convey without words how much he meant to her.

They made it back to the city in good time. Though it was late, Ayla felt wide awake. As Noah parked his bike on the street outside her apartment, she took off her helmet and handed it to him. She followed it with a tender kiss.

"I'm so proud of you," she whispered.

His eyes widened. "What for?"

"For being the bravest, kindest, sexiest man I know. For being you."

He pulled her in close against him. She felt his erection through his leathers. It sent an answering surge of need rushing through her. She tightened her arms around his neck.

Their kiss was deep and passionate. He pressed against her lips, seeking entry and she willingly complied. With tongues enmeshed they kissed until they were breathless. When at last they pulled apart, Ayla's heart pounded with desire.

"Let's go inside," she whispered.

Noah locked up his bike and then gathered up the helmets. With his free hand in hers, they walked inside together.

Up three flights of stairs and into her apartment. They'd barely cleared the door when Noah took her in his arms. With their lips joined, he walked her backward down the hall, depositing the helmets on the couch as they went. His glasses went next. Then he bent and picked her up and cradled her against his chest. She tilted her head upwards. Unerringly, his lips found hers again.

He placed her gently on the bed and followed her all the way down. With his body pressed against hers, she kissed him for all she was worth. She still marveled that he was such a newcomer to the ways of making love. He was so natural, so graceful, so in tune with her body. It was the same way when they danced. She should have known making love with him would be just as special, just as connected, like they were one.

Tugging gently at her clothes, he undressed her with tenderness and care. As each new patch of skin was exposed, he kissed it. Finally she was naked beneath him. He looked at her with such love, it snatched her breath away.

She reached up and pushed a lock of hair out of his eyes. "I love you, Noah Craigdon."

His eyes flared wide with emotion and he bent his head back down to hers. Their lips touched and melded. Impatient to feel his nakedness against her, she reached for his jacket and slid open the zipper. She pushed it off his shoulders. Next came his T-shirt. It went the same way as the jacket and she started in on his pants.

The soft leather felt good beneath her fingers. She circled his erection and caressed him through his pants. He groaned.

"Do you like that?" she asked.

"*Mm*, I like it a lot."

Knowing she had the power to turn him on sent heat rushing through her veins. Her nipples pebbled, her core tightened. Need burned heavy, low in her stomach.

"I want you," she whispered.

"I want you, too."

Frantic now, she undid the button on his pants and slid the zipper down. He shoved the leathers down his hips, taking his boots, socks and underwear with them. At last he was as naked as she. When he came back and lay down beside her, she sighed from the sheer bliss of feeling his bare skin.

Reaching up, she threaded her arms around his neck and brought his head down to hers. They kissed like two people in love. With her heart thumping and her breath coming fast, Ayla rolled away and then pushed him down on his back. Climbing astride him, she ground her pelvis against the hot hardness of his cock.

Noah moaned in appreciation. "Oh, God. You feel so good."

Reaching over, she opened the bedside drawer and pulled out a condom. With her legs still straddling his hips, she sheathed him. Staring at him, she raised her hips and guided him into her entrance. Sinking slowly down on him, she gasped at the feel of him swelling and stretching inside her.

"Noah!"

His eyes were glazed with desire. He stared at her, but didn't speak. It was almost like he was beyond words. She knew how he felt. Slowly, slowly she began to move, relishing the feel of his cock. It filled her like no other had and like no other would again.

Noah wasn't her first lover, but he was the first to steal her heart. Now she knew what it felt like to be in love. Sweet, sensual, sexy Noah. The best thing was, he was hers. As she reached her climax, she cried out from the sheer exhilaration of it. She wanted to cling to that feeling forever.

Noah felt Ayla's inner muscles contracting around his cock and it was all he could do not to come there and then. He still couldn't believe how magical it could be between them. For so long, he'd worried he wouldn't be good enough for her. That he'd disappoint her in bed. Looking back, he couldn't believe he'd spent even a minute worrying about that. The reality couldn't be further from the truth.

Though she was his first and only lover, he couldn't imagine it could be better with anyone else. What he shared with Ayla was perfect. Even better, she accepted him for who and what he was. And that was even more important. She knew him inside and out, as intimately as another person could, and still she loved him.

Unable to hold back another moment, his body picked up the pace. Desire burned through his veins, setting him on fire. His cock throbbed. His balls ached. With a cry of triumph, he reached the peak and with Ayla still perched above him, he took her by the hips and held her still while he poured himself inside her.

It was a long time later that he caught his breath enough to kiss her and draw her close. She snuggled in against him.

"So, there you have it," he murmured against the softness of her skin. "You know all of my secrets. And some of my family's, too. Are you still sure you want to hang around?"

She smiled softly and moved even closer. She pressed her lips against his in the sweetest of kisses.

"Of course I am. No one's family is perfect."

"So you're happy to have me, warts and all?"

"More than happy. Warts and all. I love you, Noah Craigdon."

"I love you, too."

With that, he took her properly into his arms and kissed her like it was the first day of the rest of their lives together. And it was.

I do hope you have enjoyed reading Noah and Ayla's story. If you've enjoyed this book, I would really appreciate it if you could leave a review at Goodreads and your favorite digital retailer. Every review increases visibility and helps other readers to find books they enjoy.

Receive a free book when you sign up for my newsletter if you like to receive news on upcoming stories, release dates, book launches and other snippets. I love to receive feedback from my readers. Please feel free to contact me at chris@christaylorauthor.com.au.

Logan is the next book in the Craigdon Family Dynasty series.

Keep reading below for a sneak peek at Logan:

Chapter One

The third week of January was always painful for Logan Craigdon. Mainly because it brought back memories of the accident that had changed his life forever. He'd been competing in a sailing regatta. They were more than halfway through the day's races and were well ahead on the leaderboard when tragedy struck. The wind had gotten up and the water was choppy. Not that it was a challenge for an experienced sailor like him, but then an unexpected squall had taken the whole crew by surprise. Logan was hit hard by the boom and knocked off his feet. He fell awkwardly. Even now, three years later, he could still hear the snap of broken bone and feel the immediate rush of pain and nausea that had filled his gut.

He'd fractured both shin bones in several places. They hadn't mended well. He'd spent weeks lying supine in a hospital bed and then even more weeks doing rehab—and still he'd been left with a permanent limp. But the worst of it was he knew he'd never sail competitively again. All the hopes and dreams and aspirations he had of being number one in the world of sailing disintegrated before his eyes. And there was nothing he could do about it. He was all of twenty-two years old and his life was over. He'd never sailed again. That is, not until now.

Logan frowned darkly at the ten sailing dinghies lined up side by side on Balmoral Beach. This was the last place he wanted to be. He was only there because his cousin, Callum, had badgered him into it. Callum, the guy who'd been on his way to becoming a priest and was now happily married to the love of his life. He might have given up on serving God as a priest, but he sure as hell hadn't given up on being a do-gooder.

He'd approached Logan a couple of months earlier with the idea of running a sailing school for disadvantaged kids. Apparently there were plenty of them in Sydney. Kids who had no hope of ever knowing what it was like to sail. Or do anything exciting, as far as Callum led him to believe. Number one was their lack of finances, but more importantly was the lack of people willing to offer them experiences like that.

Though offering sailing classes for anyone was the last thing Logan wanted to do, Callum had been persistent. In the end, Logan had agreed simply to get his cousin off his back. And here he was. Day one of a five-day course. Ten kids filled with excitement, looking to him to make the experience something they'd never forget.

Logan's lip curled up in disgust. *Great. Just great.*

Unfortunately, he'd left it too late to make his escape. Some of the kids had already arrived. They had wide grins and were chattering among themselves with nervous excitement. Logan closed his eyes and prayed for the strength and patience to get through the next five days.

As if sensing his discomfort, Callum jogged over to where Logan stood with his arms crossed over his chest.

"You want to make sure the wind doesn't change," Callum teased. "I'd hate for you to have to go through life glaring like that."

"Fuck off, Callum." Logan took the sting out of his words by offering his cousin a half-smile. It felt more like a grimace.

Callum touched him on the arm. "Hey. I just want to say thank you again for doing this. I can tell it's not easy for you to be here. I'm guessing it brings back a lot of bad memories. That's what makes me even more grateful. And for you to be volunteering too… I just want you to know your sacrifice hasn't gone unnoticed."

Logan's frown deepened. "I should be in my office, finishing the design on my latest super yacht, not wasting my time out here."

Callum's expression remained calm and filled with understanding. "It's not a waste of time. Once you meet these kids… You'll see what I mean."

Logan grimaced. "Right. I'm doing it for the kids."

Callum nodded. "Right. And they're going to love you."

Damn Callum for guilting me into being part of this. I haven't been sailing since the accident. There's a reason I've stayed away from the water for so long. It hurt too much to remember all I could have been and all I'd lost.

"Hey! Logan! You ready to get started?"

Logan was pulled from his black thoughts by his brother, Noah. Both Noah and their oldest brother, Flynn, stood together, surrounded by a bunch of noisy kids. Though Logan had reluctantly agreed to be part of the Tackers program, he'd done it on the condition his brothers come along and help out. He was glad to see they'd kept their word. With a heavy sigh, he muttered a disgruntled farewell to Callum and started walking toward the shed where everyone had gathered.

Ten pairs of eyes filled with a combination of excitement and apprehension watched his approach. Logan came to a halt a few yards from the group and clapped his hands to get their attention. Within seconds, silence descended. Logan nervously cleared his throat and forced a smile.

"Hi. I'm Logan Craigdon. Welcome to the Tackers program. Thanks for showing up. I'm betting most of you have never sailed before. Am I right?"

His question was met with nervous laughter and a few nods and uncertain grins. Behind the children stood a handful of adults. Mostly women. Moms of the kids, no doubt. They looked almost as nervous as the participants. Logan felt an instinctive need to reassure them. He might have given up sailing three years ago, but he was still more than competent to teach. No one was going to drown on his watch.

He offered a few words of reassurance to the parents. He even managed to throw in a joke. He saw them visibly relax.

"For those of you who don't know anything about the Tackers program, let me explain. In a few words, it's a sailing school for beginners. We utilize a poly-plastic sailing dinghy. It's a simplified version of the international Optimist sailing dinghy."

"Never heard of that," a chubby kid in the front row muttered.

"That's cool," Logan responded with a grin. "I don't expect any of you to have heard of that. The main thing to know is that the type of dinghy we use is a small, single-handed dinghy that is very kid-friendly. It's one of the most popular sailing dinghies in the world."

He looked around the crowd. Some of their nervousness seemed to have dissipated. They stood in silence. Their wariness had been replaced by a mixture of curiosity and impatience.

"Right. A few things to remember before we start. You're going to be split into three groups." He pointed toward Noah. "This here is my brother, Noah. He's in charge of the first group." Logan then directed his attention toward Flynn. "And this is my other brother, Flynn. He's in charge of Group Two. I'm going to take the last group."

Logan scanned the crowd. The kids were still paying attention.

Good.

"Now, it's really important that you listen to your teacher. If everyone does as they're told, we can hopefully avoid accidents, including anyone getting hurt. No one wants that, right?"

There was a murmur of agreement, mostly from the adults at the back.

Logan nodded. "Good. Now, the most important thing to remember is to have fun. Are you ready?"

His question was met with cheers of excitement. Logan smiled and then addressed the parents.

"We'll take good care of them, I promise. You're welcome to stay and watch. Otherwise, we'll see you back here in an hour."

As the adults began to disperse, Callum moved up beside him. "Thanks again, Logan. You're doing great."

Logan shot him a level look. "It's fine, Callum. You don't have to look so worried. I agreed to do this and I'll see it through. I understand a lot of these kids belong to people who frequent your soup kitchen and that's why you're so concerned, but I promise to show them a good time." He shot his cousin a disparaging smile. "Who knows? They might even learn to sail."

Callum merely smiled in that calm way of his and slapped him on the arm in a friendly show of support before moving away. For a moment, Logan watched as his cousin approached some of the women. He greeted each of them by name. Their faces lit up as he spoke to them. Callum was one of those guys who was good and kind and compassionate all the way through. For a second, Logan felt almost wistful that he wasn't more like that.

Wake up to yourself, Craigdon… You haven't got a hope of being the kind of man Callum is. You're way too damaged for that…

With a sigh of irritation, Logan turned away and joined his brothers who were surrounded by excited children all keen to start. He'd gone through their applications a week earlier. Of course, he'd received ten times as many as he could handle. It had surprised him a bit. Then he'd put the matter out of his mind. He'd agreed to one class. That was it.

He'd culled the applications ruthlessly. First to go were those kids who couldn't swim. Though everyone wore a lifejacket at all times, there was no way he was going to complicate things by taking on non-swimmers. Next were the kids who were on medication. It was tough, but he wasn't a doctor and he didn't want to have to deal with some kind of medical emergency in the middle of the ocean. He was doing this as a favor to Callum. A quick, five-day sailing school. In and out, get it over with. And then he'd return to his cave to dwell on the unfair hand life had given him and to lick his wounds in private.

After hours of culling, he'd gotten down to the chosen ten. Then he sorted the kids into groups. As the more experienced sailor, Logan would take four kids under his wing. Flynn and Noah each had three. Unfortunately, they were limited by the number of dinghies they had. It had been mighty decent of the Balmoral Sailing Club to loan them the ten. That was all the club had.

It was Callum who'd approached the club president and explained the situation. It didn't surprise Logan that the president had immediately come on board. Callum had a way about him that drew people. They wanted to help him out, do his bidding. Not many people could say no to him, Logan included.

He clapped his hands together to get everyone's attention. The kids fell silent. "Right. Who's ready to learn how to sail?"

Amelia Ivanov—Mia to her friends—kept an anxious eye on her brother. So far, Mikhail seemed to be having a good time. She'd seen the notice about sailing lessons in her local church bulletin and after a day or two giving it some consideration, she'd signed Mikhail up. Though Mia had never sailed and didn't particularly care for the ocean, her younger brother was an entirely different matter. He loved the water and was an excellent swimmer. She was sure he'd also enjoy the challenge of learning something new. Things didn't come easily for him, but he always gave it his best. Learning a new skill would be good for his esteem.

She eyed the three male instructors. Even if the one who'd introduced himself as Logan hadn't mentioned they were brothers, she would have guessed. They looked a lot alike. Flynn was taller and Logan had lighter hair, but their resemblance to each other was clear to see. All three looked strong and muscular, with broad shoulders and slim hips. Noah wore glasses and looked friendly and cute. Flynn was casual and relaxed. But it was Logan who kept drawing her gaze.

While most of the other Moms and caregivers had left, Mia had elected to stay. She was nervous for Mikhail. Though she was certain this would be good for him, she wanted to make sure he'd be okay. After all, he was among total strangers, learning to sail for the first time. And though he'd turned fourteen last birthday, he also tended to be a bit rambunctious, like an overeager puppy, and she wanted to be close by in case she needed to intervene.

She often felt this way about her little brother. He'd had a rough start in life. Through no fault of his own, he struggled with many things most people took for granted. He was born with fetal alcohol syndrome. Even thinking about it made her feel equal parts anger and sadness. One thing was for sure. She was determined he'd always know what it was like to be loved.

A surge of protectiveness went through her. She was ten

years older than he was and the only family he had left. She took her responsibilities toward him seriously. He was her little brother, her responsibility, now and for always.

Glancing toward him, she was relieved to hear his excited chatter and see the animation on his face. The mid-morning sun was warm on her skin. It sparkled off the blue waves like diamonds. She found a spot on the grassy bank above the beach and sat down, filled with a mixture of excitement and apprehension.

She watched the class from a distance. Mikhail was in Logan's group. The sun-bleached, surfer dude who looked right at place on the sand. No doubt he spent hours right here, on the beach, catching waves. She wondered what he did for a living.

As he moved from one child to the next, answering questions, showing them how to tie knots, instructing them in the ways of sailing, she noticed he limped. She wondered if it were a recent injury or something more permanent. And then she shook her head and smiled inwardly.

What do I care if the hot instructor has a limp? It's obviously not interfering with his ability to teach.

She could see her brother was watching his every move. Mikhail stared at Logan, enthralled. His eyes were bright with curiosity. He was taking everything in. Mia held her breath as he tried one of the knots. He laughed uproariously when he got it all tangled. Logan chuckled and knelt down beside Mikhail and patiently showed him again.

Mia's heart turned over. She was a sucker whenever anyone showed her brother kindness. It certainly wasn't guaranteed. Because of his age, a lot of people expected him to behave with more maturity, more self-control. They didn't know about his condition. That he couldn't process information in the same way as other teens. But Logan didn't seem to have a problem with him at all and that knowledge helped

Mia to let out the breath she'd been holding and relax.

All too soon, the first class was over. Mikhail bounded up the hill toward Mia. She got to her feet just in time before he threw himself against her, laughing.

"That was so much fun!" His eyes lit up with laughter.

She ruffled his hair. "You did so well out there, Misha. I'm proud of you."

"Logan's the best!" Mikhail smiled widely and turned back to face the beach, searching for his new hero. "There he is! Come on, Mia! Come and say hello!"

Before she could murmur a protest, Mikhail had taken her hand and began to drag her down the hill.

"Misha! Stop! Let me go!"

Her demands were met with laughter. Her brother continued to tug her along until they were face to face with the man Mia had struggled to keep her eyes off for the past hour. He was half-turned away with her, speaking to another parent, but the pull of attraction was strong and swift. Her heart leaped in her throat.

"Logan!" Mikhail shouted.

The man swung around in surprise. He was even more good looking up close. A rush of nervousness flooded through her. His eyes were an intriguing gray-green color that seemed to change depending on the light. His bleached blond hair was wet and messy and hung over his face. An attractive three-day growth shadowed his cheeks.

"Logan! Logan! This is Mia! My sister!"

Logan smiled at Mikhail and then his gaze moved to her. Mia froze. For a moment she was too mesmerized to utter a word. He was the sexiest man she'd ever set eyes on. He simply took her breath away.

Mikhail beamed, looking from one to the other. Logan held out his hand toward her. With an effort, Mia gathered her wits and managed to greet him with a handshake.

"It-it's nice to meet you, Logan," she stammered. Heat crept over her cheeks. She wished the ground would open up and swallow her.

Ignoring her awkwardness, he gazed at her with frank interest. "Nice to meet you, too. Thanks for bringing your brother along. He's a natural."

Mikhail looked at Logan with adoration. Mia's heart skipped another beat.

Good looking and kind…and interested…a heady combination.

And straight on the heels of that thought was another.

He's Misha's sailing instructor. What am I thinking!

Chapter Two

The moment Logan's gaze fell on the woman who stood beside Mikhail, it was all he could do not to do a double take. With flawless olive skin, rich chestnut colored hair and huge blue eyes that could look right into his soul, he was immediately interested. Her hair was swept off her face with a hair barrette. It only emphasized her high cheekbones, her pert nose, her luscious mouth. All he could think about was what she would taste like…

Belatedly he remembered his manners. He held out his hand toward her. After a slight hesitation, she took it. Her handshake was warm and firm and oh too brief. He wanted the contact to go on forever.

What the hell's gotten into you, Craigdon? Working with the kids have sent your brain to mush…

He shot her another quick look. Yep. Just as desirable, just as attractive as he'd thought the first time. What he really wanted was to sleep with her. Every curvy, delectable inch of her. Would it be too forward if he asked her out? She was the sister of one of his pupils. Did that matter? Did that mean she was off limits? Surely not.

Logan had a fair idea of his attractiveness to women. Despite being jilted at the altar by his long-time girlfriend and fiancée, he'd never had any trouble pulling a date. So, he'd lost count of the number of one night stands. What did that matter? He was having fun and he sure as hell had made sure his heart wasn't involved. After what had happened with Virginia, it was the only way he knew how to protect himself. There was no way he'd ever leave himself vulnerable to such hurt and pain again. That didn't mean he couldn't enjoy women and the one standing right in front of him seemed more than a tasty treat.

But something about her made him hesitate. She wasn't like the usual girl he picked up for the night. There was something about her fresh innocence that told him she wasn't a girl who did one night stands. No, women like her were looking for a life partner. They were in it for the long haul. He sure as hell didn't fit that bill and he didn't want to be the one to disillusion her or dash her dreams.

Still, as she politely thanked him for the lesson and the time he'd spent with Mikhail, he couldn't deny the pull of attraction. Mesmerized by her beauty, he mumbled an appropriate response and then watched with reluctance as she and her brother slowly turned and left.

Mia brought the last of the groceries inside and then set about with Mikhail to unpack them. He was good at stacking things such as tinned tomatoes and boxes of cereal on the shelf. He inevitably ate more of the green grapes out of the bag than what he put in the fruit bowl, but that didn't matter. She'd bought the makings of beef tacos. It was her brother's favorite meal.

All afternoon he'd been talking non-stop about the sailing class. She was thrilled he was so engaged with it, but it kept drawing her thoughts back to the hot instructor. *Logan Craigdon.* He was the sexiest surfer dude she'd ever met. Even hotter than the men on the TV show, Bondi Rescue. When she'd signed Mikhail up for the course, she'd had no idea the instructors would be so good looking. This was going to be even more fun than she'd imagined. She couldn't wait for the next lesson tomorrow.

It was lucky she'd already negotiated with her assistant, Katerina, to come in to the bridal store an hour earlier each day to allow Mia to take Mikhail to his lesson. At the time she'd done it on the chance Mikhail might need her close by. Now there was an extra motivation to hang around for the hour. The thought made her smile.

She also felt good about being able to spend more time with her younger brother. Between her hours at the store and the time he spent at school, they were often reduced to only spending a few hours in the evening together before Misha drifted toward the television and she spent the time tallying the day's takings, balancing the books and responding to an ever growing number of emails. She ought to be thankful she received so many enquires for the dresses that graced her shop. It gave her the financial freedom to take time off when it suited her. Like now.

Spending time with her brother was even more important now that it was school holidays. They still had ten more days of summer break. Then it would be shopping for school things—shoes, uniform, backpack, lunchbox. Misha loved to start off a new school year with new things. It was fortunate, thanks to their father, she was able to indulge him.

Still, there was nothing more precious than creating memories together and providing him with interesting and challenging activities. The pediatrician she regularly took him too continued to emphasize how important it was for Misha to gain new skills. That was one thing she hoped to achieve with the sailing classes. If she got to ogle a sexy sailing instructor along the way, all the better.

Logan busied himself dragging dinghies out of the shed and pretended he wasn't waiting for a glimpse of Mia. Every time a car pulled up on the promontory above them, he glanced up and felt his gut drop with disappointment when it wasn't her. It was Day Two of their five-day course. Surely Mikhail hadn't thrown it all in already? He'd appeared to have a good time the day before. Still, there was no telling with kids. Some of them surprised him with their lack of resilience. He couldn't remember being like that when he was a kid.

"Logan! Logan! Logan! I'm here!"

At the excited sounds of Mikhail, Logan looked up and smiled. Mikhail was bolting down the incline at full speed, his focus only on arriving at his destination. He threw himself at Logan and hugged him around the waist. With any other kid, Logan might have felt embarrassed, but with Mikhail, it felt just fine.

Logan looked over Mikhail's head and spotted Mia walking toward them. She looked just as stunning as she had the day before. This time she wore a white tank top and navy-blue cotton pants. Her lips were covered in some kind of pink, shiny gloss.

She smiled at him as she drew closer. Though her eyes were concealed behind huge sunglasses, his heart still skipped a beat. He was sure he could feel the warmth and appreciation in her gaze. He immediately scowled with annoyance.

What the hell? We've only just met… Why's my heart beating like I've just finished an offshore sailing event? Who cares if she's gorgeous? She's just another woman…

He didn't even know her. Knew nothing about her, save her name and the fact she had a brother. Mikhail was dressed in black and green Billabong board shorts and a long-sleeved rash shirt. He greeted Logan with a toothy grin.

"Hi, Logan. Can we go sailing now? Can we go sailing now?"

Mia ducked her head and gently touched her brother on the arm. "Misha," she said quietly. "Slow down, mate. We've only just arrived. Logan has to wait for all the other kids. You're not the only one in the class."

Logan's heart thumped at her nearness. A waft of her exotic perfume reached his nostrils, sending his pulse into overdrive. He forced his gaze away and then chuckled at the look of disappointment on Mikhail's face.

"Hey, buddy. It's all right. I'm sure the others will be here soon. Let me tell you, I love your eagerness. It's great. So, what can you tell me from yesterday? Do you remember what we learned?"

"Of course I do! I'm not stupid."

"No, you're not stupid. In fact, I think you're one of my best students. Are you sure you haven't been sailing before?"

"No." The boy's brow furrowed in thought. "At least, I don't think so." He turned to his sister who stood a short distance away. "Have I, Mia? Have I been sailing before?"

She gently shook her head. "No, Misha. This is your first time. Well, second counting today."

Logan ruffled the boy's blond hair. "Then that means you're a natural, Mikhail. The very best kind to teach. It makes my job kind of easy and so much fun."

Mikhail's wide smile reflected the pride on his face. Mia shot Logan a soft smile of gratitude. His heart lurched.

"Thank you," she mouthed.

He gave her a wink and when her face suffused with a delightful pink his body hardened instinctively.

God, she's so beautiful.

And so not for him. She was fresh and sweet and innocent. Way too good for the likes of him. He'd be wise to keep his distance. It would be best for both of them.

The classes began to fill as the rest of the students arrived. Flynn and Noah led their groups away. Logan did the same.

Callum wasn't there yet, but no doubt he'd show at some point. He wanted to do his bit to help out and reassure the parents all was well.

Throughout the lesson, Logan did his best to ignore Mia. She was perched up on the grassy knoll commanding a good view of the beach and the activity below. Though her gaze was still concealed behind sunglasses, he had the feeling her attention stayed on him and her brother.

More likely her brother. That's who she was there for, after all. Logan was an idiot to think she might share his interest. Then again, she appeared to be as aware of him as he was of her. She'd blushed when he'd teased her, hadn't she? That had to be a sign…

Logan made a sound of impatience in the back of the throat. Since when did he waste time wondering whether a woman was into him? It was ludicrous. If he wanted a willing woman for the night, all he had to do was walk into a bar and find one. There were usually plenty to choose from. He didn't even have to try.

And that was the problem. It was all so easy. A smile, a wink, an offer to buy a drink. A few anecdotes, a joke or two. A couple of well-placed questions. It was all so predictable and boring. He wondered when he'd become so jaded.

He looked across to where Noah and Flynn were teaching their groups. A few of the kids had already started to get the hang of it. It didn't surprise him. Logan and his brothers had learned to sail from the time they started school. It had been something their father enjoyed. A fun way to spend a Saturday afternoon. For Logan, it had become much more than that and at the age of eighteen, he'd turned professional. At nineteen, he was selected on the Australian Olympic team. They hadn't won gold, but they'd gone close.

Logan assumed he'd spend the rest of his days sailing competitively around the world. But it wasn't meant to be.

Life and a nasty accident had other plans. Everything he'd taken for granted was now up in the air. He'd been forced to reevaluate his future. To say he'd struggled to readjust was an understatement.

"Logan! Logan! Look at me!"

Mikhail's excited cries broke into Logan's depressing thoughts. He looked across at his young student and grinned. Mikhail was in his dinghy hanging onto the rope for dear life. Logan grinned. The Tackers program usually catered for beginners who ranged in age from eight to twelve. At fourteen, Mikhail was the oldest of the group, but he didn't seem to notice or mind. Instead, he happily listened to everything Logan said and obediently followed all instructions.

The wind caught Mikhail's sail. It snapped taut. His yelp of joy could be heard clear across the harbor.

"Way to go, Mikhail! Hold her steady now. You're doing great!"

Logan threw a quick glance over his shoulder in Mia's direction and was disappointed to see her still seated on the grass above the shoreline, engrossed in her iPad.

What did you expect? That she'd be glued to your every move? She's here for her brother, you idiot. No one else. And a good thing, too. She's so not for you.

He had a momentary frisson of alarm when Mikhail failed to tack in time and the sail shifted, taking him with it and plunging him into the water, but Logan was soon put at ease when the boy surfaced with a grin from ear to ear.

"It's freezing, Logan!" he chimed, pulling a face.

Logan laughed and made his way over to where Mikhail clung to the side of his sailboat. Logan helped the boy back into the dinghy and settled him on the seat.

"There you go. The wind took you by surprise, that's all. That will happen many more times yet before everything starts to fall into place, I promise you. But you're only on your second lesson. You can't expect to know everything just yet."

"But I want to be the best, Logan!"

The earnest look on Mikhail's face tugged at Logan's heartstrings. His chest tightened on a sudden rush of emotion. He could still remember feeling exactly like this when his father first taught him to sail. He'd been a few days past his sixth birthday.

A rush of warmth and sentimentality flooded through him, catching him off guard. It had been so long since he'd associated sailing with anything other than negativity. Three years, in fact. Three long years when he'd hated the thought of anything to do with the sport because every time his mind drifted in that direction, he was cruelly reminded of how much he'd suffered and lost.

As if on cue, a familiar shaft of pain arced down his leg and momentarily stole his breath. He winced and closed his eyes until the feeling had eased. It wasn't always like this, but the pain made itself known enough times a day for him to be tired of it. He yearned for the time when he'd be pain-free. If that day ever came.

"Logan! Logan! Look at me!"

Once again, Mikhail's cries of excitement dragged him from his sad reverie. He looked up in time to see Mia's brother sail his little boat expertly across the water, his sail full of wind. A moment later, the wind turned and the sail collapsed, along with Mikhail who toppled once again into the water. He came up laughing like he'd done the last time and Logan chuckled with him. Wading over to where the boy was, Logan helped him up again.

"Good job, Mikhail. You're really getting the hang of it."

Mikhail beamed up at him. Logan high fived him and then turned back to the rest of the group. "Okay, guys, let's head back to shore. Class is over for today."

The rest of the group slowly made their way back,

accompanied by Noah and Flynn. Most of the kids had climbed out of their dinghies and were pushing them back to shore. Once all of his students were safely out of the water and the boats, lifejackets and other equipment had been stowed away, Logan gave them all a few words of encouragement before dismissing them.

From the corner of his eye, he saw Mia stand and dust off her pants before heading down the hill. Turning away, he busied himself with the equipment.

"Mia! Mia! Mia! Did you see me? I was sailing!"

"You certainly were, buddy. Good job!"

Logan continued to pack away the last few ropes and life jackets that had been left on the shore. As hard as he tried to ignore her presence, it proved impossible when she stopped a few feet away from him.

The first thing he noticed were her shoes. She wore hot-pink converse. An unusual choice this close to the beach, but whatever. The color was sexy. His gaze drifted slowly up her crisp navy-blue cotton pants, across the white tank top and finally came to rest on her face. Her eyes were still hidden behind her oversized sunglasses, but a friendly smile turned up her lips. Despite his best efforts, his heartrate kicked up a beat.

"Thank you for another great day Logan," she said.

"All good," he muttered, staring at the ground.

"It was all Mikhail could talk about last night. He couldn't wait to get here today."

Logan smiled involuntarily. "He's doing so well. He's a great kid."

"Yes, he is."

Suddenly, Logan was filled with curiosity about Mia and her brother.

Does she still live at home with him? Where are their parents? Why is she the one bringing him to a sailing lesson? Is she his primary carer?

He opened his mouth to ask one of the many questions

circling in his head, but then closed it again. It was none of his business. *They* were none of his business. He'd agreed to teach the class of keen young sailors only because Callum had hounded him into it. The class was set to run each afternoon for a week. Five lessons in total. And then he'd be done. Once he'd completed his obligation to the kids who'd signed up for the course, he had no intention of returning to the water again and he was even more determined to steer clear of the likes of the woman who stood before him.

"Um… I was wondering…um… Would you like to grab a coffee?"

From the expression on Mia's face, he could only guess the invitation that came out of her mouth had surprised her as much as him. All the reasons why he should decline crowded his mind, but he found himself nodding.

"Yeah, why not? Sounds great."

"Yay! Can I get a milkshake?" Mikhail asked her.

She laughed and ruffled his hair affectionately. "Of course. Chocolate, right?"

"Right!"

He turned and started running up the grassy bank that led to the carpark. Logan had a quick word with his brothers and updated them on his plans. They agreed to pack away the last of the gear. He caught up with Mia and together they followed Mikhail at a more leisurely pace.

"So, do you live nearby?" he asked, filling the silence.

"Not too far away. We live in Mosman."

She mentioned an affluent, lower north shore suburb about five minutes' drive away. "Nice," he responded. "I live just down the hill, right here in Balmoral."

"Balmoral's a lovely spot."

"Not too shabby," he agreed.

"Mikhail loves to come down here for a swim."

"Yes, I can tell he's a water baby. Have you been in Mosman long?"

"Long enough. I've lived there most of my life. My father was in…the construction industry. He built our house. When he died, he left the house to me."

"Oh, I'm sorry."

She compressed her lips. "That's okay. He passed away a bit over a year ago."

"You must miss him."

She shrugged. "Living in my family home reminds me of him every day. He was also responsible for a lot of the apartment blocks you see on the lower north shore. You could say he left a substantial legacy."

"Nice," Logan responded. "My uncle was also in property development. It's been nearly twelve months since he died. He left his company to me."

She smiled. "So you're a property developer. I can imagine that keeps you busy. Especially around these parts. How are you able to volunteer your time to a project such as this?"

They'd reached the carpark, saving him from having to respond. He didn't feel like explaining he was there under sufferance and would never have agreed to be part of it if it hadn't been for his cousin's constant badgering.

"This is me," he said, indicating the steel gray CLA 250 coupé Mercedes.

"Nice," she repeated, a cheeky expression lighting up her face.

His heart somersaulted. "You know cars?" he teased.

She indicated a shiny black Tesla. "This is me."

"I'm impressed," he said.

"Good." She winked at him.

Mikhail bounced up and down on his feet, waiting impatiently to climb in. Mia pressed the button on her remote and the doors came open, lifting out and upwards like the car out of the Back to the Future movie Logan had seen many years earlier and still loved. With a brief wave, she turned and walked around to the driver's side and slid behind the wheel. "I'll meet you at Café 2088," she said, mentioning a popular coffee shop in the heart of Mosman's shopping precinct.

"See you there," he murmured and did his best to ignore the acceleration in his heartbeat. They were two new friends sharing casual conversation over coffee. Nothing more.

Yeah, right.

Chapter Three

Mia wiped her sweaty palms down the sides of her pants and tried to quell the nervous excitement that coursed through her veins. She found a parking spot within walking distance of the café and, together with Mikhail, made her way down the street. Café 2388 was one of her favorite places to hang out. It was only a few doors down from her bridal shop. This time of day, the breakfast crowd had dissipated and the lunch goers were yet to materialize. It was the perfect time to be there. The owner, Joanna Penberthy, greeted them with a smile.

"Hi, guys! It's good to see you. What are you up to?"

"We just thought we'd pop in for a coffee," Mia replied.

"Let me guess: One skinny latté and a large chocolate milkshake." She winked at Mikhail. "Am I right?"

"Yay!" Mikhail cheered.

"And a short black, thank you," Logan added, stepping inside the shop and closing the door behind him.

"Oh, I'm sorry, I didn't see you there," Joanna said, blushing.

Logan waved away his embarrassment. "It's no problem."

Mia made the introductions. "Joanna, this is Logan Craigdon. He's been teaching Mikhail to sail."

"Oh, that's wonderful. I think I saw something about that

in our local church bulletin." She smiled at Logan. "It's a great thing you're doing."

Logan shrugged and looked away, a flush of embarrassment staining his cheeks. "Thanks," he mumbled.

Mia indicated a table by the large bay window that looked out onto the street. "Should we take a seat?"

Mikhail bounded over and sat down. Mia and Logan followed. The table was only big enough to seat four people. With Logan's shoulders broader than the average man, all of a sudden it seemed much too small to seat them. He sat opposite her and seemed to dominate the space, so close she suddenly found it hard to breathe.

He was so good looking. She barely even noticed his limp. It certainly didn't seem to hamper him in the water. During Misha's sailing lesson, she'd done her best to remain immersed in dealing with her email, but the truth was, she'd been hard pressed to keep her attention on anything but the Adonis in the harbor.

Logan shifted his weight on the chair and then winced. She was overcome with curiosity about his injury and wondered if it was recent.

"What did you do to your leg?" she asked.

His expression went blank and his eyes shuttered. "I broke it."

"How long ago?"

"Three years."

She raised her eyebrows in surprise. "It must have been a bad break."

"Yep. And it's breaks. Plural."

"How did it happen?"

His eyes flashed with annoyance and his lips compressed. It was obvious he found her questions irritating.

"It doesn't matter." His tone was brusque, closing down any further discussion.

She bit her lip and nodded. It was none of her business.

She hardly knew the guy. She had no right poking into his life. Tension now reverberated off him in waves. His expression was taut. Gone was the easy-going sailing instructor of a few minutes earlier.

Okay, so even after three years, he's still sensitive about his accident. She burned with curiosity to know what had happened but was wise enough not to push it for now.

For now? What am I thinking? Am I hoping this is only the first of many personal conversations we might share?

Of course she was. The man who sat before her was tall, broad-shouldered, sexy. He was also kind and thoughtful and funny and treated her brother like he was just another teenager. The latter was more important to her than any of the other, but there was no denying he ticked a lot of boxes. The romantic in her couldn't help but dream they might have a future.

Good God! You're being ridiculous! You've only just met the guy! Give it a break!

To her relief, Joanna arrived with their order and she was forced to put a hold on her wayward thoughts. All three of them murmured their thanks and then started in on their drinks. Mikhail slurped noisily through his straw and both she and Logan laughed.

"Good?" he asked Mikhail with a smile.

"Good. I love chocolate and milkshakes are the best!"

Logan laughed. "You won't get an argument from me, buddy. Although I usually go for caramel."

"I like caramel, too," Mikhail replied. "But chocolate is the best!" He laughed boisterously and Logan joined in.

She took another sip from her coffee. Logan continued to regard Mikhail with curiosity. Mia could see the questions in his eyes, but he either wasn't as curious as Mikhail as she was about him, or he had more self-control. Either way, he remained silent.

"So, what made you think about starting the sailing class?" she asked, unable to help herself. She had an innate curiosity about people and right now she wanted to know everything about him. It was almost a physical yearning.

Logan set his coffee cup down and shook his head, a rueful expression flooding his face. "You have my cousin to thank for that. Callum Craigdon. He used to be a priest. Now he runs a soup kitchen in the city and is in the middle of constructing affordable housing. He's always had an active social conscience. He thought a class like this one would be a good idea."

"Well, I'm certainly grateful to him. This has been great for Mikhail and it's only the second day. When I saw the notice about it, I just had to check it out."

"I'm glad you did."

"So am I."

Their gazes caught and held. Mia's heart skipped a beat and then galloped away so fast she felt breathless. With an effort, she looked away and did her best to regain control over her speeding pulse.

"You mentioned your shop," Logan continued in such a smooth voice she could only assume he hadn't been as affected as she had by their prolonged exchange.

She blinked to clear her thoughts. "Yes. I-I own a bridal wear shop in Mosman. It's right on Military Road. *Wishes and Dreams*. Do you know it?"

Logan stared at her in horror. *Did she just say she owned a bridal wear shop? Oh, God. This was worse than he thought!* He should have followed his instincts and stayed the hell away from her. She was as fresh and innocent as he'd imagined. She owned a bridal shop, for God's sake! She believed in love, in happy-ever-afters... Oh, God. This couldn't get any worse.

Despite everything, he'd managed to ignore the warnings in his head and accept her invitation to coffee. The truth was, he liked her and his cock had been hard from the very first moment he'd spied her walking toward him from the carpark near the Balmoral Beach wharf. She was an incredibly attractive woman and he was only a flesh and blood man.

But then he'd talked to her and had realized she was the exact opposite of the women he usually flirted with and who he eventually took home to bed. And yet, here he was. Sitting across from her, sharing conversation, getting to know her and wanting to know her a hell of a lot more.

I need to get out of here…

Almost clumsily, he pushed back his chair and stood. He glanced at his watch and then at Mia. "I'm really sorry. I just remembered a meeting I have scheduled. A…staff meeting…at Craigdon Enterprises. I…usually leave them to my cousin, Nicholas, but I promised to be there today. I'm sorry. I'm really sorry."

She blinked away her surprise and merely offered him a genuine smile of disappointment. "Don't be silly. Go. There's no need to apologize. It's been fun, hasn't it, Mikhail?"

Her brother turned to look at Logan and gave him a wide grin. "Yes! Fun, Logan. See you tomorrow, Logan!" Mikhail waved enthusiastically and Logan half-heartedly waved back.

"See you tomorrow," he mumbled and feeling like the coward he was, he threw down enough money to cover their drinks, then spun on his heel and left.

"Turn off the TV, Mikhail. It's time to go to bed." Mia braced herself for the familiar argument.

"But, Mia! It's only nine o'clock! Just another hour!"

She remained firm. "No, Misha. It's bedtime."

"But it's holidays!"

"Exactly! You're normally in bed by eight."

When her brother looked like he was about to argue further, Mia took his hand and pulled him off the couch.

"You have to go sailing again tomorrow. You don't want to be all worn out before you get there."

His expression brightened. "Sailing! Yay! I love sailing!"

His wide grin lit up his face, making him look even younger. Tenderness surged through her. She drew him close and hugged him. A few seconds later, her wriggled out of her embrace.

"Will Logan be there again tomorrow?"

She nodded. "Yes. He's your instructor. You'll have him all week."

"Yay! Can we invite him again for a milkshake?"

Mia laughed at the eagerness on Mikhail's face. "Maybe."

Her brother punched the air. "Yes!"

She chucked him gently under the chin and chuckled. "I don't know which one you're more excited about—spending time with Logan or having another milkshake."

Mikhail grinned. "Both!"

She laughed and walked down the hallway toward his bedroom relieved when he followed without further protest. She turned down his bed and fluffed his pillows. He walked in behind her.

"Don't forget to brush your teeth," she reminded him.

With a sigh, he went into the adjoining bathroom. She heard the water running and the sound of him brushing his teeth. A few moments later, he walked back into the bedroom and climbed into bed. She perched on the edge beside him.

"Did you have a good day today?"

He smiled happily. "Yes. A good day. Tomorrow will be even better!"

She leaned over and brushed a lock of hair out of his eyes and winked. "I'm sure it will be."

He let out a huge yawn. She smiled. "Goodnight, Misha. Have a good sleep. I'll see you in the morning." She stood and kissed him on the forehead and then leaned over and switched off the bedside light.

"Goodnight, Mia. I love you."

Her heart clenched at the sweetness of his words. "I love you too, Misha." With that, she turned and left the room, leaving the door to his bedroom open.

Making her way back to the living room, she poured herself a glass of white wine and settled on the couch. It had been a tiring day. Even though Mikhail was fourteen, he was closer to a mental age of ten. She wasn't game to leave him at home alone all day so during school holidays, when she was working she took him with her. She was fortunate she owned the business and this option was available to her.

Mikhail spent hours in her office at the back of the shop, mostly playing games on his iPad or watching Netflix. He rarely complained, accepting without protest that he had to stay there. Occasionally she let him walk to Café 2388 and do a coffee run. He also got to buy himself a milkshake.

She took a sip from her glass and sighed quietly. It was these moments after Mikhail had gone to bed that she treasured. Though she loved him unconditionally and never got tired of taking on the responsibility of raising him, it was always nice to have some quiet time to herself.

There were only ten years separating them, but more often than not she felt more like his mother than his sister. She supposed that was only natural. She'd been taking care of him all his life. Their mother had died when he was seven, but even before then Mia had been his caregiver.

Their mother's parenting skills had been non-existent and with their father absent more times than he was present, the responsibility of seeing to her brother's daily needs had inevitably fallen to Mia. Not that she resented the intrusion.

He was her brother and she loved him. It wasn't his fault their mother had been an alcoholic and drug addict from before he was born. It wasn't his fault his physical and mental development had been impaired as a result. It made Mia all the more determined to give him the life he deserved. She refused to allow anything to hold him back. Signing him up for sailing lessons was a perfect example of that.

Just like that, her thoughts returned to Logan Craigdon. She groaned aloud in renewed embarrassment. She still wasn't sure what she'd said to frighten him off, but she guessed it had something to do with the mention of her bridal wear shop. She'd barely finished speaking and he'd torn out of there like his pants were on fire.

Did he think I was angling for a husband? Is that what it had been about?

She'd done a bit of research on social media the night before. She'd discovered Logan was well known on the social scene. According to the Internet, he partied long and hard and was currently single. No doubt a man with good looks, charm and money was a much-sought-after prize for the women of Sydney.

Perhaps he assumed I was of the same vein?

In that case, she couldn't blame him for his hasty departure. It was a shame he hadn't hung around long enough for her to assure him that owning a bridal wear shop didn't mean she was looking for a husband. She might be an incurable romantic who believed in love and happy-ever-afters, but she was also a pragmatist. After all, nearly half of all marriages ended in divorce. That was a sobering statistic.

Of course, no doubt someone like Logan was propositioned more times than he could count. After all, he was a good catch. Most everyone in Sydney had heard of the Craigdon family. They were one of the richest families in the state, with much influence and standing in both business and political circles. Before his death, Henry Craigdon had headed a multimillion dollar property development enterprise. Apparently the same business Logan had just inherited. No wonder he was antsy when he came into contact with females of marriageable age, and even more so when said female owned a bridal wear shop.

She sighed and took another sip of wine. It was getting late. She ought to go to bed, read for a bit and then call it a night. Mikhail had always been an early riser, which meant she was an early riser, too. It was always hectic in the mornings, getting breakfast for the two of them, packing his school bag, including his lunch and making sure he could find his shoes. Normally she'd then drop him off at his very expensive, very prestigious school and head off to work. At least during the school holidays, she was spared that part of the routine. Doing the school run during peak hour traffic was never fun.

Signing her brother up for sailing lessons had been a stroke of genius. Not only did it get Mikhail outside and learning a new skill, it was just down the road from where they lived. A five-minute drive. How good was that? And Mikhail was having fun. Watching him laugh and learn and splash in the water was a nice distraction from her usual work day. And then there was Logan.

An even nicer distraction…

With an impatient sigh, she forced her mind away from the too-handsome-for-his-own-good Logan Craigdon. She'd spent way too much time thinking about him already. It was time to give it a break. After all, there was always tomorrow…and another sailing lesson. With that thought in mind, she finished her wine and with a smile tugging at her lips, she switched off the lights and headed for bed.

LOGAN is available for preorder at all of the digital retailers. It will be released on 13 June, 2021.

About the Author

Chris Taylor grew up on a farm in north-west New South Wales, Australia. She always had a thirst for stories and recalls writing her first book at the ripe old age of eight. Always a lover of romance and happily-ever-afters, a career in criminal law sparked her interest in intrigue and suspense. For Chris to be able to combine romance with suspense in her books is a dream come true.

Chris is married to Linden and is the mother of five children. If not behind her computer, you can find her doing the school run, taxiing children to swimming lessons, football, ballet and cricket. In her spare time, Chris loves to read her favorite authors who include Richard North Patterson, Sandra Brown, Kathleen E Woodiwiss and Jude Devereaux.

You can find out more about Chris and sign up for her newsletter at her website:

http://www.christaylorauthor.com.au